WINGS

OF

SNOW

BOOKS BY KRISTA STREET

SUPERNATURAL WORLD NOVELS

Fae of Snow & Ice

Court of Winter
Thorns of Frost
Wings of Snow
Crowns of Ice

Supernatural Curse

Wolf of Fire
Bound of Blood
Cursed of Moon
Forged of Bone

Supernatural Institute

Fated by Starlight
Born by Moonlight
Hunted by Firelight
Kissed by Shadowlight

Supernatural Community

Magic in Light
Power in Darkness
Dragons in Fire
Angel in Embers

Supernatural Standalone Novels

Beast of Shadows

Links to all of Krista's books may be found on her website:

www.kristastreet.com

WINGS OF SNOW

fae fantasy romance

FAE OF SNOW & ICE

BOOK 3

KRISTA STREET

WELCOME TO THE FAE LANDS

Wings of Snow is book three in the four-book *Fae of Snow & Ice* series, which is a slow-burn, enemies-to-lovers, fae fantasy romance.

This book takes place in the fae lands of Krista Street's *Supernatural World*. Although Krista's other paranormal romance books also features the fae lands, the *Fae of Snow & Ice* series is entirely separate so may be read before or after her previous series.

Solis Continent

Brashier Sea

Ice Caves
Pentlebim

Kroravee

Isalee

Solisarium

Floating
Meadows

Prinavee

Gielis

Highsteer
Castle

Osaravee

Duval

Murlands

Hanivel

Guxbee

Bay
of
Korl

Barvilu

Tala Sea

Glassen
Barrier
Islands

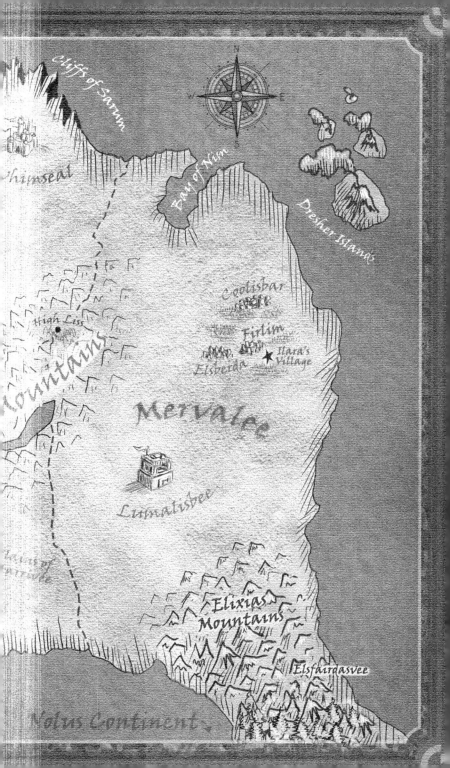

GLOSSARY

<u>Territories of the Solis Continent</u>

Harrivee – the middle southern territory, coastal cities often fighting with the Lochen fae. Territory color is yellow.

Isalee – the northernmost territory, Cliffs of Sarum on its northern peak. Territory color is white.

Kroravee – the northwestern territory, most reclusive territory, very unwelcoming even to other Solis fae. Territory color is purple.

Mervalee – the easternmost territory, richly blessed with *orem,* borders the Nolus continent. Territory color is green.

Osaravee – the southwestern territory, coastal cities often fighting with the Lochen fae. Territory color is red.

Prinavee – the central territory, where Solisarium, the capital of the Solis continent, resides. Territory color is the royal palate: blue, black, and silver.

❄

Seas of the fae lands

Adriastic Sea – the ocean to the west of the Nolus continent.

Brashier Sea – the most northern sea in the fae lands, large icebergs often present.

Tala Sea – the ocean to the south of the Solis continent.

Terms

Affinity – the magical ability that each Solis fae develops at maturing age. Maturing age happens around thirteen years of age in the hundreds-year-long life span of a Solis fairy. A Solis fairy's affinity can be common or quite rare, weak or very strong. Most Solis fae only have one affinity. Very powerful Solis fae have more than one.

Archon – a fairy that holds power over a village, city, territory, or land. There are tiers of archons, and the more land that an archon manages, the more politically powerful that archon is. The most powerful archon on the Solis continent is King Novakin.

Blessed Mother – a magical life force of the fae lands that nurtures growth and life among the fae. The Blessed Mother is not a goddess but a force from nature that is similar in strength and power to the gods. The Blessed Mother is believed to reside deep within the land at the heart of the planet. This belief is unique to the Solis fae.

Channa – intrinsic Lochen magic that keeps Lochen fae warm no matter the climate.

Defective – a Solis fae who is magicless and never develops an affinity.

Full season – the equivalent of one year.

Ingamy – a derogatory word for a Solis fairy.

Millee – the Solis fae unit of measurement, the equivalent of one mile.

Orem – the magic that infuses the Solis continent, allowing plants and crops to grow in freezing temperatures. *Orem* is replenished by celestial events and comes from the gods.

Salivar – a Lochen fae concubine.

Solls – a term Solis fae use when they clink glasses to celebrate, like Cheers.

Fae races

Solis fae – the Solis fae reside on the icy, most northern continent of the fae lands planet. Solis fae have silvery white hair, crystalline blue eyes, and wings. They typically live for thousands of years.

Nolus fae – the Nolus fae reside on the central continent. They often have various shades of colorful hair, pointy teeth, glowing skin, and otherworldly strength. They typically live three hundred years, but royal Nolus fae live for thousands of years.

Lochen fae – the Lochen fae reside on a southern continent, islands, and in the seas throughout the fae lands. They can morph into fish-like creatures, similar to mermaids, but they can also walk on two legs and live on land. There are subspecies of Lochen fae that live in fresh-water rivers, lakes, and ponds. The Lochen fae typically have green eyes and varying skin shades and hair colors.

Silten fae – the Silten fae reside on a separate continent across the Adriastic Sea, west of the Nolus continent. They have animalistic features: horns, scales, hooves, and tails, and they are the most varied in how they appear. Most live in underground dens, hollow logs, or wooded forests, but Silten fae with more human-like bodies reside in cities.

Fae plants and food

Acorlis – a root vegetable, sweet flavor with an orange skin, similar to a sweet potato.

Cottonum – a plant similar to cotton.

Leminai – a bright-green alcoholic drink common throughout the fae lands.

Nightill – purple and black wildflowers.

Salopas – a fairy version of a bar with no serving staff. There are magically enchanted trays that serve patrons.

Fae animals

Colantha – a large cat that resides in jungles.

Domal – an animal similar to a horse but more intelligent.

Feerily – a deadly sea creature. As a form of execution, the Lochen will feed a fairy to a feerily.

Ice bear – a large bear with a naturally white furry coat and six-inch claws, which stands eight feet tall on two legs. An ice bear's coat can change color to match its surroundings.

Snowgum – the most feared ice creature whose magical ability allows it to become invisible for short spans. Snowgums resemble a large feline.

Tilamy – a sea creature that's lively and non-threatening. They're sometimes kept as pets by the Lochen fae.

Trisilee – a tiny bird with wings that flap hundreds of miles per hour, like a hummingbird.

PRONUNCIATION GUIDE

Names

Ilara Seary – Ill-are-uh Seer-ee

Norivun Achul – Nor-ih-vun Ah-cool

Cailis – Kay-liss

Krisil – Kris-ill

Evis – Eve-iss

Sandus – Sand-us

Balbus – Bell-bus

Patrice – Pah-treese

Haisley – Hay-slee

Nuwin – New-win

Daiseeum – Day-zee-um

Novakin – Naw-vah-kin

Lissandra – Li-sahn-druh

Drachu – Draw-koo

Michas – My-kiss

Sirus – Seer-us

Meegana – Mee-gah-nuh

Georgyanna – George-ee-ah-nuh

Matron Olsander – May-tron Ole-sand-err

Sabreeny – Saw-breen-ee

Tylen – Tie-len

Priestess Genoova –Gen-oo-vuh

Bavar – Bah-varr

God Zorifel –Zorr-ih-fell

Goddess Nuleef – Null-leaf

Goddess Verasellee – Vair-uh-sell-ee

Fae Races, Territories, Seas, & Cities

Solis – Saw-liss

Nolus – Naw-luss

Lochen – Lock-uhn

Silten – Sill-tun

Harrivee – Hair-uh-vee

Isalee – Iss-ah-lee

Kroravee – Quor-uh-vee

Mervalee – Merr-vuh-lee

Osaravee – Oh-sar-uh-vee

Prinavee – Prin-uh-vee

Glassen Barrier Islands – Gloss-en

Adriastic Sea – Aid-ree-ass-tic

Brashier Sea – Bra-zhee-err

Tala Sea – Tall-uh

Derian Forest – Dare-ee-un

Wisareian Forest – Wiss-are-ee-un

Isle of Malician –Muh-liss-ee-un

Pasibith – Pass-ih-bith

Solisarium – Sole-liss-are-ee-um

Vemil Brasea – Vem-ill Bra-sea

Vockalin – Vock-ah-lynn

CHAPTER 1 - ILARA

My sister, Cailis, and I stood on the black sand shores of the Glassen Barrier Islands. Jutting fjords rose steeply on each side of the northern-most island as millions of stars twinkled in the galaxy above. Tall trees and thick vegetation covered in frost obscured most of the land, and a cool breeze billowed over my cheeks.

The Lochen fae king, Drachu, stood before us, his eyes glittering in the night as the Tala Sea rolled in waves behind him. The moonlight illuminated his thick muscles and minimal clothing. He was toned everywhere, his muscles thick and defined. He only wore a strip of green fabric that covered his groin and upper legs while his dark hair fell in tangles to his shoulders. Like Prince Norivun, Drachu had a build that was seasoned to fighting.

"Will you keep us safe?" I asked.

Drachu's lips curved. "The Lochen will guard you with our lives."

Cailis squeezed my hand once. *Truth.* The fae king wasn't lying.

"And you won't keep us as prisoners or use us for your personal gain?" I pushed.

His eyebrows drew together. "Don't insult me. You are a queen, and you will be treated as such."

Cailis's lips tightened, and her forehead furrowed. Her hand still held mine, but it took a moment before she squeezed once. Under her breath, she said, "I think."

Confusion filled me. I wasn't a queen. I was a farm girl from Mervalee, but Drachu had always looked at me as if I was so much more.

I studied the necklace he wore again, wondering what it did.

"Thank you," I finally replied. "For giving us safe haven."

Drachu grinned, the smile transforming his face into one of savage beauty. "Of course, *Krelahala.* I've been waiting for you to join my clan and for you to learn who you really are."

Krelahala? Join his clan?

I started as he prowled softly toward me. The sea lapped at his ankles until he stood only inches away. His sheer size dwarfed my frame, forcing me to tilt my head back as nerves fluttered through me.

I swallowed the knot in my throat as the green light in Drachu's necklace flared. Shells, gems, and teeth from predators in the Tala Sea hung from the intricate jewelry, but the center pendant—a large stone—throbbed with an emerald light, illuminating his brown skin.

"I've been waiting for you." Drachu's lips peeled back.

Rows of straight teeth and two pointy incisors appeared in the moonlight.

"You have?" I cocked my head as Cailis's breath hitched.

My sister squeezed my hand again. *Truth.*

I frowned. "How did you know we were coming?"

Drachu's grin broadened. "I know many things."

My sister squeezed again. *Truth.*

Frowning more, I asked, "Why did you call me Krelahala? My name's Ilara Seary."

"Krelahala is my clan's name for your kind."

"My kind? As in Solis fae?"

He threaded his fingers through my ebony hair. "No, *your* kind."

I cocked my head. "Do you mean my black hair?" Other than me and the queen, no Solis fae had black hair.

His expression turned knowing.

"Do you know why I have black hair?" I pressed.

"Like I said, I know many things."

Another squeeze. *Truth.*

My heartbeat ticked steadily faster, and I tried to calm it. I didn't know Drachu. I didn't know if his riddles were what one always encountered with him or if he was toying with me, perhaps manipulating me in a subtle way to draw me in and make me curious, skirting Cailis's truth affinity in the process.

The fact that Drachu was here and not in the sea told me that, on some level, he had to know we would be arriving. He wasn't lying in that aspect, and Blessed Mother, he'd pretty much confirmed that.

But how? He might be a Lochen fae who carried magic that allowed him to shift forms, since he currently walked on two legs and wasn't in his fish-like body, but Lochen fae couldn't see the future.

Or could they?

Drachu's commanding aura did remind me sharply of the crown prince's. Perhaps he was like Norivun. Perhaps Drachu also carried immensely powerful gifts like my mate.

It would explain why Drachu was king, and it would explain his cryptic words and uncanny knowledge of my arrival. It might even explain why he claimed to know what I was.

Or maybe not, and it was all to deceive me.

Ock, Norivun, I wish you were here. My breath hitched when I thought of my mate. It'd only been a few hours since I'd last seen him, but already it felt like winters. My entire being ached for him.

Shoving that reaction away, I concentrated on the present.

Regardless of my regret over all that had transpired, we needed Drachu's help right now because something in the Isalee field had tethered my affinities. I needed to free them, and the only way I could do that was if I was somewhere safe without the Court of Winter's politics deciding my fate.

If Cailis and I hadn't left, I would be shackled to the castle. My wedding planning to the vile Lord Arcane Woodsbury would be underway. I would have no time or resources to discover what happened to me or find a way to undo it.

But now I was free with rulibs hidden in our bags. My

sister and I could seek the answers I sought. And once my magic had recovered, I would return to the Solis continent to fight the king and marry who I truly belonged with—the crown prince of the Winter Court.

Drachu canted his head, his smile disappearing. "Does the death warlord know that you're here?"

Another arrow pierced my heart at the mention of the prince. "No. I imagine he knows that I've fled, but he doesn't know where we went."

I tried not to worry that we'd used our one and only potion to mistphase to this island. Until my magic was no longer suppressed and I could mistphase reliably on my own, we were stuck here.

"Come." Drachu turned and began to walk toward the trees, away from the sea and into the thick forest. Despite frost coating all of the leaves on the island, the plant life was thriving.

Sand shifted beneath my feet as I followed him, my sister just behind me.

Overhead, the northern-most star shone its brightest. It was the Eve of Olirum. Magic pulsed through our atmosphere from the small celestial event, yet nothing about this night felt magical. I'd lost the Trial. I'd fled from my home. I'd left Norivun behind.

My heart squeezed again so tightly that my breath shuddered. *Norivun, my mate, my love. When will I see you again?* The band constricting my breath cinched more. Just thinking about the time ahead, potentially weeks, months, perhaps full seasons, in which I wouldn't be at his side, made my heart feel like it was shattering all over again.

But I'd had to do it. Even the queen had agreed that I'd needed to leave until I could effectively fight the arranged marriages the king wanted to force upon Norivun and me.

Reality set in more and more with each step that I took. Nausea roiled my gut when I thought of the potential fate that waited for my mate. Norivun was supposed to marry Georgyanna, the spiteful Kroravee witch who'd beaten me in my weakened state during the final test in the Rising Queen Trial.

We'll find a way, my love. We'll find a way to change the paths forged by your father.

And we had to, because even though I'd refused to submit to the fate that King Novakin demanded, I was still bound to the prince, not only by our mate bond but by our bargain.

That single petal that had burned into my skin, then disappeared when we'd been sealed by the gods in a fairy bargain, had yet to make an appearance again, but I knew it would if I failed to uphold my end of our agreement.

I *had* to find a way to continue healing the dying crops, lest the gods punish me. But what I'd done previously couldn't reliably save our land. Only two days ago, I'd visited a field in Isalee that I thought had been healed, but the plants had turned black again and the soil gray. Even more bizarre, when I'd dove my affinity into the land, it had felt as though a veil had been buried deep within the ground. As though that veil had coated the *orem,* and somehow that strange veil had latched onto me and was now encapsulating the power within my gut.

I picked at my fingernails as my feet met firmer soil near the forest. Once again, I tried to access my magic. It rumbled in my belly, still there, but as before, when I tried to coax it upward, it halted when it hit an invisible barrier. A barrier that perhaps wasn't of the gods making at all.

My brow furrowed as I recalled a theory that Norivun and I had come up with—that the netting I'd encountered had come from fae, our theory leaning toward Lord Crimsonale or Lady Wormiful as the culprits.

A twig snapped, jolting me from my thoughts.

"Are you all right?" The fae king glanced over his shoulder as we approached the thick forest. He still hadn't paid my sister any attention, and if I wasn't reeling from all that had happened, I would have taken offense.

"I'm fine."

He inclined his head toward the fjord. "It's a steep walk to reach our land-dwelling city on this island," Drachu said, his voice as deep and rich as his mahogany hair. "Once we arrive, you may rest and recover."

"Why would we need to recover?" Cailis asked, her tone wary.

Drachu smirked. "Your sister's magic is weakened. She needs much recovery."

Cailis and I shared a sharp look.

"How did you know that?" I asked.

"I told you I—"

"Know many things." I sighed. "Yes, you've made that rather apparent."

His sharp canines made an appearance again when he grinned. Smoothing that expression, he lifted an icy branch when we reached the trees. Towering trunks with frosted leaves hung everywhere. It was a plant species I was unfamiliar with, and the more I looked around at the darkened landscape, the more I realized that we were truly in a foreign land.

An instinct begged me to drop to my knees and push my palm against the sandy soil to see if this land also held magic within its depths, but I didn't. I already knew what would happen, and it was too devastating to once again feel my affinities tethered within me.

And it seemed that Drachu apparently knew of my caged power.

An ominous feeling slid through me, but I reminded myself that the fae king had nothing to do with the diminishing *orem* on my home continent.

At least, I didn't think he did.

Heavy breaths soon lifted my chest as we began to climb the landscape, moving higher and higher up one of the steep fjords.

Strange bird calls filled the sky, and it struck me that no other Lochen fae had joined us.

"Where's your clan?" I gripped a slick branch to steady myself on the steep terrain.

"Some in the sea." Drachu's deep voice cut through the

night, his breathing steady and even. "And some are here on land, living in Vockalin."

"Vockalin?" Cailis panted at my back, also struggling with the climb. "Is that the name of your city?"

"It is. We shall be there shortly, if you can manage the climb."

I gave my sister a guilty look. She could have, of course, flown to wherever we were going, but I knew she wouldn't since that would require leaving me and my wingless form behind.

Gulping in air, Cailis asked, "Why would a sea-fairing race build their city so high up a mountain? Wouldn't you want it closer to the water?"

Drachu shook his head. "The climb is needed for our legs when we emerge from the sea. It activates the magic more, making us fully shift into our two-legged form."

My eyes widened. I didn't know much of the Lochen fae, only that they commanded the oceans. "Truly? How many fae in your clan are in Vockalin?"

He shrugged and stepped on a large rock. "I would imagine several hundred, but we shall see when I arrive."

"Do you have many cities?" I asked.

"Of course. We have as many as the Solis, but half of ours are underwater."

"Does that mean there are as many Lochen fae as there are Solis fae?"

Drachu eyed me over his shoulder once more, his green eyes glittering. "If not more."

One look at Cailis confirmed that Drachu had spoken the truth about all that he'd just revealed.

Millions of Solis fae lived on our frozen northern continent, but like the Lochen fae, the Solis were prideful, often ignoring the other fae races in our realm. I couldn't recall finding any books in the castle's library that spoke of the Lochen, Nolus, or Silten fae, at least none that I'd seen. I knew some texts had to exist. We weren't entirely ignorant of one another, but none of my studies when I'd been in school as a child had taught us of our fae neighbors.

All I knew of the Lochen was that they lived in the sea and called most of the islands in our realm home. They also inhabited a small continent, far south of here, and if they stayed submerged in the sea for months on end, they would turn into fish-like creatures. But on land, they appeared as Drachu did—like all fae with pointed ears and two legs. But Drachu's teeth were sharper. His two distinct canines were something no Solis had, and he lacked wings, although I could relate in that aspect. And unlike the Solis, the Lochen weren't bound to white or silver hair and blue eyes. The few Lochen I'd met had varying hair and skin colors, but they all had green irises.

Drachu moved swiftly through the forest, climbing the steep fjord as though it were nothing. Unlike Cailis and me, he wasn't panting.

We climbed and climbed as the night grew darker around us. Sweat dripped between my breasts despite the cool temperature, and even though I'd been training intensively for the past three months with Sandus, one of Norivun's personal guards, the climb wasn't easy.

The fjord finally began to level out as the tip of the mountain neared. Lights flared through the trees.

Cailis and I both stopped, winded, as the fae king halted before a thick curtain of vines.

He draped it to the side, and my eyes widened as the Lochen king grinned. "Welcome to Vockalin, city of sea and sky."

CHAPTER 2 - NORIVUN

"Where did she go?" my father demanded as I stood before him in the throne room of the Court of Winter. Only hours ago I'd been subjected to the insufferable dinner following the Rising Queen Trial, and now I had to listen to this. All after my mate had fled, leaving me to fight in her stead.

Outside, the moon glittered at the late hour. Magic rumbled through my limbs as I waited at the bottom of the throne's stairs. Not because I feared the tyrant wearing the crown, but because the next words I spoke were true. "I already told you. I don't know."

"My guards said she disappeared from her room when they arrived, she and her commoner sister. And in the past few hours, none of my seers have been able to lock firm visions on her." The king ground his teeth. "And scrying hasn't worked either. Nobody can see her."

My father glared at me, but I hid my emotions behind a

steely expression. While I was partly thankful that Ilara's whereabouts were hidden, since it meant she was safe from the Solis king's wrath, it also caused a vicious tide of violence to rise within my soul. Because the male who'd sired me was the cause of my mate's disappearance. He was also the cause of my mate's fear of her future.

King Novakin seethed as veins protruded in his neck. Gray hairs streaked through his mussed white hair at his temples, and the wrinkles around his mouth deepened in his anger. "She's to marry Lord Arcane Woodsbury as I commanded. She's to birth him children to strengthen our race. She *will* do as I demand." He leaned forward more, drumming his fingers on his armrest. "And don't for a moment think I'm believing you. She's your mate, isn't she? Can't mates feel one another? You should know where she is even if nobody else can. You are to bring her to me."

The dragon inside me roared as his fire heated my blood. Nostrils flaring, I drank in my father's scent. Not one trace of terror coated his emotional flavor. Instead, smug satisfaction not only rolled across his expression but also drenched his smell.

Fucking tyrant.

I kept my expression carefully schooled, not allowing even a hint of the animosity I felt to leak onto my face. "We're not fully mated. I can't feel her. So I'm afraid I'm no more inclined to know her whereabouts than you are."

His scowl turned glacial as my mother's back grew rigid. Her fingers curled around her throne's armrests so tight that her knuckles grew white.

"You lie." King Novakin's scowl strengthened. "I know she's your mate."

"Indeed she is, but we're not fully mated, so even you should know what that means."

He scoffed. "You never bedded her? You truly expect me to believe that she never spread her legs for you after what I witnessed on that dais following her first test? Her arousal ran so high I could have scented it a millee away."

It took everything in me not to clench my fists. Fury boiled within me as the mate bond sang.

Kill.

Destroy.

Avenge.

The bond vibrated so palpably within my chest that it felt as though I'd channeled a demon who demanded the king's head.

My dragon snarled in agreement as visions of shifting and snapping the king's body in two nearly made me smile. But I couldn't kill him. I couldn't do anything.

I took a slow, steady breath so as not to let my chest rise too high, then I blew my Outlets open at my back to slightly alleviate the rising magic that was coursing through my veins.

The guards standing near the doors far behind me shuffled nervously. They stood too far away to hear what we spoke of, but they undoubtedly felt my power swirling through the room at my back, but at least my father couldn't.

I couldn't blow my Outlets wider for fear of alerting the king to how much his statement had affected me. So I called upon decades of learned practice at controlling my responses as I smashed the mating instincts down that were threatening to consume me.

After taking one last deep inhale, I inspected my fingernails. "So what would you have me do, Father? Would you like me to scour the continent for her? Perhaps fly back and forth over our vast terrain until I spot her black hair? Surely, that won't take too long. No more than several hundred winters if I'm thorough."

"Watch your tone, Norivun." The king's eyes turned glacial, so cold it was a miracle frost wasn't nipping his eyelashes.

I met his stare, unflinchingly. "She's gone, Father. You chased her away when you demanded she marry a pedophile. I doubt she'll be returning."

He laughed, the sound quick and sharp. "Do you truly expect me to believe that? You're her *mate*. She'll be back to see you sooner or later, even if she's not fully bonded to you. Or, the bond will force *you* to find her. Either way, I will have her back in this court giving me the offspring our continent deserves, and I expect *you* to find her."

I bowed slightly, mockingly. "As you wish, my king, although I cannot promise when this will occur. Ilara is nothing if not stubborn. She may be in hiding for many full seasons before I'm able to track her down, *if* I'm able."

"If you can't do so in a timely manner, then perhaps I shall have to get creative in ways to motivate you." He stretched his arm to the side, then laid his hand atop my mother's. He stroked the back of her hand languidly. "Surely, you can find it in yourself to search faster for her, Norivun.

With your affinities and fully born mate bond, there's no one better suited to the task."

My mother sat completely rigid on her throne, not one muscle moving. My jaw worked, and I nearly broke my composure. My father would probably beat her tonight, perhaps using a whip or chain to make the process more painful. All to prove his point—that he could, and it would be far worse if I refused his command.

The king had made my mother bleed and suffer so many times I'd lost count, and his abuse only strengthened until I did as he wished.

But the look on my mother's face now—the way she regarded me with absolute steel in her eyes—made me pause.

Her expression practically screamed at me to defy the king.

I knew she'd helped Ilara escape only hours ago. I knew she'd used the only potion she possessed to give my mate a way out. And now . . .

I had a feeling she would rather suffer under my father's malicious hand than allow me to bend to his will.

Frustration threatened to make me snarl because I couldn't bear to see him abuse her, and he knew that.

If only her affinities weren't tethered, she would be able to reach into my mind and tell me what she was thinking, but whatever spell the king had cast upon her all those winters ago kept her caged. As it was, her magic was so stifled that at best she was able to pick up hints and feelings in others, occasionally able to decipher someone's thoughts. It was nothing like what she was truly capable of when her affinities weren't suppressed.

Bowing again, I gave my father the answer he wanted. "Very well, Father. I will endeavor to find Ilara and bring her back."

If nothing else, my ruse would buy me extra time while I considered my next move.

King Novakin smiled smugly and removed his hand from my mother's. "See to it that you do. You have one month to have her bowing before me, Norivun. One month or your mother will fall under *unfortunate* circumstances."

I stilled. "My wedding to Georgyanna is in one month."

"Exactly." The king gave a triumphant sneer.

"You want Ilara present to witness my marriage to another."

"Perhaps. It would be the least she deserves for defying me."

My nostrils flared as hatred burned a fiery path through my insides while vicious magic flooded my limbs. The king threatening me by using my mother was nothing new, but now his threats were also extending to my mate. He wanted Ilara returned to the court so he could not only control her, but so she would be forced to witness my marriage to Georgyanna.

Sadistic bastard.

Seething, I turned on my heel and strode toward the throne room doors, keeping my wings tucked in tight and pulled up high. Tension radiated down my spine.

Go to the training room.

Sparring with my guards was probably the only thing that would keep me from blowing up the entire castle in an explosion of power. Following that, several strong glasses of leminai or whiskey were in order.

It would have to do, for now, even though what I truly needed was to feel Ilara's silken skin sliding beneath my fingertips, to hear her laugh when I tickled the sensitive area beneath her ear, and to bask in the fierceness of her love that was only the tip of the iceberg of what I felt for her.

She might not be fully bonded to me yet, but she was my love. My mate. My queen.

I would die before I allowed my father to hurt her, which meant I needed to find her not because I was willing to bend to my father, but because I needed her warned of what was to come.

Unbeknownst to Ilara, my father was going to hunt the realm for her. He wasn't going to let her go quietly. And that was something my mate had never thought he would do.

It gave me pause, though, his undo interest in her. It was one thing to want her bred, but it was another thing entirely to spend every second since her departure demanding that she be found.

The king was up to something.

But I didn't know what.

The guards opened the doors seamlessly when I neared, and my swift movements made the letter Ilara had written me shift in my pocket. It was carefully tucked within my tunic and under a thick illusion spell so that no one could see it, even if my tunic were ripped off me.

I cherished the feel of it pressed to me now. I wouldn't fail her.

A malevolent smile lifted my lips. I would suck my father's soul from his body, shred it into ribbons, then pitch it down to Lucifer in the underworld before I ever allowed the king to lay a hand on my mate.

"MY PRINCE!" Georgyanna called. "Can you believe this? How could I possibly be married in fabric this dreadful? Do come and look at this material. And to think this *lady's servant*"—she sneered the words—"thinks this is suitable material for a wedding gown. It's preposterous, don't you think?"

My nostrils flared when Georgyanna's prideful scent hit me. *Wedding gown material? Already?* Mother Below, I hated this witch. My mate had only been gone hours and already Georgyanna had taken over Ilara's chambers and was planning our fucking wedding.

My betrothed sat on the couch in the Exorbiant Chamber. The stars glittered outside, above the courtyard, on this Eve of Olirum.

Georgyanna's lithe figure was stretched out. Silver hair, pinned back with sparkling clips, glittered in the light. It was the hair choice she often wore, and my guess was that she knew it amplified her delicate features and full lips.

I still thought she looked hideous.

Daiseeum kneeled in front of her, and all I could think

was that the Kroravee female was sitting in my mate's seat, and it was enough to drive me fucking mad. If Meegana or Beatrice had resided in this chamber it wouldn't have bothered me nearly as much since they were Ilara's friends, but instead, the other two Rising Queen Trial participants were to continue occupying their previous chambers while they awaited their arranged marriages. Only Georgyanna had been moved at my father's insistence, right after Ilara had fled nonetheless.

Truth be told, I wasn't even sure how I ended up in the Exorbiant Chamber. I'd been on my way to the training rooms following the disastrous conversation with my father when I'd been told I was needed here, so I annoyingly ventured to this part of my wing only to realize it was because Georgyanna wanted me to look at wedding dress material. Already.

The floorboards vibrated beneath my toes as I opened my Outlets more.

"Prince Norivun?" Georgyanna called again. "Do come see."

"I'll have to pass," I said, striding toward the door as Daiseeum held up another roll of fabric, her lips wobbling in a plastered smile as she presented a third swath of fabric to the manipulative witch.

"What do you think of this one, my lady?" Daiseeum asked in a trembling tone.

Georgyanna rolled her eyes and swatted it away. "Truly, you can't be serious? Is there anyone in this castle that knows *anything* about fashion?"

Daiseeum's lips pursed tightly as color coated her cheeks, but she set it down and forcefully pulled out another roll of fabric as I stalked from the room.

I cast a sympathetic look at the servant before leaving.

"Waste of my fucking time," I said beneath my breath as I exited to the hallway. I needed to find my guards so I could spar and work off this steam. It was the only way I would be able to think clearly, because I needed to figure out a way to keep my mate safe.

CHAPTER 3 - ILARA

The city of Vockalin sat atop the flattened mountaintop as the forest fell into a lush carpet tumbling down the mountain's sides. A glittering array of rock-like homes with textured siding filled our view. Above, the three crescent moons glowed with pearly light as the night sky shone so brightly that it felt as though all one needed to do was lift a finger to touch the stars.

The northernmost star shone so brightly on this magical eve. It was even more stunning this high up. My thoughts drifted to my mate again. *Are you looking at the night sky too right now, Norivun?*

That band threatened to squeeze my chest again. I took a deep, shuddering breath and forced myself not to dwell.

Distant waves crashed on the beach below, and faint beating music strummed toward us, as though someone was playing drums of various depths and cadences.

The hypnotic waves and drumbeat made me want to shift

and sway. The sound was truly mesmerizing as we stepped onto a path leading into the city. I focused on the music, using it to help alleviate the ache cleaving my heart in two.

Magic swam in the air, heating our surroundings. No snow lay on the ground, and the frost-nipped leaves had vanished to reveal iridescent grass and bare petals of soft pink, bright turquoise, subtle lilac, and translucent green. *Orem* either existed within this soil, or the Lochen fae had their own magic to keep their land blooming in the midst of winter.

Ahead, Lochen fae walked about, their legs no different than mine or Cailis's. Some carried baskets as they dipped between shops and eating establishments. Others carried sleeping children on their backs as they hung laundry to dry in the warm evening breeze of their small yards.

The females appeared as the males, scantily clad in only strips of fabric, but their breasts were covered, and long hair hung down their backs.

"Do you not feel the cold?" I asked as we moved closer to the outer buildings.

Drachu shook his head. "No. Our *channa* heats our blood, keeping us warm in the most frozen of seas and coldest of lands. Clothing isn't necessary. We've merely adapted it as customary among other fae."

"What's *channa*?" Cailis asked curiously.

"Intrinsic Lochen magic. Other fae do not possess it."

My nose twitched when sizzling scents of cooking food wafted to greet us. It smelled foreign and fragrant, and I wondered what the Lochen's diet typically consisted of.

Despite Vockalin being small, it was a vibrant city full of life if the bustle was any indication. And to think that this was only one of many island cities the Lochen called home.

"Where would you like my sister and I to stay?" I asked when Drachu led us deeper into the mountainous village.

"At my residence," Drachu replied.

Several Lochen stopped to watch us, their brows furrowing as they assessed Cailis's wings. All of them wore minimal clothing, had green eyes, and varying skin shades. A few gawked, and more than one scowled in our direction.

"Do you live here when you're on land?" Cailis tucked her wings in tighter when a child ran up behind her and tried to run his finger across her wing's leathery black membrane.

The child's mother snatched him away, then bared her sharp canines at us.

Drachu's lips downturned as he assessed the growing crowd. "These females are my guests. I expect them to be treated as such."

The female smoothed her lips, hiding her teeth, but it didn't stop her glare before she led her child away.

Other Lochen around us all stepped back, most of their angry and distrustful expressions faltering as Drachu strode forward. The Lochen king nodded to the fae who made eye contact with him, but he didn't introduce us or tell them more about why we were here.

Also surprising, no one bowed to Drachu as the Solis did to King Novakin. Instead, each fairy we passed brought a thumb to their mouth before bringing their thumb to their forehead. I wondered if it was the same as when Solis brought a fist to one's chest before bowing—a sign of respect.

"To answer your question, if I'm staying on this island chain, then yes, I stay here," the king said over his shoulder after we passed the crowd. "I have homes on most of our lands."

My eyes bugged out. "How many homes is that?"

"Forty-two." His lips twitched. "Are you unfamiliar with what island chains we call home? We also have a continent south of here, and then there are the cities beneath the waves. I have many areas of residence."

My cheeks reddened that I was so ignorant of the Lochen, especially since their king had offered us refuge.

"Sabreeny!" Drachu called.

Ahead, a female straightened near a home. Long brown hair tumbled down her back, and a simple band of cloth covered her full breasts while a short skirt—if it could be called that—concealed her lower half. The minuscule attire left an abundance of her creamy flesh on display.

The house behind her was small and simple and rose from the mountain as though cut from the rock itself. Vibrant purple shells covered the home's entire exterior, and upon closer inspection, all of the other houses and buildings also had outside walls covered with shells or sea rock.

Millions of seashells had to be in this city, and each home seemed inclined to favor a shell of a single color. Some were as bright as the purple ones before us. Others were green, yellow, red, and every shade in between, but some were more subdued, favoring shades of white, gray, or black.

Cailis fingered one of the violet shells on the corner of Drachu's house. "Is this from the Tala Sea?"

"It is," Drachu replied.

The female Drachu had addressed earlier, Sabreeny, cut Cailis a sharp look when my sister's fingers continued to trail along the home's exterior. Sabreeny said something to Drachu in a language I couldn't understand. In response, Drachu scowled at her and said something just as sharply in return. But instead of the female dipping her head in acquiescence, she merely gave the king her back and stalked into the house.

"You'll have to excuse her," Drachu said, his tone irritated. "She's my newest *salivar,* and she doesn't want any other females in my home."

Cailis and I shared a look before I said, "Salivar?"

"What do you Solis call them? Let me think." He cocked his head. "Ah yes, concubine, or is it mistress?"

I blushed, my cheeks flaming. "Ah, I see."

Drachu laughed, a rich, booming sound. "I forget how squeamish the Solis can be when it comes to fucking. I should share with you now that I bed many females in my clan and have dozens of salivars. I would also be more than willing to bed you if you so desire." His eyes heated, and my stomach dropped.

I took a step back. "I'm mated to the death warlord."

His eyebrow arched. "Is that true?" He inched closer to me, his nostrils flaring. "I don't detect his scent on you."

My sister cleared her throat, and I couldn't tell if she was trying to suppress a laugh or smother a snort.

"Our bond isn't completed." I ran a hand through my hair, wishing I could sink through this mountain. "But he's my mate. He's fully bonded to me."

Drachu cocked an eyebrow. "I take it you're giving me fair warning what he would do if he learned that I fucked his mate?"

Cailis did snort this time, and one look at my sister told me she was definitely trying to keep from laughing.

At least one of us was enjoying my humiliation.

I glowered at her, and she finally smoothed her expression. While I wasn't a virgin, I wasn't exactly experienced, and my sister knew that.

I forced my posture to straighten as I looked Drachu in the eye. "I will not be bedding you, my . . . err, my king. But we haven't come unprepared. There's no need for us to inconvenience your salivar." I gestured toward the pack Cailis carried that held all of our carefully stowed items that we'd acquired during the past few months, just in case we ever found ourselves in the position we were currently in. "We are just as happy to pay for accommodation at an inn or for a room in someone's home."

Drachu waved a hand. "Nonsense, you are my guests. I shall have Sabreeny ready the guestroom for you, and then in the morning, we shall endeavor to discover what's trapped your magic so that it may once again be freed."

My jaw dropped as my heartbeat sped up. "Do you know how to do that?"

"Perhaps."

Hope surged through me. Maybe I could reacquire my

affinities quickly, which meant I could return to Norivun much sooner than I'd thought possible. "And you would really help me free my affinities?"

"Of course."

But just as quickly as my hope appeared, a moment of apprehension filled me. "Why would you offer to help me like that?"

But instead of answering, Drachu merely called out something to Sabreeny in their language before waving Cailis and me forward. "Come. The night grows late."

CHAPTER 4 - ILARA

"Drachu! Aww, *siv*, Drachu! *Siv!*"

I looked at my sister lying in the bed across from me in the guestroom at Sabreeny's residence. The dark night sky glittered through the window as the distant sound of crashing waves reached my ears. Well, they reached my ears when Sabreeny wasn't moaning or screaming.

Even though the hour was late and exhaustion made my eyelids heavy, it was rather hard to sleep with the racket from Drachu's bedroom chambers. The occasional rumbling walls from his power didn't help either. Although, I had to admit, the fae king had stamina. They'd been going at it for at least an hour as Sabreeny got plundered senseless by the Lochen king.

Trying to ignore their carnal exuberance, I rolled on my side to face my sister. "Why do you think Drachu is so willing to help me?"

She sighed. In the shadows, I could barely make out her features. "I don't know. I've been wondering the same."

"Are you certain that he was being honest when he said he'd give us safe haven?"

Cailis straightened her wings more behind her, grumbling when they hit the wall. Lochen beds were definitely not made to accommodate wings. "Yes, he was being truthful as far as my affinity could tell. But when you asked him about using you for his personal gain or keeping us prisoners, his aura bled slightly gray."

A shiver ran through me. "What do you think that means?"

"I'm not sure, but I don't think his intentions are entirely noble."

I nodded as Sabreeny let out another long wail. "I don't think so either. Why would a king be waiting for me and bend over backward to help me? And what did he mean about me joining his clan? I don't intend to stay here indefinitely. I'm still Solis and want to return home. I *will* help Norivun replenish the *orem* and defy the king's arranged marriage demands."

"I know you will, which means we need to be careful. I want to think we can trust Drachu to help us, but I think being wary is the smarter plan." Cailis let out an aggrieved sigh when another loud moan followed by a magical tremor rattled the windowpane. "Blessed Mother. Do you think she's always this loud? The female screams more than a babe upon being born, and it's non-stop. You would think she would have lost her voice by now."

"She's probably doing it so we know why Drachu's allowed her to live here. He did say she was a new salivar. Perhaps she feels threatened by us."

"Do you think if I tell her we're not a threat, that she'll give it a rest so we can get some sleep?"

I muffled a laugh, then slammed my pillow to my ears when the concubine let out another piercing sound of ecstasy. "Something tells me she won't take kindly to that."

Despite the humor in the situation, my heart cracked, and not for the first time since their noisy lovemaking had started, agony cut me deep. Hearing them reminded me of what I'd left behind, and the weight of what I'd lost threatened to consume me once more.

Norivun and I were supposed to be doing exactly what Drachu and his concubine were currently engaging in. If the Rising Queen Trial had gone the way it undoubtedly would have if my affinities hadn't been suppressed, I would have won the final test and been engaged to the prince.

At this very moment, I could have been bedding Prince Norivun as the bond fully tethered itself to me. I would be feeling his emotions, would be able to detect where he was in the realm, and his scent would have collided with mine, letting all other fae know that we were mated.

The crushing realization of what I'd lost hit me all at once.

Tears filled my eyes. I hastily turned away and wiped them before Cailis could notice.

Thankfully, blessedly, Drachu's roar broke through Sabreeny's screams a moment later. A gigantic shudder vibrated the entire home, and then the house fell silent as their mating session *finally* came to an end.

"Wow," Cailis whispered. "I definitely need to find a male who's capable of that. I had no idea sex could last that long."

"And to think I could have been experiencing something like that," I whispered to myself, but Cailis still heard me.

"Ock, I'm sorry, Ilara." My sister's sorrowful tone cut through the shadows in the room. "But don't lose faith. We'll figure out a way to untrap your affinities, and then we'll discover what it was you felt in that Isalee field. Like you said, I think that's the key to this. And once that's sorted perhaps the king will see that you truly are the strongest female fairy on our continent and *you* should be the one marrying the prince, not Georgyanna."

I nodded and used that reminder to pull myself from the melancholy that was threatening to overwhelm me. Maybe my sister was right. Maybe there was still hope that I could marry the prince.

Because I was convinced that whatever netting had been buried deep within the soil was causing our crops to die. It'd felt as though it were encapsulating the *orem*, which meant everyone had been wrong. The *orem* wasn't vanishing. It was being contained or perhaps buried so far that it couldn't find its way to the surface. And if I could figure out how to free it, maybe King Novakin would decide I was the better match for his son.

I nibbled on my lip as my thoughts drifted back to the

field and the deeply buried veil, as a singular question probed my mind—*where* had that veil come from?

Sᴀʙʀᴇᴇɴʏ ᴡᴀs sᴛᴀɴᴅɪɴɢ in the kitchen when I ventured out of our guestroom the next morning. Her long brown hair hung to her waist, and her sharp green eyes darted to me the second I stepped into the room.

Bright sunlight streamed through the window overlooking the sink. The kitchen was small with only the basic necessities, pretty much the exact opposite of the Solis king's castle.

"Good morning," I offered.

She sneered, not gracing me with a response. She continued making tea before pouring it into a single cup. Beside the teapot was a plate of white fish with a few slices of bread and what I guessed was a fruit. The purple flesh had black seeds in the middle and was a species I didn't recognize.

"Are you preparing breakfast?" I inched closer to her and made sure to keep my voice friendly. "I would be happy to help."

Sabreeny whirled around. "And allow a wingless *ingamy* to touch my king's food?" She scoffed and grabbed the plate off the counter before carrying it along with the teacup right past me. Her shoulder knocked into me, and the movement took me so much by surprise that I slammed into the wall behind me.

"Ouch," I muttered, rubbing my shoulder.

But Sabreeny just stalked back through the living area, passing my sister on the way, before disappearing into the hallway that led to the bedroom chambers.

"What was that all about?" Cailis asked, coming up to my side.

I rolled my eyes. "Since I'm a wingless ingamy, I guess I'm not worthy of touching anything Drachu consumes."

"Ingamy?" Cailis went to the counter and grabbed two cups off a shelf. "What's that?"

"I'm assuming it's a derogatory word for Solis fae."

"You would be right," a deep voice said from behind me.

I whirled around, my heart thumping since I hadn't heard anyone approach.

A male Lochen fairy stood at the kitchen's threshold. Blond hair covered his head, and his bright green eyes assessed me. Like Drachu, his skin was brown but a shade lighter than the king's.

"Oh, good morning," I said, my hands fluttering self-consciously to my hair since he'd caught me so unaware.

He smirked. "We don't wish each other good morning in the Lochen culture. It beckons bad luck."

"It does?" My eyes widened. Of course, that was probably one more reason Sabreeny hated me.

The male drifted past me, moving silently until he reached Cailis's side, where he lifted the teapot. "Wishing someone a good morning is believed to anger the gods. The gods determine what our mornings will bring. Not fae."

I offered a weak smile. "I apologize. I'm afraid I'm ignorant of your ways."

He inclined his head. "Naturally. My king tells me you're mated to the death warlord."

"I am, sort of."

He arched an eyebrow, and I blushed.

"The bond's not fully sealed," my sister clarified with a barely controlled smile. "But *he's* fully mated to her."

I cast Cailis a side-eye. I knew she hadn't added that remark offhandedly. She wanted to ensure the Lochen understood that if something happened to me, the Bringer of Darkness would be who they answered to.

"Ah." The male dumped out the old tea and proceeded to make a fresh pot. "So you're saying that sooner or later, he will show up on our shores."

I resisted the urge to pick at my fingernails as the male set the teapot over a small fire in the tiny hearth. What I wouldn't give to know how Norivun was doing or what the Solis king was up to. But I didn't even want to think about Georgyanna or the wedding preparations that were undoubtedly underway. Just imagining her smug satisfaction made my blood boil, not to mention the threat she'd given me at the end of the final test—a threat I had no doubt she would enthusiastically pursue.

"May we help?" Cailis said when the male pulled a plate from the shelf. "And I'm Cailis Seary by the way, and this is my sister, Ilara."

Both of us automatically brought fists to our chests before we bowed.

Surprisingly, the male mimicked the Solis gesture before saying, "Tylen. It's a pleasure to make your acquaintance."

I cocked my head. "Do you have a last name, Tylen?"

"No, unlike the Solis royals, we don't feel the need to add a dozen names to our first one."

My eyes widened. "You're royal?"

"Indeed. Drachu is my father."

"Apologies," I murmured as we both dipped into curtsies.

Cailis canted her head. "So you're a prince?"

Tylen arched a blond eyebrow. "Technically, yes, but I share that title with over fifty other males."

"Fifty?" Surely, I'd misheard him. "You're telling me that there are fifty other princes? But that would mean that Drachu's sired fifty males with the queen."

That had to be impossible. Fae were lucky to birth more than half a dozen children in our lifetimes, and the Nolus fae birthed even less in their short lifespans. Female cycles could be sporadic, and conception wasn't guaranteed even if one had a fertile womb. The fact that Cailis, Tormesh, and I had been born so close together was nearly unheard of.

"The queen didn't birth most of my father's children. Many of his concubines did." Tylen began to strain the tea and pour it into cups. "My mother lives on an island far south of here. She's been a concubine of Drachu's for over seventy seasons."

Cailis and I shared a surprised yet intrigued look. I nibbled on my bottom lip, not sure how to ask what I was wondering. But I decided I was never going to learn the

Lochen culture if I didn't voice my curiosities. "So . . . even children sired from a concubine are considered legitimate?"

Tylen's lips twitched, and I was glad he found my question amusing versus offensive. "Indeed. 'Tis another way we differ from the Solis in addition to our lack of names."

Cailis frowned as her wings caught the sunlight, making their black shade appear brown. "But how do you keep everyone straight without more than one name?"

"Because each name in our culture is unique. Nobody shares names."

Cailis snorted. "How's that possible?"

Tylen poured tea into three cups and smirked. "Creativity."

Curiosity again getting the better of me, I joined him at the counter as he pulled white fish from the same small jar that Sabreeny had used and began dispersing it onto three plates. The delicate meat was stored in a salty-smelling liquid, and surprisingly, the scent wasn't bad even though I'd never been fond of sustenance from the sea.

"Surely, there are some Lochen fae with the same name, perhaps named the same by accident?" I asked.

Tylen placed slices of fish on the plate, then grabbed a large black-skinned fruit from the counter. He cut through it with a sharp knife, revealing the same purple flesh and black seeds that Sabreeny had prepared for the king.

"No, nobody shares a name in our culture. When a babe is born, they're brought to Vemil Brasea, where the parents present them, along with the name they've chosen, to the palace's scribe. If that name is already in existence in our records, the request is denied and the parents must choose a new name. Until they do, the babe remains nameless."

"Where's Vemil Brasea?" I asked as he gestured to the table and chairs near the far wall.

"It's beneath the waves in the Adriastic Sea. Vemil Brasea is our capital."

Cailis and I both shared a fascinated look and pulled out chairs to sit beside Tylen. As we sipped on tea and ate the sweet purple fruit, nutty bread, and flaky fish that was surprisingly tasty, we asked Tylen relentless questions. It helped that he was so willing to answer, something that I found not only perplexing but unusual. Normally, fae of the different races weren't welcoming nor willing to appease guests on their continents or islands. Sabreeny's reaction to me was more on par with what I would expect. Not Tylen's easy smiles and open responses.

Of course, halfway through our conversation, Sabreeny's moans began again, and the house shuddered from time to time with Drachu's power. Doing my best to ignore the carnal sounds coming from down the hall, I concentrated on everything Tylen was saying.

"So, since Drachu has so many children, there are over one hundred princes and princesses vying for his throne?" I asked as I popped the last bite of bread into my mouth.

"No," Tylen replied. "Just because I was sired by Drachu does not make me in line for the throne, nor does his oldest child automatically wear the crown when my father steps down. Even the 'legitimate' children, as you call them, those born by the queen, aren't in line for the throne. Our king is chosen by the Lochen, not by who births them."

My jaw dropped until it felt as though it hit the floor. "You're telling me that when Drachu steps down, *any* Lochen fairy may become the next king? But how? How can that possibly be?"

An amused smile tilted his lips as he began to clear the dishes. It wasn't lost on me that there were no servants here despite the king being in residence. "The Lochen fae value strength, courage, and a cunning mind. Just because I was born from a male who possesses such traits doesn't mean that I'll bear them as well. So, to keep our kingdom strong, an election is held when each king passes or steps down. Those placed on the ballot are chosen based upon whether or not they're of good health, how they've acted in battles, the deeds they've done that show they possess the wit and cleverness to lead such a mighty race, and so forth."

Cailis looked as bewildered as me when she asked, "So any male can be king?"

"Correct, and any female can be queen. We aren't exclusive to genders. If a female possesses those characteristics above a male, she may rule our race."

My shock was so complete that for a moment, I couldn't speak. My sister seemed to be in a similar state because she gaped like a fish.

"I've never heard of such a thing," I finally said.

Tylen shrugged. "I'm not surprised. We don't often have other fae races venture to our shores. Our way of life is too difficult for the land-dwellers. Besides, you wouldn't survive the journey to our oceanic cities as you cannot breathe under water."

I shrugged. "True, but—"

"Ah, I see that you're all awake." Drachu strode into the kitchen, a loose robe covering his body. It was partially draped open, revealing his strong muscular chest beneath. "Tylen, have you informed them of what we'll be doing today?"

Tylen shook his head and leaned against the counter, crossing his arms. His blond hair shone like gold in the sun. "Not yet. We became caught up in questions about our culture."

Sabreeny sauntered into the room behind Drachu, her hips swaying provocatively. Mussed hair trailed around her shoulders, and her lips appeared swollen as she placed a hand possessively on Drachu's shoulder. Daggers practically shot from her eyes when she glared at me and Cailis.

"Sabreeny, fetch me my shoes, will you?" The king ran a hand along her plump bottom and squeezed.

She nipped his ear, her tongue sliding out to graze the skin before she purred, "As you wish, my king."

She flounced down the hall, and I glanced warily toward where the salivar had disappeared to.

"So, what are your plans today?" I asked the king as I began to contemplate what Cailis and I would do from here. Regardless of what Drachu and Tylen were planning, I needed to find a way to recover my affinities, with or without their help.

"We're venturing to the Adrall Temple," Drachu replied.

"May I ask why you're going to a temple?" Cailis's eyebrows rose.

"Not just Tylen and me are going. *All* of us will venture there." Drachu smiled. "And we're going there to help Ilara. You do want your affinities freed, correct?" He gave me a pointed look.

My brow furrowed. "Yes, that's of utmost importance, but how is a temple going to help that?"

Drachu smiled, his canines glinting in the sun. "Because at the Adrall Temple, we can call upon the gods. If God Zorifel will heed our plea, I believe he may help with unlocking your magic."

CHAPTER 5 - NORIVUN

Early morning clouds swirled above me as I paced in the courtyard outside of the front gates of the castle. Dawn had arrived, the sun cresting the horizon, and cold air blew around me. I'd barely slept. Last night, I'd found my guards, sparred with them, and done my best to work off the heightened energy that had been spiraling through me following the encounter with my father and Georgyanna, but it hadn't been enough.

Tension still radiated along my wings. I couldn't stop thinking about my father's undue interest in Ilara. It quite simply didn't make sense.

The castle's commander had his guards practicing drills nearby. Every now and then, the commander glanced my way, but the darkness gathering around my shoulders seemed to deter him from conversing.

Good. I didn't want anyone's company right now. I needed to find a way to protect my mate. And I hadn't the slightest idea how to do that since I knew tracking her wasn't an option, thanks to the potion my mother had given her.

Turning, I strode back toward the far wall when a shuffle of feet came from behind me.

"Pacing a path into the snow, my prince? Is your morning already off to that bad of a start?"

My lip curled when Michas Crimsonale's comment flowed through the breeze. Wheeling around, I smirked. "Nothing better to do with your free time than bother me? Why am I not surprised?"

Michas leaned against the outer stone wall and crossed his arms. Thick, wide wings were tucked into his back, and his round eyes practically alighted with glee. "Am I bothering you, my prince? I do apologize."

I growled. "Fuck off, Michas." I swiveled on my heel and paced the other way.

"Does your disagreeable mood have anything to do with Ilara's disappearance?"

My dragon snarled inside me, and it took all of my control not to let his smoke puff through my nose. Facing the despicable fairy, I said quietly, "What did you say?"

Michas pushed away from the wall and sauntered toward me. "I hear that Lady Seary left you." He buffed his fingernails on his tunic. "Such a pity. I did enjoy her company."

In a blink, I was standing right before him. "Mind your tongue, Michas. That's my mate you're speaking of."

He arched an eyebrow. "Yet you're to marry Lady Endalaver."

I fisted my hands, and a dark curl of pleasure rolled

through me when I imagined punching his straight nose right down his throat.

Michas sighed. "Such lack of control. What's happened to you? You were never this easy to rile before."

For the briefest moment, the young lord's tone changed, as though he was contemplating my reaction versus reveling in it and was actually disappointed that I wasn't harder to provoke.

I sighed. "What do you want, Michas?" I turned away, having no intention of waiting for his response.

"I had an interesting conversation with your mate on our last Trial date," he called.

Something in his tone made me pause. Stiffening, I didn't face him, but I cocked my head to listen.

"She said something that was quite surprising." His tone lowered, his words barely a whisper. "She hinted that perhaps neither of you is loyal to the king. I thought she'd been playing a game, but after seeing what the king is planning to do to you and her by marrying you to others, I'm starting to wonder if perhaps it wasn't."

My attention pricked to the castle commander and guards, but they were practicing aerial maneuvers, too high in the sky to hear our conversation even if one of them had a sound sensory affinity. Still, not taking any chances, I called upon my air element and formed a silencing Shield around us. Turning, I faced Michas squarely again.

"Ilara told me about your conversation," I replied.

Michas studied me, his expression guarded. "What did she say?"

Frowning, I searched his expression, looking for a hint of deceit or possibly malicious intent, yet I found none, and I remembered what Ilara had said, that even though Michas was a prick, she thought in this aspect, he wasn't being a trickster. Inhaling, I scented his emotions.

Wariness, nervousness, and . . . hope.

Interesting.

I took a deep breath and said quietly, "Ilara told me that she was hoping you would open up to her and share what you know of the crops and the future of our kingdom."

I waited on bated breath. To think I'd just revealed that to Michas Crimsonale of all fae was appalling, but Ilara had been insistent that Michas seemed genuine in this aspect—something I'd never been inclined to believe.

Michas cocked his head, his expression still closed off. "It is peculiar, don't you think, that the crops dying has led to talks of invasion?"

My nostrils flared. "An invasion your father supports."

"True." Michas nodded. "But invasion was not something we'd ever supported until the state of our land came into jeopardy."

I canted my head. The Crimsonales had always craved power. That was nothing new, but they were still proud Solis fae as Michas was implying. They always had been, and like most Solis, they hated the thought of depending on others.

I stepped closer to him and narrowed my eyes. "What are you alluding to, Michas?"

The young lord glanced over his shoulder, toward the commander and guards, but they were still in the sky.

I crossed my arms. "I cast a silencing Shield. They can't hear us."

"You did?" Michas glanced upward, and I smirked.

"You can't see it."

Glowering, he replied, "I'm just saying that it's strange for our crops to die so suddenly, something that's never happened in the history of our land. It does make one wonder *who* is truly behind it. At least, that's what my father and I are starting to question."

"You're saying it's not the gods killing our *orem*?"

He shrugged. "It could be, I suppose, but when have the gods ever failed us in that aspect?"

"Never."

"Exactly." He turned on his heel and began to stroll away, then called over his shoulder, "Like I said, it does make you wonder."

I watched him until he disappeared, for the first time really reconsidering everything I'd ever felt and thought about the Crimsonales while also recalling what Ilara had told me he said on their last date.

Afterward, she'd told me Michas had been on the verge of revealing something to her, that Lord Crimsonale—the archon of Osaravee Territory and Michas's father—had concerns about something, but then Georgyanna had interrupted them.

I placed my hands on my hips as Michas's form grew distant. Snow began to fall, collecting on the ground in white puffs.

My brow furrowed, and I wondered if the theory Ilara

and I had come up with—that Lord Crimsonale and Lady Wormiful were behind the dying *orem*—was untrue. Why else would Michas share all of what he had if his father was trying to hide his involvement.

My frown deepened. Perhaps Ilara and I were wrong. Maybe it wasn't the Crimsonales at all, and instead was someone else entirely.

But then the question became, *who?*

THE MID-MORNING SKY shone brightly through my window as I paced my bedroom chambers, my mind buzzing with barely contained magic. I'd been pacing most of the morning, even more so after that strange conversation with Michas, and I'd barely been able to sit still at the morning council meeting.

It didn't help that I was on a deadline. It only added to my agitation. *One month.* I had one month to present my mate to the king, or I would have to watch my mother suffer from unspeakable torture.

Because I had no doubt my father would sink that low if I failed to find Ilara.

But why did he want Ilara so badly?

I tore a hand through my hair as everything swirled through my mind like black smoke. My father's obsession with Ilara's disappearance wasn't like him. Last night, following Ilara's escape, it'd been all he'd talked about. My father had even spent the entire council meeting this morning discussing how she could be found. And during that meeting, Lord Crimsonale had given me peculiar glances more than once, making me wonder if Michas had told him about our conversation at dawn.

I concentrated on my father's obsessive interest in Ilara again. Hundreds of fae had managed to avoid King Novakin's wrath before. It was inevitable with a continent as large as ours that it would happen, but whenever that had previously occurred, the king had sent court guards to find the fleeing fae, or if their crimes were great enough, he would send me and have me kill them on sight.

In the interim, while we were searching for the fairy, my father would typically forget about the matter until the guards returned with the criminal.

With Ilara, though, it was different, and I didn't think it was just because she was a powerful fairy. He'd had powerful fae thwart him before, and he'd never shown an extreme reaction.

Yet, with Ilara, the king was beyond livid that she'd fled, so much so that he hadn't been able to control his rage when Lord Crimsonale had mentioned at the meeting that perhaps it was best that she'd departed since she and I were mates. He'd actually empathized at having to watch a mated male and female be wed to others.

Blessed Mother, Lord Crimsonale had actually sounded *sympathetic*.

The king, however, hadn't been. My father's face had mottled in rage at that comment, something that rarely occurred. To the public, the council, and the nobles of our court, my father always wore his mask of a strong, unfailing leader. His sadistic, controlling side was never on display.

But it had been this morning.

Because of Ilara.

My nostrils flared as I thought back to everything that had been occurring of late. I replayed every conversation, every council meeting, every moment that the king had heard and learned of what Ilara was and what she was doing over and over in my mind, looking for something that would give me a clue as to what was really going on.

And Michas's comment earlier this morning kept coming back to me.

"When have the gods ever failed us in that aspect?"

He was right. They never had failed to replenish our *orem*. Not until lately.

"What else do you know, Michas?" I mumbled to myself then blazed a path toward the door.

Striding from my room, I burst down my corridor on a gust of my air affinity. I didn't stop until I reached the wing where archons and nobles stayed while they were at court.

When I reached Michas's door, I pounded twice on it.

Footsteps reached my ears, letting me know wards didn't surround his room.

The second his door cracked, I pushed through it.

"Excuse me," Michas said indignantly.

I didn't reply and instead closed the door behind me, then cast a solid air Shield around us so nobody could hear our conversation.

"Tell me what you know," I all but growled. "Tell me what you know of the vanishing *orem*. All of it."

Michas's mouth opened and closed like a fish. He was in fencing clothes, and I guessed he'd been about to venture to the training rooms.

"Please," I added when he remained silent. "It's important." When he continued to study me, I said in a rush, "I don't ally with the king. I never have. If I could force my father off the throne, I would."

Michas's eyes widened, and he cast a frantic look around.

"My air Shield is keeping this conversation quiet. Nobody can hear anything we say."

His chest rose quickly, but when he reached a hand out and encountered a solid wall of air, some of the tension radiating on his face lessened. Dropping his hand to his side, Michas said, "Do you truly mean that, about the king?"

"I do. My father's a tyrant. Only most don't know that."

Michas's lips thinned. "He's more than a tyrant. My father heard—" He paused and glanced around the room again.

"What? Tell me?"

Michas studied me again. "You truly aren't loyal to the king?"

"No," I snarled. "Now fucking *tell me* what you know."

The young lord took another deep breath. "I'll deny this conversation if it ever comes back to me."

"Noted."

"You can't pin anything on me."

"I know, and I don't plan to. I just want to know what's happening with our continent."

Michas gave a curt nod as sunlight shining through the window glinted off the curls in his hair. "My father overheard King Novakin one night, over a full season ago, speaking to someone in the hall when the king didn't know he was near. It was late, almost the middle of the night, and everyone had retired to their chambers hours before, but my father couldn't sleep so had gone down to the kitchens to get some warm milk. He'd taken a servant passage since it was faster, a hall typically only used during the day, when he overheard the king talking to someone in hushed tones near the bottom of the stairwell. He was telling whoever he was talking to that *it needed to die*, all of it. He didn't outright say the *orem*, but he said until it was dead, his plans couldn't begin."

My breath stopped. "Are you saying the king is behind the dying *orem*?"

Michas raked a hand through his hair. "I don't know, but it was a strange enough comment in a strange enough circumstance that my father remembered it. And then a month later, the first report came in from Isalee that a field had died."

I placed my hands on my hips. "Who was the king speaking to in that stairwell?"

Michas shrugged. "We don't know. My father was afraid of the king learning of his eavesdropping, so he went back the way he came and returned to his chamber, but—" He shook his head.

"What?"

"It's probably nothing, but my father also said the

strangest smell was in the air during that moment. A smell he'd never detected before."

I frowned. "What kind of smell?"

"Like . . . rot. It stood out enough and was pungent enough that he couldn't help but notice it."

Rot? My thoughts flashed back to a night Ilara had scented something similar. "Do you know anything else?"

"No, but that's what I was going to tell Ilara the night of our date. I was going to tell her what my father suspected of the king and the *orem*."

I mulled over what he'd revealed. "So you truly think my father is behind the dying crops?"

"We do."

Still stunned, for a moment, I couldn't move, but then I shook myself and said, "Thank you for telling me."

Michas's nostrils flared, and he eyed me coldly. "I'll deny any of this if you betray me or tell the king."

"I won't tell the king anything."

We studied each other, the distrust still flowing between us so strongly that I could taste it, and since it didn't seem our childhood rivalry was ending anytime soon, I added, "So you and your father, even knowing the king may be behind the dying *orem*, have decided to support an invasion anyway versus getting to the bottom of how the king's doing it?"

Michas's lip curled.

I scoffed. "Still hoping to capitalize on this, I see. Some things never change."

Michas toed closer to me. "Your father has been on the

throne for hundreds of winters. Sometimes drastic measures are needed to disrupt power."

"And you were hoping to claim the throne during an invasion the second a moment of weakness appeared. Why am I not surprised?"

Michas snarled. "That time could still come. One of these days, you may find yourself bowing to *me*."

"If that day ever comes, Michas, it'll be when my dead body's before you, and you're forcing it into a bow."

I dispersed my air Shield and gave him my back as I strode to the door. "Enjoy your sparring, Lord Crimsonale."

He gave me his pinky finger just as I closed the door behind me, and even though a part of me raged at the Crimsonales' greed for power, I also knew that Michas had taken a chance by confessing what he knew to me.

Seething, I stalked down the hall. I had no idea how my father could have killed the *orem*, but one thing I did know, I wasn't surprised in the slightest to learn who the real mastermind was behind this.

CHAPTER 6 - ILARA

"How are we to travel to the Adrall Temple?" I asked Drachu as he plucked a piece of purple fruit from the counter and chewed it languidly.

His throat worked when he swallowed, and his sharp canines glinted in the morning light. "This is how."

He slipped a hand into his robe's pocket, then opened his palm to reveal several tiny metallic keys. They were minuscule, each one only the length of his knuckle, but he displayed them so proudly that I had a feeling they were much more than they appeared.

"What are those?" Cailis asked.

"Portal keys," Drachu replied. "They were invented in that *other* realm and are frequently used by the Nolus fae. Seeing as how I recently visited the Nolus continent and had the pleasure of meeting with their king to discuss some unfortunate raids that have occurred on their shores of late, their king was kind enough to gift me with an entire jar of these."

I snorted because I had a feeling that the Nolus king's "kind" gesture was more of a bribe to get Drachu's clan to back off and stop raiding the Nolus's coastal cities. I was quickly coming to learn that the Lochen fae thrived on thievery. And I could hardly blame them. With the seas under their command and their unique ability to shift forms that allowed them to travel swiftly on land or in water, I couldn't fault them for using that to their advantage.

"So what do these keys do?" I asked, arching an eyebrow.

Drachu jiggled them in his palm, grinning. "They've proven quite useful. They allow any recipient to travel from one area of our realm to another nearly instantaneously, similar to Solis fae who can mistphase."

My eyes bugged out. "Truly? These allow *anyone* to mistphase?"

"Yes, although technically it's not mistphasing. It enacts a different kind of magic and was created by a species I'm unfamiliar with who live in that *other* realm, but these keys will allow us to travel to the temple easily."

I eyed the keys as my magic pulsed in my gut. Similar to yesterday, it didn't rise when I commanded it, and most likely, the farthest I could mistphase on my own would be to another area in this house or within Vockalin. If I was really lucky, I would be able to mistphase down to the beach, but I had a feeling my trapped magic wouldn't be able to handle anything beyond that.

"Cailis and I better get our things before we go."

Drachu inclined his head. "I shall dress while you're preparing. Tylen shall also be joining us."

I didn't ask why the king's son had been added to our party, but the conclusion that Cailis and I had reached last night, that on some level Drachu must have an ulterior motive for helping us, made me pause.

Nodding once, I beckoned my sister, and we hurried back to our room to collect our belongings.

Once our door was shut behind us, I clawed at my magic, siphoning it through the netting inside me until I was able to form a silencing Shield, but *Blessed Mother*, did it take concentration and extreme effort.

Once the wall of air was formed, I said, "Do you think we can trust those keys?"

She shrugged. "At this point, Ilara, I don't know. My affinity didn't detect any deceit in him, but Drachu is a fae king. Who knows what his magic is or what he's capable of. It's possible he's only allowing me to see what he wants revealed."

I picked at my fingernails. "Do you think the Lochen have Shields like we do, and you're unable to see what's a truth or lie with him because of a Shield?"

She lifted her shoulders again. "I don't know. If they do, I can't detect their Shields, not like I can with our kind."

I sighed. "Well, that's not comforting. It sounds like their magic is too different for your affinity to truly work."

Her nose scrunched up. "I know. I'm sorry. I wish I could be more confident in my affinity."

"Ock, Cailis, it's not your fault. If anything, all of this is *my* fault. If I hadn't been so intent on trying to understand what's buried deep within Isalee's field before my final test, none of this would have happened."

She curled her arm around me, and her wing brushed my side. "There's no point in wishing things can be different. They are what they are. At least we can take some comfort knowing that Mother, Father, and Tormesh continue to be protected in the prince's refuge."

I hugged her back. "You're right. It could be worse. Thank the Mother they're safe." Releasing her, I ran a hand through my hair, my fingers getting caught in a snarl. "I'm going to clean up quick in the bathing chambers, then I'll be ready to go."

I left the room to head down the hall, and my pulse fluttered the entire time. We were now leaving this island to go to some temple with Drachu. We would be even farther away from our continent, and we'd be entirely dependent on the Lochen king to bring us back here if my affinities continued to be trapped.

Unless I can steal some portal keys. I groaned at that thought. *Is that what I've been reduced to? Stealing because my magic is trapped?*

But the thought of thievery stayed with me, because essentially, we were growing more and more dependent on Drachu, and nothing about that sat well with me. I picked at my fingernails again when I entered the bathing chamber, then closed the door to clean up.

❄

WHEN I FINISHED BATHING the traditional way, since using my magic to self-cleanse required too much work, I opened the door to find Sabreeny waiting in the hall.

The salivar wore a mesh-like dress that stopped just below the juncture of her thighs. It was partly see-through, revealing the roundness of her breasts and toned skin along her abdomen. I couldn't help but wonder if all salivars dressed this provocatively at all hours of the day.

Before I could step aside to give her space to enter the bathing chamber, she was in the room with me, and the door slammed closed.

It all happened so fast that for a moment I didn't move.

In my next blink, she shoved me against the wall and brought a knife to my throat.

I froze.

She pressed the blade harder into my neck. "Because of you, my king is leaving me." Fury flashed in her eyes, and the knife burned across my skin. "If I kill you, I can throw your worthless body to the sea, letting the *feerily* devour you, and then my king will stay."

"Sabreeny, *stop*." I held up my hands, finally gaining control of my limbs. "He's not leaving you. He's just taking us somewhere." I tried to inch out from under her grasp, mindful of where the knife grazed my skin, but she pinned me harder to the wall.

Breath sucking in, I stilled, and a rumble of magic stirred low in my gut.

"Lie!" she hissed. Hatred flashed again in her eyes. "I'll

kill your sister next, throwing both of your bodies in the sea. You'll be devoured by the feerily, and no one will ever know what happened to you."

"Sabreeny, this is madness." I tried to keep my position non-threatening. A tiny scar running along her chin was plainly visible. Mother Below, she was completely in my face. "Nobody is trying to steal the king from you, and the last thing Cailis or I want is to take your place."

"As if you could!" she spat. Her teeth flashed, her canines glistening, and a course of power abruptly zinged from low in my belly through my limbs, but it was gone in a heartbeat.

Sabreeny's wrist flicked, and the knife cut me.

I sucked in a breath as pain zinged through me, and that strange pulse low in my belly increased.

Blood dribbled down my neck, a drop landing on the floor, and my eyes widened in disbelief when she whipped her hand to the side.

In that second, I knew she was truly going to slit my throat. She would kill me before allowing Drachu to leave prematurely.

Oh gods. Magic roared in my gut, as though trying to erupt from even lower in my abdomen than what I was used to, but it slammed into that veil suppressing my affinities as my arm shot up to dislodge her hand.

I ducked just as she stabbed at where my eye had been only a second prior.

Sandus's training roared through me, and Sabreeny shrieked when my elbow jerked up and caught her in the chin. I swiped my leg out, catching her unaware, and hooked her behind the knee, buckling her entire body.

She spun sideways with a scream. I punched out at her chest, hitting her right in the breastbone. She launched across the room and landed with a crash against the sink while her knife clattered to the floor when she crumpled.

I was on top of her, pinning her to the ground just as Cailis appeared in the doorway. Shock flashed across my sister's features as her wings flared.

"What in the realm is going on?" she yelled.

Drachu and Tylen appeared behind her, not even a blink later.

Magic again pushed and shoved against the veil within me, but all of my concentration lay on keeping Sabreeny restrained.

The salivar thrashed beneath me, but I kept her pinned using Sandus's techniques, not allowing her to rise.

"What in the seas?" Drachu growled. "What are you doing, Ilara?"

"Your salivar just tried to murder me!" I shot him an accusing glare as my chest heaved. I suddenly regretted coming here. We never should have trusted the Lochen king or any fae other than our own.

"Sabreeny!" The king's sharp call had her frantic movements stilling. "Is this true?"

"Of course not!" She hissed and looked at me with pure malice. "I was simply dressing in here when she barged in on me. It's *she* who tried to kill *me*!"

"What?" I jumped to a stand as if burned. "I did not!"

Sabreeny also stood, all lithe grace and fluid limbs. Her dress had ridden up, revealing a strip of cloth covering her womanly area. Even caught in such a state, she didn't appear ruffled, and if anything, her haughty glare was back before she gave the Lochen king a pleading stare. "My king, as your salivar, you're bound to protect me. Please, banish this ingamy from my home."

"But I didn't do anything!" Frustration threatened to boil up inside me as my trapped magic rattled and vibrated so strongly that I thought I was going to be sick. That strange pulse throbbed in my lower gut again as electric shocks traveled down my limbs, causing painful bursts and jolts. "She slammed me into the wall when I opened the door, then brought that knife to my throat. I was simply defending myself. See?" I pointed to the knife that still lay discarded on the floor, then to the puncture wound on my neck.

Drachu cocked his head and stepped closer to me.

His gaze narrowed as he assessed my throat. Eyes darkening, he picked up the knife, studying the hilt. Jewels were embedded into the sheath, and the blade glinted in the morning sunlight. "This weapon was a gift to me from the chancellor of Pasibith. I was keeping it in the nightstand near our bed." He brought the knife to his nose and sniffed. "That is indeed Ilara's blood coating the blade."

He set it down on the bathing chamber sink, and power began to ripple around him as he faced Sabreeny. "You tried to kill a guest in my home?"

His voice was so quiet, so lethal, that even I shivered despite his question being directed at his concubine.

Sabreeny's chin lifted as her hair tumbled down her back. "No! She's lying. I didn't—"

"You dare lie to me again?" The entire house shook with the strength of Drachu's magic, and my breath sucked in.

"My king," she pleaded. Her lips quivered as her creamy complexion paled. "I serve you and only you." She fell to her knees, bowing her head as she curled her hands around his legs. She ran her palms up his thighs, and her fingers disappeared under the fabric covering his groin.

He let out a low growl when she began stroking him, and Cailis and I shared a wild look. *They were actually conducting an act like this now?*

But just as Drachu began to lengthen in her hand, his arousal evident beneath the fabric for all of us to see, he flicked her palm away and snarled deeper in his throat.

"You are no longer my salivar. Out. *Now.*"

Sabreeny's lips parted, and she desperately moved closer to him, bringing her mouth to his half-formed erection. "Please, my king, let me remind you how much I can pleasure you."

"Out!" he roared when she tried to lift his clothing and bring him to her mouth.

My heart beat like a beast in my chest when Sabreeny's eyes dipped. Such a crestfallen expression fell over her face that I actually felt sorry for her when she rose. But that feeling only lasted a split second and was doused when she shot me a murderous stare.

The salivar gave her king one last pleading look, but the

absolute steel in Drachu's expression had cut his features into unrelenting stone.

With an enraged shriek, she ran from the room, then the distant sound of a door slamming reached my ears.

Breathing hard, I glanced between Drachu and Tylen. Tylen's eyes were hard, as were Drachu's.

"Are you hurt?" Tylen asked.

I fingered my throat, but the blood had already clotted. "No. I'm fine." I went to the sink and splashed water on my injury until the blood was gone.

"I apologize for that," Drachu said, his magic still filling the space as he glared toward where Sabreeny had fled.

"We need a minute." Cailis grabbed my hand and pulled me toward the guestroom.

Once our door was closed, I yanked on my magic until I was able to form another silencing Shield around us, but dammit, it was difficult.

Panting from the effort, I nearly screeched, "What in all the realms was that?"

Cailis was breathing just as hard. "Right? Did she actually try to kill you?"

"She did. She said if we were gone, Drachu would stay here with her. She blamed me for his plans to depart."

"Blessed Mother." Cailis shook her head as she fumed. "These fae are . . . unhinged. Their behavior is so bizarre." Her cheeks flushed. "And Sabreeny was going to suck Drachu's"—she gestured to her groin—"right in front of us. It's so . . . brazen."

"Or desperate." I shook my head as adrenaline from

Sabreeny's attack still raced through my veins. "We need to do something to protect ourselves better. If we go with Drachu to that temple, we need to leave some kind of message behind describing where we went, just in case we never return to the Solis continent, and just in case Drachu does decide to keep us prisoner." I closed my eyes, thinking of the letter I'd written my mate, telling him to wait for me. But I knew, *knew* to the marrow of my bones, that if I didn't return in the near future, the crown prince would look for me.

I scoured my thoughts with how to let him know where we were going, then realized there was only one solution. "I'm going back to the beach. Prince Norivun knows that Drachu offered me refuge if I ever needed it. If Drachu truly has dishonorable intentions, then I need to leave something on the shore that only Norivun can find. Considering that the potion the queen gave us makes it impossible to track our whereabouts, this may be the only way he could ever find us."

"But how are you going to do that?" Cailis nibbled on her lower lip.

"Did you pack any parchment or quills?"

She nodded and grabbed the bag, rummaging around until she found the supplies.

I hastily wrote down where Drachu was taking us, then rubbed the paper all over me, again and again, until every portion of its surface had come in contact with my skin.

Cailis wrinkled her nose. "What are you doing?"

"Coating this letter with my scent. Norivun has a scent-sensory affinity. He'll be able to detect this if he ever comes to this island." Once I was certain that my essence thoroughly covered the page, I took a deep breath. "I need to mistphase down there. It's the only way I can make it there and then back without Drachu suspecting that we don't trust him."

"Do you think you'll be able to?"

"I must."

CHAPTER 7 – NORIVUN

I found all four of my guards in the training rooms. Each was hard at work using the weights in the corner or sparring on the mats. My guards exercised daily. It was a rare occasion when they weren't honing their skills or strengthening their muscles. The last time I remembered any of them taking a day off from strength training was when Sandus's niece, Harpelin, had been born. Prior to that, it'd been months. They even trained on their days off.

"Nori, good day," Nish called out when I strode into the room.

I gave him a curt nod as Haxil and Sandus lifted weights, their reps swift and blurred at times they moved so fast. Ryder, the cheeky bastard, used Nish's momentary greeting to me as an opening to clock the surly guard right on the chin.

Nish went down with a groan, but when Ryder waved a greeting to me too, Nish swung his leg out, knocking the long-haired fairy to the floor with him.

"Are you two done with the cheap shots?" My lips twitched in amusement. I crossed my arms as my wings settled between my shoulder blades when I snapped them in tight.

"Depends. Are we leaving for a job?" Ryder asked as his long braid whipped around his shoulder when he dodged another blow from Nish.

"We are. Ilara needs to be found."

All four of them stopped, their movements freezing so completely that it was as though Verasellee, the Goddess of Time, had descended from the universe and exacted her monumental power.

"Truly?" Haxil asked in a hopeful tone.

My power rumbled at his growing smile. I knew he and Ilara were nothing more than friends, but I still had to quell the possessive aspect of the mate bond every time I saw him smile at her, or worse, when she smiled at him in return. It was a juvenile response. I knew that, but fuck if I could stop it.

Raking a hand through my hair, I gave a curt nod even though I wanted to punch him in the jaw. "As I told you last night, my father gave me a month to present Ilara to him before he does something truly unspeakable to my mother."

Sandus's eyes flickered. "He's a despicable tyrant. So what do you suggest we do?"

"We find Ilara, discover how to unlock her affinities, and then discover if the dying *orem* truly is of the gods' doing or someone else's."

All four of them frowned.

"You're saying that the gods and goddesses aren't behind the dying *orem*?" Ryder's expression turned shrewd.

"Possibly."

"What in all the realms are you talking about, Nori?" Haxil asked.

I cast a silencing Shield, then told them what Michas had revealed to me this morning, how the Crimsonales suspected that somehow my father was ultimately behind the dying *orem*.

"Truly?" Nish's eyebrows shot up.

I gave a curt nod. "The more I think about it, the more inclined I am to believe it. Ilara felt something in that Isalee field, buried deep within it. She was convinced that it wasn't natural, which means it wasn't of the gods doing and could very well be because of something my father's done."

"But why would he do that?" Haxil asked.

My lip curled. "Because it's created support for a war. It's created support for our continent to march on the Nolus fae and try to steal their land, and we all know someone who craves power more than anyone else on this continent."

All of their eyes widened when understanding hit them.

"The king," they replied in unison.

"The one and only."

"But he's been so adamant that the crops will return to life if we just give it enough time," Sandus countered.

"He has, and what's gone on in the interim as he's been adamant all will be fine? Unrest. Concern. The council pushing for us to invade the Nolus continent. War. He now has an entire continent brimming with barely leashed violence and the demand that we march upon our southern neighbors, and all the while, he looks like the innocent party who never wanted war in the first place. Our fae continue to love him."

"But why would he do that?" Ryder pushed.

"Power." I placed my hands on my hips as I mulled everything over again. I'd suspected my father might be behind the missing fae in the castle, since I knew he'd wanted to stop the talks of unrest, but I'd never suspected that he'd actually wanted the unrest to continue and was murdering fae as a way to mask his involvement. It was so manipulative and was such a calculated move—exactly something like my father would do. "I've always known that my father is power hungry, but I hadn't thought he would move beyond our border. For the past several hundred winters, after he'd conquered all of the territories and united them under his rule, he's been content according to my mother, but now, he's not. He's dominated the north, and now he craves the south. But how could he convince our fae to start a war? They wouldn't support him simply because he wanted to expand his reach, but they *would* support him if their survival depended upon it."

"Blessed Mother," Nish whispered.

Ryder crossed his arms. "What if you're wrong, and it's not him?"

I shrugged. "I could be, but then you tell me who else on this continent has the power and means to find a way to douse the *orem*?"

They all eyed each other, then Ryder nodded. "You're

right. I suppose it's possible a council member would have the means, but nobody else would, and your reasoning for it being the king makes the most sense, as disgraceful as that is." He sneered. "But it is in line with his character."

Haxil shook his head. "But *how*? How did he kill the crops?"

"I don't know." I scowled. "But he's done something, and given what Lord Crimsonale overheard, he's hired help. Someone who would know how to kill the *orem*."

"Who in all the realm has enough power to do that?" Sandus's confused expression looked exactly as I'd felt since this morning.

"That is what I still don't know."

Nish scowled. "Ock, it would explain why the king wants Ilara so desperately. If she's the only fairy who's been able to stop whatever it is he's done to the *orem,* by using her affinity to allow the crops to grow despite this poisonous veil, then she poses a threat to everything he's been working toward."

"Exactly," I said with a nod. I'd reached the same conclusion after speaking with Michas. "And I think that's why my father's so desperate to find her. He wants her found so he can control her. If she's in his court, he can either stop her from visiting the fields, or he can keep tabs on which ones she's healing so he can sabotage them again."

Haxil's eyebrows shot up. "Which is what he did to the Isalee fields right before Ilara's test!"

I nodded again. "Yes."

"That's why the crops died overnight. He must have done something that killed them a second time." Haxil's glare turned deadly. I had no doubt he, a son of Isalee, was taking that affront personally.

"I believe so too," I agreed, "but if Ilara can free her affinities, and if we venture to Isalee once more, then we stand a chance at figuring out what my father's done."

Ryder frowned. "But whatever is in the land punched out at her and trapped her affinities. Who's to say that won't happen again even if we find a way to untrap her magic."

"It did." My blood boiled just thinking about it, but I also knew that my mate was strong, stronger than any female I'd ever met, perhaps even stronger than the queen. "But if Ilara knows what to expect and can avoid what she did the first time so the veil won't target her, perhaps she'll be able to figure out what it is, and then we can discover a way to dismantle it, perhaps even destroy it completely."

"Which would stop any further talks of war. If the crops return to normal, the king will have a hard time drumming up support for an invasion." Sandus nodded. "Sounds like a solid plan."

"And Georgyanna?" Haxil raised his eyebrows. "What of her? Your wedding is only weeks away."

Power rumbled down my limbs all the way to my toes. "Georgyanna can go fuck herself."

Nish snickered.

Ryder crossed his arms. "And what of the queen and how she'll fare when you defy the king's command and don't turn Ilara over?"

"I haven't figured that one out yet."

Ryder arched an eyebrow. "What if we find Ilara, and the

king manages to get his hands on her despite us trying to protect her?"

I stroked my chin. "Ilara's affinities are strong enough to tear through mine. Unless he finds a way to subject her to the same spell he forced upon the queen, Ilara can handle herself, as long as we find a way to unlock her magic."

"Agreed." Sandus grunted and crossed his arms. "Ilara's a true warrior even if she hasn't manifested that affinity."

"This will be seen as treason," Ryder warned, "if the king discovers that we're actively working against him."

"I'm aware," I replied dryly.

"And your father will punish the queen so severely for your actions that she may be permanently marred, even injured beyond repair," Ryder added.

My jaw worked. "I know. I've already considered that, but I'll find a way to prevent that from happening."

"And the Solis citizens may see your actions as being entirely despicable, since it flounces their beloved king's new law enacting the Olirum Accords in his face. They may demand your head for it."

Nish rolled his eyes. "Truly, Ryder, such a ray of sunshine you are."

Ryder shrugged. "Just making sure our prince is prepared for whatever comes."

Magic simmered along my limbs, and the wall vibrated behind me. "I appreciate your council, Ryder." Of all my guards, the long-haired fairy had the most cunning mind. "I'm aware of all of that, but the citizens also know that Ilara is my mate. Those who were present after the first test saw us kiss, and they felt our bond. I plan to use that knowledge to my advantage. Even Crimsonale was sympathetic to our plight at the last council meeting. Once word spreads that I rejected the king's command to marry Georgyanna because Ilara's my mate, I'm hoping they'll understand."

Ryder inclined his head. "True. You're probably right in that aspect."

"So now what?" Nish propped his elbow against the wall of weapons. "How do we find Ilara?"

I smiled and the mate bond rumbled inside me. "We search every possible place she could have gone, and we start with her village."

Ryder laughed. "Surely, she wasn't foolish enough to have gone home."

I smirked. "Of course not, but the king will still search there. I'm not naïve enough to think he hasn't already sent other search parties to hunt for her. He knows I have the best chance of finding her, but he won't leave it just to me. He doesn't trust me enough to reliably do his bidding, not with Ilara being my mate."

"So why are we going to her village?" Sandus asked.

"To fuck with the king." My lips curved in a malicious smile. "Ilara's village archon may have abused her, but she told me the rest of her village fae had grown loyal to her. If they know the court is hunting her with the intention of hurting her, and they learn that I'm her mate and I'm trying to keep her safe, they'll do what they can to thwart the king's attempts."

Nish laughed. "They can send the king's fae off on a wild goose chase."

I grinned. "With any luck, yes."

THE FIVE OF us mistphased to the heart of Ilara's village. The second we appeared, a shriek reached my ears, and a female with a young child scurried out of the way. She disappeared behind a shop before I could tell her that we hadn't come to apprehend anyone.

My guards surveyed the remaining fae with annoyed glares as the villagers fled from the central area.

Nish kicked at the snow crusted on the street. "How are we supposed to convince any of them that we're here on Ilara's behalf if they're all running from us?"

"Perhaps if you tamed that scowl of yours, they'd be more inclined to listen." Haxil patted his shoulder.

Nish curled his lip at him. "I'm not scowling."

Sandus patted Nish's other shoulder. "You are. 'Tis how you usually appear, so perhaps today, you can do your best to seem more cheerful."

The twisting of Nish's mouth into what he probably thought was a smile was so hideous that I would have laughed if this visit wasn't so serious.

Since it was, I ignored his attempt and strode down the street, intent on reaching the fields just beyond the town's borders.

"According to what Ilara's told me," I called to my guards

over my shoulder, "if anyone in her village is able to spread word fast and keep the tongues wagging, it's the two cooks that serve the laborers each day—Evis and Krisil. She said they're the biggest gossips this side of the Gielis Mountains and are constantly in everyone's business."

Snowflakes flew in the sky and covered all the roofs in white as my guards followed me. Seeing the simple shops and single lane running down the village reminded me of the humbleness of Ilara's upbringing. It was very similar to my mother's.

Several shops we passed had small fires roaring inside, and smoke curled from the chimneys. Burning wood scents drifted in the air along with the distant crops' blossoms tinging the breeze. It smelled of health and life. It smelled of my mate.

I continued toward the barn as the mate bond billowed inside me—the strength of it aching so strongly that I nearly roared in frustration at everything that'd been done.

Cold air nipped my skin when we rounded the final turn to the field barn. The brisk wind increased, turning frigid, once the shops no longer provided protection against the elements.

I called upon my air affinity and created a protective Shield around us. The wind died, and the silver strands of my hair that had been whipping around my face settled on my shoulders.

We reached the barn a few minutes later, and shook the snow from our boots before entering. A sense of déjà vu filled me when the door banged open. This was where I'd first met my mate. I crossed the threshold, my heart squeezing at the memory of seeing Ilara seated upon a wooden bench with her head bowed and a scarf covering her hair.

The two cooks twirled toward us when our presence filled the room. Evis squeaked and immediately dipped into a deep curtsy. Her entire frame wobbled as the scent of fear rose from her.

Whereas Krisil nearly dropped the ladle she was using to transfer broth between pots. "Ock. What a surprise . . . err, Your Highness." She also curtsied.

Both females kept their attention on me as Haxil, Ryder, Nish, and Sandus spanned out on my sides. The cooks stayed dipped in submissive positions. Sour scents rose from them as their terror grew. I could practically hear the questions screaming from their minds. *What's happened now? Is he here to take another one of us away?*

I suppressed an irritated snarl and wished my mother was here. If she was, and her affinities weren't being suppressed, she could tell me exactly what they were thinking.

"Stand," I said in a clipped tone. "You have nothing to fear."

Krisil and Evis bumped into one another in their effort to move upright.

"Are you both well?" I asked.

Their eyes widened, and I had a feeling the last thing they expected was for me to ask of their well-being.

Krisil bobbed her head, as did Evis, but their lips remained pressed into tight lines.

"You needn't fear our visit. Truly." I offered a reassuring smile.

Evis tugged at her apron, then began balling it in her fist. "My prince, may I ask where Ilara is?"

Krisil kicked her in the shin, but Evis merely scoffed in return. "He's here without her, Krisil," she hissed to the other cook. "You're telling me that's not cause for concern?"

"Actually, the fact that Ilara isn't with me is why we're here," I cut in. "We need your help."

"Oh?" Krisil's eyes widened, and curiosity puffed from her scent in stringent waves, overriding her previous fear.

I tucked my hands into my trousers' pockets. "I come because Ilara has fled the continent, and what I'm going to ask of you could determine her fate."

Krisil dropped her ladle in the pot, then took a step around the stove. "What's happened, my prince?"

As quickly as I could, I told them what Ilara had become during her time at the Court of Winter. Her affinities, the Trial, the magic that had suppressed her power, and the king's plan to wed her off to a disgusting pedophile.

Evis's nose scrunched up when I revealed that. "Truly, my prince? That's absolutely ghastly."

"Indeed, especially considering Ilara's my mate."

Krisil's mouth dropped open so far that Nish snickered behind me.

Evis cleared her throat. "Come again, my prince?"

"You heard me. Ilara is my mate. The gods chose her for me and me for her."

They shared a wide-eyed look, and the excitement that

grew on their faces told me that Ilara had been right about them. With this kind of information, they would be dying to share it with anyone who would listen.

"Which brings me to the point of my visit," I said before either of them could completely forget themselves and scurry off to the first fairy they could find. "My father doesn't approve of me marrying Ilara."

Krisil brought a hand to her chest, her expression stewing with indignation. "Ilara isn't good enough? Dear, sweet Ilara, who has given everything she's had to our village, never once complained, and still worked as hard as she could despite everything that's happened to her family in the past year?"

As if realizing that *I* was what had happened to her family, Krisil drew up short.

They both seemed to reach the conclusion that Ilara was mated to the murderer of her family at the same time—well, they thought I'd murdered her family. Neither of them knew the Seary family still lived in my hidden village on the Cliffs of Sarum.

Complexions paling, the cooks backed up, horror descending upon their features.

I locked my jaw. "There is much you don't know nor understand, but please believe me when I say that I would die for Ilara and would never harm her. Ever."

"Of course not, my prince," Evis squeaked.

"Now, it's important that you listen and heed what I'm going to ask of you. Ilara's survival depends on it. Can I trust you to do as I say?"

They both nodded.

"Good. First off, has anyone from the court arrived in town inquiring about Ilara or Cailis?"

They both shot one another surprised looks before Evis said under her breath, "As a matter of fact, we did have two strange males in the village just last night."

I stilled. "Oh? Did they say what they were here for?"

Krisil shook her head. "Not outright, but old Nevis said they stopped at his house, asking if anyone had seen the Seary girls, and after that stop, they pounded on both Finnley's and Birnee's doors."

My magic rumbled along my limbs. So my father knew who Ilara's friends were. He'd taken more of an interest in her than I'd realized. "What did Nevis, Birnee, and Finnley tell them?"

Evis wrung her hands even more in her apron. "That both Cailis and Ilara were at the Court of Winter. That none of us had seen them in months."

"Do you know where these males are now?"

Krisil nodded. "Staying at an inn, just outside of Firlim is what I heard."

"I'm going to need you to go to Firlim and tell them that you've heard whisperings of where the Seary girls are." I pulled a few rulibs from my pocket and gave them the coins. "For your time and effort."

I spent the next hour helping the cooks weave out a tale that would keep my father's males searching far and wide for Ilara and her sister in an area of the continent that I knew they would never venture to. The area I chose was filled with forest sprites, creatures my mate hated above all others. If

Ilara had fled anywhere in the realm, the last place she would have chosen would have been there.

When I finished, the cooks' eyes grew even wider, and a buzz of excitement filled their tiny auras. I knew that of all the fae in this village, these two would ensure the males hunting for my mate would never find her.

A smug smile covered my face when we mistphased back to Solisarium. Now, the time came for *me* to find my mate while my father's males found nothing.

CHAPTER 8 - ILARA

My magic swelled and pulsed in my gut, but *Blessed Mother*, trying to pull it through the veil that contained my affinities was no easier than it'd been the night following the attack in Isalee. It didn't seem that time affected whatever was suppressing my power. The thickness and strength of the veil covering my magic hadn't diminished in the least.

Similar to how I'd struggled when I'd mistphased back to my room the morning of my final test, I was nearly groaning with exertion as I attempted to do it again. Slowly, *so* slowly, the realm began to disassemble around me.

I moved through the realm in mist and shadows, air and wind, as I concentrated completely on the black sand beach at the base of the fjord.

Minutes ticked by before I reappeared with a jolt, my heart thudding with how much of a struggle it'd been to accomplish such a short mistphase.

"Mother Below," I whispered when the salty air whipped around me, and cool waves lapped at my boots.

Panting, I scoured the beach, looking for any fae who might be about. I searched the sea too, but there weren't any bobbing heads at the surface watching me from afar. Once certain nobody was nearby, I searched for a safe place where I could store my letter while making sure the ocean waves didn't hit it.

I ran along the shore. Scattered rocks covered the beach and dug into my soles. Farther up the shore were outcroppings of rough boulders near the tree line. The waterline didn't reach that area.

I scrambled toward the rocks, then searched for a hidden area.

After moving a large stone, I tucked the parchment carefully between two rocks and felt confident neither the wind nor the sea would reach it.

Panting, I closed my eyes and concentrated again on mistphasing back to the king's residence.

The realm disappeared as slowly as it had the first time. I was moving even slower than Lord Pinebeer had when we'd all mistphased to the Bay of Nim at the second test. My near-instantaneous ability was gone. All of the months I'd been practicing my mistphasing to make it so accurate and reliable felt wasted.

Groaning in frustration, I finally disassembled, and when I reappeared, my eyes widened at the unfamiliar room around me.

It smelled of sex, and when I spotted Drachu's discarded

robe at the end of a bed, horror filled me. *Ock, I mistphased to the wrong room!*

A rumble of voices came from down the hall. I slapped a hand to my mouth as it hit me that I was in Drachu and Sabreeny's bedroom chamber—the very chamber she and Drachu had been intimate in not too long ago. No wonder it reeked.

"Fiddlesticks in domal dung!" I crept toward the door, hoping nobody was in the hall so I could sneak back to the guestroom undetected, but a flash of something caught my eye. Frowning, I spotted a chest near the far wall. It was opened slightly, allowing me to see something bright and sparkling inside.

I was about to scamper out of the room, but voices coming from down the hall grew louder until thudding footsteps headed this way.

I hurried away from the door and flung myself into the only hiding spot available—the closet. I was in the process of sliding the door closed when Drachu entered the chamber.

"Have you alerted Priestess Genoova?" Drachu asked whoever he was with.

I stopped all of my movements, not making a sound.

"I have, Father. She's expecting us this morning," Tylen replied.

"Good, the last thing I need is another subject who displeases me." Shuffling came from the room, as though Drachu was walking across the floor.

Tylen chuckled. "Sabreeny seemed like a frisky *tilamy* in bed. I'm surprised you banished her so easily."

Drachu chuffed. "I might regret it. That female knows how to suck a cock, but I can't have a salivar whose jealousy controls her. I knew she wouldn't like having Ilara and Cailis in these walls, but I thought she'd tolerate them, not attack one." He released an irritated sounding breath. "It was probably for the best. If Sabreeny had learned that I'd planned to visit Xanimy in a few days' time, she may have followed me there to claw the female's eyes out."

"Ah, Xanimy." Tylen laughed softly. "I've had the pleasure of her ass on my cock a few times." A growl came from Drachu, then Tylen said in a hurry, "I haven't fucked her, but she likes to flirt during the times I've visited, and she seems to enjoy sitting on male laps and rubbing herself on them."

A second growl came from the king. "I'll have to speak with her about that," Drachu muttered. "But if you think her ass feels good, you should feel her scales. She's even more delectable to take beneath the waves."

I blanched. Mother Below, these males spoke of females as though all we were good for was sex, and the number of concubines that Drachu had was so numerous it only strengthened that belief.

I held my breath as the males made no attempt to leave. One of them moved in the room again, and since the closet was dark with a sliver of light coming in through the cracked door, I shifted silently and peered out of it.

Drachu had walked to the chest near the wall and was leaning over it, its cover fully open. My eyes widened at the plethora of jewels and gems within the huge chest. The sparkling stones were so large that some were as big as his fist.

He held one up, inspecting it, before he placed it into the necklace around his neck, right next to the green stone.

The large emerald seemed to *swallow* the other one, and my eyes widened even more when a burst of magic puffed around the fae king. It stayed like that for a moment before the pulsing emerald dimmed. Drachu closed his eyes, his head tilting back.

"That's better." When he opened his eyes, a faint green light shone from his irises before they returned to normal.

My lips parted in surprise and curiosity. The necklace was magical, I knew that much, but as for its purpose, I could only guess.

"Do you think they're ready?" Drachu asked Tylen. He grabbed another stone off the table near the bed, just a plain rock from the looks of it, before he slipped it into his pocket. "They're certainly taking long enough, and I haven't heard a word from either of them since they disappeared back into the guestroom."

"Would you like me to check on them?" Tylen asked.

"Yes, we should really get moving. The gods are always easiest to appease midday, and Genoova will need to finish last minute preparations once we arrive."

Tylen walked toward the hall, and my heart thudded that he was about to retrieve me from the guestroom, not realizing that only Cailis was in our chamber.

Mother Below! I closed my eyes, and panic made me tug on my magic so hard that a thick ribbon streamed through the netting. I concentrated entirely on mistphasing to my room just down the hall.

I disappeared much faster than I had when I'd ventured to the beach, thank the Mother.

Cailis let out a cry of surprise when I reappeared beside her a second before Tylen opened the door.

I plastered a smile on my face while Cailis looked like she'd seen a ghost.

"We should get moving." Tylen glanced between the two of us, and I did my best to make my expression appear normal. "All ready?"

Cailis stiffly shouldered our pack. "Yes, whenever you are."

"Excellent." Tylen opened the door wider, and I knew any chance of telling Cailis what I'd seen the king do with his gemstones wasn't happening. "The temple awaits."

We followed him out of the house through the back door. Nobody was about except for Drachu who was waiting for us. The Lochen king's long dark hair tangled in the wind, and he smiled wide, his canines so sharp they reminded me of blades.

I glanced at his necklace, toward the center stone, but it appeared of the same size and color as it had the first time I'd seen it. *How strange.*

"We need to join hands for the portal key to transport all of us at once." Drachu held his palm out to me, but I clasped my sister's hand first before taking the king's.

Drachu's skin felt warm and dry, but stiff, not like the supple skin of the crown prince's.

An ache so sharp punctured my breath that it felt as though the wind had been knocked from me. *Gods, I miss you, Norivun.* Even though it'd only been a day since we'd fled our continent, I missed my mate so acutely that it was a physical pain in my chest.

Cailis squeezed my hand, probably sensing my reaction. I forced my breathing to slow as Drachu pulled one of the tiny portal keys from his pocket, the same pocket that he'd tucked that rock into.

"Open key for thou, I ask. I need a door for this new task." He whispered that strange statement, then squeezed my hand harder.

The realm disappeared around us in a wink of magic.

CHAPTER 9 - ILARA

Portal keys were nothing like mistphasing. It felt as if I was being pulled apart and squished back together all within the same breath. By the time we reappeared on a solid surface, my stomach was tumbling, and it felt as though I was going to be sick.

"Blessed Mother." Cailis dry heaved beside me, and Tylen winced.

Drachu chuckled. "The keys can be a bit jarring. Did I not warn you?"

"Funny how you forgot to mention that," Cailis grumbled.

I took another deep breath, thankful that my breakfast stayed in my stomach, but despite the portal key transfer being a million times worse than a natural mistphase, it had indeed moved us across the realm.

Straightening, I took in the vast view. We stood on the

top of a high mountain, sheer drops on all sides. A temple made of white stone rose just behind us. Stairs cutting into the rock climbed to it. The temple was a simple design with a circular floor, domed ceiling, and columns supporting the structure.

Since we stood just beneath it, I couldn't see if anything was inside the open structure, but if there was, it had to be low to the ground. Open air swirled through the columns.

A fierce wind tangled my hair, sending black locks thrashing around my eyes as I scanned the terrain's descending slopes. Hundreds of feet below us, the ocean crashed against a pale sandy beach as a warm, salty breeze flowed over my cheeks, and a clear pale-green sky stretched above.

And the landscape . . .

My mouth dropped at the lack of snow and ice. Everything was vibrant, warm, and so very alive. Emerald-green, bright-blue, and magenta leaves coated the island's plants. Not one speck of snow or frost was anywhere.

"Is this the Adrall Temple?" I asked.

"It is." Drachu pointed toward the sea. "And if you look that way, you can see our continent. It's just south of here."

My attention whipped south, and my jaw dropped at the huge land mass glimmering in the distance. Blessed Mother, we were in an entirely different *hemisphere*.

Cailis gaped.

My heart pattered even harder. We were likely thousands of millees from our northern continent.

A chill raced down my spine, but before I could regret this decision entirely, a soft female voice carried to me on the breeze, distracting me. "King Drachu. You bless me with your presence."

I whirled around to see a female at the top of the temple's stairs. Like all Lochen fae, she had startling green eyes. Dark hair, a shade lighter than mine, hung in ringlets to her shoulders. She walked slowly down the steps, her movements graceful and light. The sunlight shone off her umber-brown skin, then caught on the pendant hanging from her neck.

Like Drachu, she also wore a necklace with shells and gems, but unlike the fae king's, there wasn't a central stone throbbing with light.

When she reached us, she brought her thumb to her mouth, then to her forehead.

"Priestess Genoova." Drachu inclined his head.

"I'm prepared and ready for your arrival. Is she the one you spoke of?" The priestess turned to me, her malachite eyes sharp and assessing.

"Indeed." Drachu smirked.

Cailis and I shared an apprehensive look as Tylen stood behind his father.

My throat bobbed in a swallow when Genoova stepped closer, then brought her palm to my chest. The unsolicited contact took me so much by surprise that I stepped back, but she moved with me, her hand never leaving my body.

Warmth bloomed across my chest, and a wide smile danced upon her lips, revealing small canines. "She's perfect."

"Perfect?" I repeated. Even though some might think that was a compliment, something told me it wasn't. "Perfect in what way?"

"The power you carry is as my king described. Come." She gestured toward the stairs and began to climb them.

"Wait." I planted my feet to the sandy rock as Cailis plastered herself to my side. "What is it you want from me, and why exactly are we here?"

"I told you," Drachu replied in a patient tone. "We're going to attempt to free your trapped power, but to do that, we need God Zorifel's help."

Cailis scowled. "How do you know he will free it?"

The king shrugged. "I don't, but it's worth trying, isn't it?"

Cailis's hand slid down my arm until her hand clasped mine. She gave two squeezes. *Two.*

Mother Below. Drachu was lying.

I took another step away from the temple, and my sister moved with me, our bodies glued together. If Drachu was lying, then he knew that whatever they planned to do with me would either indeed free my affinities, or it would do something else. Something I wasn't sure I wanted to know.

"I'd rather not." I lifted my chin, holding eye contact with Drachu.

Something flashed across his features, but then his easy smile returned. "I promised you that we would treat you as a queen, did I not?"

"You did."

"Yet you still balk at my trying to help you. How do you intend to be queen if you are as weak as a babe?"

"I . . ." But I didn't have a response for that. I had no idea how I would ever be worthy of being the Solis queen in my current state, but allowing them to conduct a ritual, or gods forbid a sacrifice, didn't seem like the wisest option either. Because the truth was, I had no idea what they intended to do with me in that temple.

"What will occur up there?" I nodded to the columns.

Genoova clasped her hands in front of her, her posture demure. "We shall call upon God Zorifel and beg for his help. As the God of Power, he may respond. Drachu was right about you. You carry strong magic inside you, Krelahala."

"What does Krelahala mean?" Cailis hissed.

"Krelahala is what we call a female who possesses intensely strong magic." Tylen stepped closer to us, breaking his silence.

Cailis squeezed me once. So, Tylen was telling the truth.

"You have a name for fae like me?" I cocked my head.

"We do," Drachu replied. "It's very rare to wield as much magic as you do. Few of our clan have ever possessed it to that extent. Those who have, have risen to be queen and advanced our race. They ruled like no other leader. They were all queens."

My eyes widened. For Drachu to admit that queens prior to him were stronger leaders than him took a level of humbleness that wasn't something I'd expect in a king. I could never see King Novakin admitting to something like that.

But Cailis had still detected a lie from him when he'd said they didn't know if they could free my trapped affinities.

"Do you know what will happen to me if I do what you're asking?"

"It's quite simple," Genoova replied. "God Zorifel will either respond and bless you with his gift, or he won't." She shrugged as though it were really that easy.

I looked to Cailis, and she squeezed once.

Deep breaths lifted my chest as I felt for my magic again. Something still covered it, smothered it, and made it nearly impossible for me to access. Considering that Murl, the head healer at the Court of Winter, had been as stumped by it as me, I knew my options for freeing my affinities were minimal at best. And considering time was not in any way weakening whatever was dousing my magic, I was beginning to believe that it would forever taint my abilities if I didn't do something drastic.

Perhaps this was the only way for me to regain my affinities, or maybe it wasn't, and I was making a huge mistake.

Mother Below, it's not like I have many options. I was thousands of millees from home. King Novakin would either execute me if I returned or force me to marry Arcane Woodsbury, and in my current state, I was nearly as helpless as I'd been before Prince Norivun had entered my life.

I stepped away from my sister and looked to the top of the stairs and prayed to Nuleef, the Goddess of Luck, that I was making the right choice. "Okay, I'll do it."

Priestess Genoova gave a wide smile and ushered me toward the stairs. I climbed them slowly, each step feeling like an anchor around my ankles.

When we reached the top, I could see that it was indeed

an open design. There wasn't any furniture or altars. Thank the Mother. It was a simple circular dome supported by columns, and the stone flooring was covered in intricate designs. The most powerful constellations in our galaxy had been etched into the stone, rimming the rock, and at the center of the temple was a carving of the supreme symbol that united all of the gods and goddesses—a circle with an array of connecting swirls and stars.

"Drachu?" Genoova said, holding her palm out.

Startling me, the brush of the Lochen king at my back had me nearly pitching forward. He'd climbed the steps so silently behind me that I hadn't heard him.

The king extracted something from his pocket and then handed it to her. Stiffening, I realized it was the rock that I'd seen him place in his pocket when I'd been hidden in his closet, the same small stone that looked as though it'd been picked up on a nameless beach somewhere.

Genoova took the small rock to the center of the temple, then placed it directly in the middle, right in the center of the star.

"Please stand here." She gestured to the central symbol. "Place your feet in the slots."

The rock that Drachu had handed her waited between the two divots, and the fact that there were grooves for a fairy to stand in gave me pause and comfort simultaneously. It meant others had done this before me, but whether they'd endured a bad outcome was something to be determined.

"Will this hurt?" I asked.

Genoova shook her head as Cailis and Tylen ascended the steps to stand beside Drachu, just outside of the temple's columns. "I shall be summoning God Zorifel, which requires nothing of you. All I ask is that you close your eyes and clear your mind."

I took a deep breath and studied my sister. Worry lines puckered her mouth, but she gave me a single nod, probably because it wasn't uncommon to summon the gods and goddesses when our kind was in need. Sometimes they answered—most of the time they didn't. Who knew if God Zorifel would heed Genoova's plea. It was possible I would simply stand there, and nothing would happen.

No harm in that, I suppose.

Moving to the center of the temple, I stepped onto the divots. I could have sworn that a wash of magic brushed over my skin like a gentle caress. Closing my eyes, I stood still. The temple's stone floor felt smooth beneath my soles, and it almost felt as if the minuscule weight of the stone Genoova had placed on the central star between my feet called to me.

I waited for something to happen. Waited for a shift in the realm or something otherworldly to occur as the wind lifted my hair, and the sound of Cailis tapping her foot filled the open space.

"All right, clear your mind and breathe." Genoova began to chant in a language I didn't understand. It didn't have the same cadence and notes of the language I'd heard Drachu and Sabreeny speaking. Perhaps it was another dialect of the Lochen's unique tongue, or maybe it was more ancient.

Regardless, I did my best to empty my mind of any thoughts or feelings. I breathed deeply in and out as the priestess's chants grew stronger and faster until they blended into a song that spun around me.

Time seemed to slow as I stood there. The breeze stopped whipping against my cheeks. The scent of salt in the air dimmed. The sunlight piercing my closed eyelids faded until blackness coated my sight. Even Genoova's lulling chants fell to the great beyond.

And then it felt as though I was falling.

The force of the sensation hit me like a bolt of lightning. I tried to open my eyes, tried to scream, but my body was immobilized. The sensations of the realm disappeared as I sank into a void.

Falling.

Falling.

Falling.

Down, down I went even though no air kissed my skin, and no sight graced my eyes.

Oh, Blessed Mother.

I plummeted through time and space, zinging through a tunnel of nothing and everything all at once.

With a jolting lash, the falling sensation stopped, and then I was suspended.

Darkness surrounded me, as a deep humming sensation began in my gut. It vibrated my body, pulsing and throbbing, in a way that felt akin to my magic.

Heat flooded my veins as fire coursed through my limbs while wind whipped by my ears. My skin felt as though it glowed as an otherworldly power sang through my veins, and then something was splintering inside me. I felt for my affinities. I dove my consciousness deep into my belly as I tried to stay latched to the present, to the tangible feel of my body that grounded me to my realm, because it suddenly felt as though I was being lost, pulled, perhaps even extinguished, and that my realm was no realm at all and perhaps had never been. As if everything had been an illusion. My life. My existence. The very fabric of our universe.

No. I latched onto the feel of my power, my affinities, and my magic, even though that awful veil still covered them and kept me from accessing my true potential. I would not get lost. I would not succumb to this darkness.

I would *live.*

The hot sensation increased, but I tried to buck it off while bearing down on my concentration as fear zinged through me, and that sense of detachment and non-existence grew. *Oh gods.*

A grunt came from the darkness, then a deep voice called, "Stop fighting me."

I stilled even though it felt as though flames encircled my form.

A chuckle pierced the blackness. "That's better."

I hung, suspended in emptiness as everything I'd once known fell away until nothing but my mind and power remained. If I could have breathed, shallow pants would have lifted my chest.

But I couldn't.

Because I was nothing and everything. I was born yet

deceased. Present yet in the past. A fairy yet an unknown creature.

Mother Below, what's happening?

"You're an interesting one, aren't you?"

A bolt of power slammed into me, and I screamed from the force of it.

"Yes, very interesting indeed," the male said again. "Yet, someone has tried to stop you. They've attempted to coat this lovely strength within you until it's nothing."

Someone caressed my arm, the first true sensation that I felt. I latched onto it, even though it screamed *other.*

"You like that, do you?" That stroke came again, and a shiver of want and need—a craving that commanded me to my toes nearly made me come undone.

Mother Below, that felt *incredible.*

The male chuckled again. "This . . . foreign power inside you is quite complex, not something I fully recognize." Another caress came along the netting containing my affinities, and if I could have rolled my eyes back in my head in rapture, I would have. I wanted that stroking power to keep touching me again and again.

The male chuckled once more. "You fae do love our touch."

Another caress came along the netting encapsulating my affinities, then a growl. "This is *not* of our universe. This should not be within you." A rumble of power, of angry might, vibrated through me. "What fairy would attempt such a sacrilegious act as to douse the gift I bestowed upon you?"

All I could do was exist before him as I waited, *desperately* waited, for him to touch me again.

"Hmm," the male sighed as he pried along the netting's edges. "You fae always do try to override the force I command, but I am a god. You cannot overpower *me*."

That statement hit me like a crashing wave. *Blessed Mother. I'm with God Zorifel. He answered Genoova's call. He actually came.*

No wonder I craved the feel of him. It was said that if one encountered a god or goddess, their power was so addictive that you would do anything to feel it and be touched by them.

I tried to bow, to show submission to this supreme being, but the void I was in had no ground. No walls. No substance. There was nothing for me to lean on or grasp or hold onto.

"Thank you," I whispered. "I bow to you, God Zorifel."

He didn't reply, but I could have sworn that an answer came through the darkness, like a smug purr.

"Where am I?" I dared ask as nothing but a sense of his overwhelming *otherness* surrounded me.

"Your fairy body is still in your realm, but your soul has joined me in the galaxies."

"Truly?" I didn't question him further, even though I still *felt* as if I had a body, but considering I couldn't see or hear anything other than his voice, perhaps it was my soul's way of connecting to what it knew versus a physical body that actually existed in his realm. And instead of speaking, I was actually projecting my questions.

God Zorifel chuckled again, a masterful sound that made me vibrate with longing. "Your power is truly delicious. Why would someone want to suppress that? Fools." He made a sound like a *tsk*. "You should rule with a power this bold."

Something brushed against my soul again, like a giant hand, and that blissful shiver came over me anew. Everything in me wanted to absorb the god's strength. Each time he'd touched me even in the slightest, his absolute might had called to me, begging me to submit, and *Blessed Mother*, I would give anything to feel that again.

"This might feel . . . interesting." With a rush of power, the veil covering my affinities was ripped off, and a crackling magic exploded through the air as whatever had been encapsulating my affinities sizzled out of existence.

I gasped. The annihilation of that veil within me happened so quickly that it burned.

"Be free, young one. Let them feel your might."

A crash of energy slammed into me, wrenching me apart until everything inside me compressed and imploded before a rupture of power burst to the surface. It felt as though the strength of a thousand suns, a million bolts of lightning, and the hand of a god smashed a final layer inside me containing what had been buried within me all along, before everything flooded to the surface of my skin like a geyser.

A rip seared along my back.

Power skated along my limbs.

Unfurling tendrils burst between my shoulder blades as the shell that had contained other affinities within me shattered into a million pieces as rupturing magic beneath it unlocked and exploded to the surface.

And then I was rising.

Rising.

Rising.

Rising.

Snow-flecked light glowed all around me.

I was spiraling, zooming, going up, up, up.

Rushing to the surface, I careened through the realm with the God Zorifel's power at my back, bursting me through time and space, through dimensions I couldn't comprehend as the galaxy flew past me.

And then I was slamming into something. Awareness flooded me as my limbs became whole. A gasp pierced my ears. *My gasp.*

Air rushed into my lungs. Beautiful, blessed, salty air filled me up as fire raged across my limbs, and someone else's scream pierced my ears.

Strength flooded my veins as my legs whipped out, moving me into a crouch so fast that I was poised and ready to destroy anything that came near.

A brush against my back and the spread of white along my peripheral vision had shock reeling through me as great feathery wings stretched along each side of my shoulders. Their snowy appearance reflected the light as the sense of new appendages flooded my clouded brain.

One flap, two. The rhythmic feel of them latched on to something in my brain as the need to fight and spar, destroy and swing, hit me all at once.

The warrior moves Sandus had taught me vibrated along my limbs, and a sense of absolute rightness came next. This, *this* was who I was.

"Ilara?" my sister called, her voice sounding as though it came from far away.

Through the haze of fire and air swirling around me in a powerful cyclone came the image of four fae standing just outside of my reach. Wings flapped behind me as my brain slowly calmed, and the tornado of power barreling out of me as *all* of my affinities burst free from within hit me all at once.

"Oh gods, what happened to me?" I felt air, fire, life, warrior, and . . . something else rumbling along my back.

My mind became grounded abruptly, as though my soul and body in that exact moment locked back together like a puzzle clicked into place.

I stood in a blur of speed and power, and coiled my magic back inside me, ceasing the fire radiating along my limbs and the air whipping within the circular temple. My life magic hummed through my veins, but I quickly calmed it.

Priestess Genoova looked as though she'd seen a ghost when I finally stopped the magnificent display of my affinities, but that power, that barely leashed *might,* rippled just beneath my skin, waiting to be unleashed with every breath that I took. A warrior's power.

Dear gods, Matron Olsander had been right! I'd had other affinities locked within me. I could feel the warrior power coursing through me now, just underneath my skin, and something else, something so foreign that I didn't have a word for it, heated my back.

I whirled around when that flash of white hit my peripheral sight again and gaped at the wings—*wings*—that spread behind me.

"Blessed Mother, I have wings!" They weren't Solis wings, though. Not black. Not leathery. Not tipped in talons as the prince's were.

Instead, they were beautiful white feathers that were as crisp as snow. They sparkled with magic as they lifted and swayed. They glittered like falling icicles, so mesmerizing as they shimmered in the light.

Breathing hard, I sensed that sensation again between my shoulder blades, and with a mental flick, I flapped my wings again.

I lifted a few inches from the ground.

My hand flew to my mouth as I quieted that feeling, and my wings calmed. I drifted back to the floor without a wobble as that instinctual warrior sense of balance and strength corrected any clumsiness in my limbs without so much as a flicker of thought. Sandus and Matron Olsander had been right. A warrior affinity had indeed been within me.

"Ilara!" my sister called again.

I swung to face her.

Cailis, Drachu, Tylen, and Priestess Genoova all stood outside of the temple's columns. Genoova immediately dipped into a bow when I faced her, while Tylen and Cailis wore shocked expressions.

Drachu merely grinned as a knowing light hit his eyes.

"She's been kissed by the gods," Genoova whispered as shining reverence gleamed in her eyes when she lifted her head.

"Indeed, she has." Drachu's grin never faltered, but his

eyes skated to the floor, to where I still stood in the temple's divots.

I followed his gaze, and my eyes widened when I beheld a huge glittering gemstone between my feet. Gone was the simple tiny rock that had been placed there. A massive diamond sat on the ground, so large that it had to weigh at least a stone.

Drachu prowled toward me, and I immediately sensed his aura. It slammed into me as my affinities flowed strongly within me. Air, fire, life, warrior, and . . . my breath sucked in when I felt that other strange affinity that didn't reside in my gut but instead swirled between my shoulders. My warrior affinity existed near the others, in my belly. It vibrated with leashed strength, but the other one—

I had no words for what it was, but Mother Below, it contained *power*.

I opened my Outlets more as a sense of electricity zinged along my veins, just as the Lochen king reached me.

He bent down and clasped the huge diamond, lifting it as triumph graced his expression. Before I could ask how a simple rock had been transformed into such a priceless gem, Drachu brought it to his necklace.

Similar to what had happened when he'd been in his room, the shining green stone of his pendant seemed to absorb the massive diamond.

Shock filled me when the Lochen king dipped his head back in rapture, and a flare of my affinities inside me tugged toward him. His necklace pulsed as enormous energy ripped through the air around him. When the large diamond had been fully immersed in his pendant's green stone, he opened his eyes.

Blazing emerald irises assessed me as his canines glinted in the sunlight. His smile was so wide that it radiated joy and . . . something else. Something I couldn't quite place as he gazed at me with elation in his eyes.

"And there you are, Krelahala. Born at last and ready to rule your domain. I thank you for the gift."

CHAPTER 10 – NORIVUN

My guards and I reappeared in a flash of mistphasing magic on the beach of the north-ernmost shore of the Glassen Barrier Islands, the exact spot Ilara and I had been months ago.

I'd had to transport Sandus, Ryder, Nish, and Haxil here. Their magic was nearly tapped out since we'd been mist-phasing extensively for most of the day as we searched for my mate, and I needed them to conserve what they had in case they needed their power.

We'd gone everywhere we could think of on the Solis continent without any clue as to where Ilara had gone. The only comfort I took was in knowing that if I couldn't find her, my father couldn't either.

But early this afternoon when we stood near the ice caves in Kroravee, as the black sand shifted beneath my boots, I remembered another black sand beach. A shoreline where a

Lochen king had once told my mate she could seek refuge on his land.

Should you tire of the death warlord, my shores are open to you.

I didn't know if Ilara knew of the trickery the Lochen king wove, or if she even remembered that offer Drachu had voiced, but it was worth a try to see if she'd fled this far south, especially given the implications of what would ensue if Drachu had indeed gotten his claws into her.

Magic rumbled in my gut just thinking about it.

"Ock, Nori." Nish took a step away from me. "Calm yourself, my prince. We shall find her."

My nostrils flared when I inhaled, and murderous thoughts swirled through my mind of what I would do if Drachu hurt her.

Wind whipped around us. I tucked my wings in tight as we all fanned out, walking along the beach. Afternoon sunlight shone down on us and glinted off the frost-nipped leaves of the fjord's forest. I scanned the area and scented the breeze, but no Lochen fae were near.

"Pretty quiet," Ryder remarked.

"Plenty of footprints." Sandus nodded toward the sand. Fairy prints littered the shore.

"Barefoot, though." Haxil hunched down and pointed out the distinct marks indicating webbing between the toes. That trait disappeared slowly once Lochen transformed into their land-walking form. "These are from Lochen emerging from the sea, in the process of shifting, not from Ilara or Cailis."

"He's right." I placed my hands on my hips and tilted my head back. "Let's fly up to Vockalin and question if anyone's seen the sisters."

A gust of wind shot toward us, coming from the south just as my wings spread. I let it pull me up, then flapped hard, using the current to soar upward. My guards easily kept pace as the icy forest passed beneath us in our steep ascent.

We reached the top of the fjord in minutes, and a few cries from Lochen fae pierced the skies when several of the city's residents spotted us.

We flapped to the city's center before we touched down, and when we landed, the mountain shuddered as a huge burst of power flowed out of me.

Haxil, Sandus, Ryder, and Nish flanked my sides, but none of us drew our swords. Fear filled the faces of the Lochen nearest us. Several of the males bared their teeth, hissing as they backed up.

I held my palms up, trying to appear as unthreatening as possible, just as a male shoved his way through the crowd and stormed toward us.

"You have no right setting foot on our shores, Prince Norivun!" Gray hair brushed against his ears, and his portly belly made me think he'd given up on the sea and was spending his remaining days on land until the gods took him to the afterlife. "King Drachu isn't here, and we haven't been raiding your coastal cities. You have no reason to be angry with us!"

Indignation filled his tone, yet his scent reeked of terror. The sour smell poured from him in waves even though he kept his shoulders back. Despite being old, he was brave. I gave him that.

I lowered my hands, placing them on my hips. "I'm not here to cause any strife. I'm looking for someone and am hoping you can help."

Those surrounding us released a collective sigh, but the older Lochen bristled in spite of my reassuring words. "Oh? Who is it you seek?"

"She's an unusual-looking Solis female. She has black hair and no wings. Her name's Ilara. She may have come here within the past two days."

The male frowned. "I know nobody by that name."

His scent carried no hint of deceit, and the Lochen around him all looked to one another with growing frowns. I sniffed the breeze again. Not one scent carried the trace of a lie.

Worry began pulsing through me, and my jaw locked. I scanned the crowd. "Does anyone know of her whereabouts? Any of you?" I described Ilara again and watched all of them closely.

A few of them looked down, fierce resolve in their expressions. Lip curling, I was about to stride toward the nearest one when a child ran forward and pointed at me.

"Look, mumma, he has wings like the other one!"

His mother snatched him back, but not before the scent of her hatred hit me.

A snarl worked up my throat.

The female sneered. "A few of us saw her and another

female yesterday. They were here, but not for long. They've since disappeared."

"Disappeared?" I prowled toward her but stopped short when a strange scent wafted to me on the wind. The emotional scent was filled with hatred and spite. That in itself was something I was used to since it was how most fae felt toward me, but this one was different. The subtle fragrance of my mate's roses and dew scent clung to it.

My dragon affinity instantly reared, and the urge to shift and bite off the head of whoever carried my mate's scent on their skin threatened to break my composure.

I inhaled again, then strode through the crowd as power rose around me while I followed the trail.

The Vockalin citizens parted, giving me generous amounts of space as I homed in on a female. She wore next to nothing, and her creamy flesh and soft curves were on full display. As I got closer, bloodlust began to consume me. The female reeked of not only my mate but of sex and Drachu.

Magic flooded my veins, and blood pounded through my ears.

The female peered up at me, eyes widening, but I couldn't stop my reaction. She smelled of my mate, the Lochen king, and *fucking*. If she or that king had laid a hand on Ilara in wonton longing, something I knew would have been against Ilara's wishes since she was mated to *me*, I would—

"Nori," Haxil said cautiously at my back. "Rein it in. We don't know what's happened."

His words cut through the red haze growing in my mind,

and I loosened my fisted hands, not even realizing they'd been balled or that I'd been on the verge of succumbing to my baser instincts. I took deep breaths and opened my Outlets more as the female's scent shifted to terror when she realized *she* was the reason for my growing rage.

"Why do you smell like my mate?" I growled. Somehow I managed to get the question out even though my tone barely sounded fae as a hint of my dragon rolled into it.

Her lower lip began to tremble, and she clasped her hands. "I'm sorry, my prince. I mean, I don't—"

"Let me help you out here, love," Sandus cut in. "His mate's scent is all over you, even I can smell it, and he's a fully mated Solis male. He also carries more magic and power than anyone in this village. I would advise you to answer truthfully and quickly before he levels this entire mountaintop in a single blow of power."

"Tell him, Sabreeny!" a female hissed behind her.

My attention stayed fixated on the scantily clad female quaking before me.

Sabreeny licked her full lips, eyeing Sandus again, before blurting out, "She and her sister came here asking for safe haven. They left this morning with my king." Another scent joined the others wafting around her—jealousy.

The spicy fragrance with a bitter aftertaste made my muscles flex at what that emotional scent implied.

"Nori, keep it under control," Haxil said again. "We don't know what happened."

Fuck. I was losing it.

I directed a burst of my power downward, needing to

release something, *anything* to keep from imploding. The mountain rumbled again, and a sharp cry of fear rose from several citizens, but Mother Below, I needed to keep releasing the magic heating up inside me, or I was going to level this entire damned city.

Clenching my teeth, I asked, "Why do you smell of her?"

The female raised her chin. "She spent the night in my home, I mean, Drachu's home."

I arched an eyebrow, my tone deadly quiet. "Explain."

"She and her sister came here looking for my king. Drachu knew she was coming, so he was waiting for her, and I . . ." She twisted her hands, which got a scathing look from Nish.

"Ock, out with it. *All* of it." Nish seethed.

"He invited her to stay in his home, which was also my home as his salivar." She raised her chin higher, her eyes flashing. "I did not care to have other females in my house, especially when I saw the way my king was looking at her."

Somehow I managed to keep breathing as images of Drachu trying to seduce Ilara barreled to the front of my thoughts.

"Did he touch her?" A huge gush of magic flew from me, rattling the windowpanes nearest us. Screams rose from the crowd again.

"Of course not," Sabreeny said in a scathing tone. "I took his cock three times last night and sucked him within an inch of his life this morning. I had him begging for me and not that cunt of a—"

My hand was around her throat before she knew what hit

her. "Speak very, *very* carefully. That's my mate you're disrespecting."

The bob of her throat rolled in my palm. I didn't increase my pressure, but I would if she continued. By the gods, it wasn't below me to hurt a female if it involved Ilara. I would break my code of no violence against females if my mate had been assaulted.

A brush of my death affinity wrapped around Sabreeny's soul. Her eyes bulged, and she wisely said in a more controlled tone, "Drachu didn't touch her. He was too enamored with me."

No deceit coated her scent, so I released her throat, and she hastily took a step back.

"And why isn't she here now? Where did Drachu take her?"

Sabreeny shook her head. "I don't know."

Nish *tsked*. "You sure about that?"

She bared her sharp canines at him as her breasts heaved with each breath. "He didn't tell me his plans. The king answers to no one. Not even you," she spat.

She eyed me boldly, and I couldn't decide if she was the stupidest female to ever live or the bravest.

I curled my lip in disgust, then addressed the entire city. "Does anyone know where Drachu took my mate?"

They shared confused looks, then glanced back at the king's house, the largest one in the city that was covered with purple shells and stones. It was covered so thickly with items from the sea that I knew it was channeling the power of the ocean.

I prowled toward it and placed my hand along the exterior, running my fingers down it until one of the shells pried loose in my grip.

"We didn't see him leave, Prince Norivun," a male finally answered. "They disappeared this morning. None of us know where he took your mate or her sister."

Power rumbled along my limbs as I turned to face the crowd again. I inhaled all of the scents drifting through the air. The male wasn't lying. None of them were. "*Fuck.*"

I shot into the sky, my wings flapping so violently that the air around me whipped and swirled. My air elemental affinity unleashed, and the tree branches creaked and groaned as I dove back toward the beach, then began to soar over the ocean.

I released a huge burst of magic toward the sea, and a ripple shot out across the water as I bellowed in rage.

My guards caught up with me a second later, their wings flapping so fast they were a blur as they kept pace behind me.

"We'll find her, Nori," Ryder called as his sharp cheekbones caught the sunlight.

"How?" I growled. "The queen gave her a potion that hides her whereabouts. Nobody can find her using magic, and—" My mate's scent hit me with a vengeance when we flew over an outcropping of rocks. It was so strong that I nearly dropped to the ground midflight.

Nish let out a grumble when I clipped his wing, but I was too consumed with the scent on the wind to apologize.

I landed on the shore and inhaled again, my stride eating

up the ground as Ilara's scent grew stronger and stronger as I strode toward the rocks.

My hands were buried in the outcropping before my guards could ask what I was doing. Rocks flew over my shoulder as I threw them.

A flutter of parchment appeared a second later. My mate's essence coated it. I carefully pulled the top rock off it, my breaths coming so fast I was certain all four of my guards could hear.

With shaking fingers, I smoothed the folded creases, and my heart nearly stopped when Ilara's handwriting stared back at me.

Norivun,

If you're reading this, then you've come in search of me on Drachu's shores. I don't know how long it'll be until you find this letter, but I've been with the Lochen king for two days, and he's now taking me to the Adrall Temple. He believes he can free my trapped affinities.

I'm going because I have no other options, and I'm too weak in my current state to do anything to stop your father's plans for our future, but if I haven't returned to the Solis continent, and you're worried for my safety, then please find me. It means venturing to the Adrall Temple was a mistake.

I love you,
Ilara

Pride at my mate's cleverness to leave me something she knew I could find and absolute terror at what might have happened to her hit me simultaneously.

"Fuck!" With trembling fingers, I folded the paper and tucked it into my pocket as my guards gazed at me with wild eyes.

"What is it?" Haxil asked as fear entered his scent.

My lip curled. "Drachu's taken her to the Adrall Temple. Ilara thinks it's because he's going to untrap her affinities."

The blood drained from Haxil's face. "No."

"Exactly." I wrapped all four of them in my mistphasing magic as I called on a huge dose of it. Fear at what might have already happened consumed me.

Because if Drachu took her to that temple, it was only for one reason, which meant we might be too late.

CHAPTER 11 - ILARA

ift? I stared at Drachu, wondering what he meant by that comment as I brought a hand to my gut. Power swirled beneath my palm . . . *Immense* magic, even more than I'd carried before.

I caressed the new affinity inside me, the warrior one that now resided below my air, fire, and life-giving affinities. The warrior affinity was all jagged edges and cool stone, not like my feathery air, brimming fire, or glowing life. And the affinity that nestled between my shoulder blades . . .

I assessed that next and found a tight, dense ball of startling light and cold power. I didn't know how else to describe it.

So strange.

"Are you truly okay?" Cailis asked, her gaze skating over me.

"Of course, she's okay." Drachu gave a smug smile, and something about his smile—

I drifted toward him before I realized what I was doing, then drew myself up short. "I'm fine. I just—" I brought a hand to my head and shook myself.

Taking a deep breath, I glanced back at the center of the temple. *Did I really just venture to somewhere within the galaxy and meet God Zorifel?* All of it now felt like a dream—a distant, bizarre, and very powerful dream.

Frowning, I recalled what the god had said about how the veil that had suppressed my affinities wasn't of this universe, which made no sense whatsoever, because if it wasn't of this universe, then where had it come from?

"Are you ready to see our great capital on the Lochen continent?" Drachu's question snapped me from my mulling.

"What?"

His smile didn't falter, and a little tug clenched in my chest again. Before I knew what was happening, I was walking toward him, and it was only when I stood a foot away that the urgency to be near him calmed.

So weird.

Giving Drachu what I hoped was a remorseful smile, I replied, "I'm afraid I can't. I have a bargain I must uphold, and it's already been several days since I've worked toward fulfilling it. If I wait too much longer, the gods will no doubt begin to take their vengeance." I didn't add that I also had a king to thwart. I still didn't know how I was going to do that, but somehow, Norivun and I had to discover a way to stop the Olirum Accords.

Drachu cocked his head. "I thought you fled the Solis continent?"

"I did, temporarily, but I can't stay here forever."

He closed the distance between us, and his gaze heated. "Are you sure about that?"

His tone caused a shiver to dance down my spine, and the urge to thread my fingers through his hair grew to the point of pain. I leaned into him as Cailis's eyebrows shot to her hairline. A pulsing sensation began in my chest. I wanted to be near the king, close to him, until he was wrapped around me. I *needed* it.

I whipped back just as my arm began to curl around the king. *Blessed Mother, what is wrong with me?*

Chest heaving, I forced myself to take a step back even though I really wanted to melt into the Lochen king's embrace. "I'm sorry. I don't know what's come over me."

"I do," Drachu said with a glint in his eyes.

My brow furrowed as Cailis yanked me to her side. "Ilara," she said urgently, "we must go." Her hand snaked down my arm until she reached my palm. She gave a painful, single squeeze.

Truth. Drachu hadn't been lying. He knew why I just responded as I had.

I breathed harder, and my frown turned into a scowl as I leveled him with a bold stare. But even though anger coursed through me at the wrongness of this, at the same time, I wanted to pull away from my sister and join the king again.

"What did you do to me?"

Priestess Genoova's lips upturned in a secretive, malicious smile. "King Drachu has blessed you, just as the gods have."

Fear blazed through me. I shot her a glare, then returned my attention to Drachu. "*What* did you do?"

Drachu cocked an eyebrow as a smug smile curved his lips. "I tethered you to me." He tapped his necklace. "Part of you was within that diamond. This temple has the power to channel a fairy's magic to a stone in addition to channeling the gods. And since I claimed that diamond, I now own a part of you and have the ability to channel those extraordinary affinities within your body."

My lips parted as I struggled to understand. "You *own* a part of me?"

"I do."

Mind racing, I thought back to the chest I'd seen in his room, the chest with hundreds of priceless gems just like the diamond that had appeared between my feet. Did that mean Drachu also owned other fae?

But those gems weren't in his necklace. They were in that chest in his room. So what did that mean? That the Lochen king owned *thousands* of fae whenever he fed his necklace their powers? Could he add and remove their power from his pendant at will, meaning he had thousands of fae's abilities at his disposal? I recalled how he'd fed his pendant one of those gems when I'd been hiding in the closet. *Mother Below.* Drachu *did* own that many fae's power.

"Remember what I said about how one becomes king in our realm?" Tylen said quietly, snapping me from my thoughts.

My jaw dropped when the meaning of Tylen's question

hit me square in my gut. To be the leader of the Lochen fae, one must show strength, courage, and a cunning mind.

A cunning mind.

Tears of frustration welled in my eyes as I understood what the young prince was trying to tell me. *Of course.* Drachu had thoroughly and completely tricked me. He'd never set out to help me from the goodness of his heart. On the first day we'd met, the Lochen king had felt the kind of power I had and wanted to use me, just as Prince Norivun had when he'd whisked me from my village. Drachu had even admitted that the queens before him—the ones that reminded him of me—had ruled like no other. They'd held power like mine, and now he held that kind of power too . . . by tethering *my* affinities to him.

And I'd never consented to that.

My tears vanished, and anger abruptly scorched my nerves. I would *not* be used again, especially not by a foreign fae king.

I crouched into a fighting stance as I whipped a ring of fire around me and kicked up a sharp rock from the ground in the same beat. The rock was in my raised hand, and then it was zinging so fast through the air that I doubted anyone even knew what I intended before my makeshift blade headed straight for the king's head.

Cailis's breath sucked in after the blade was already airborne. Genoova let out a startled scream, and Tylen shouted.

But just when the sharp rock should have imbedded itself within Drachu's eye, a gust of wind flung it to the side. The burst of air was so abrupt, so perfectly streamed, and a slight rise of my affinity pulsed in my gut.

My mouth opened in horror when the wind abruptly turned course and slammed into me, knocking me off my feet until my rump met the rocky ground.

"None of that, Ilara," Drachu said with a waggle of his finger. The stone in his necklace glowed, as though a sun lit it from within. "I don't want to steal your powers from you or control you with them. I merely want to borrow them from time to time as I need them. That's all. Surely, you can learn to live with that and not try to murder me every time you see me."

"You vile, loathsome, horrible—" My chest was heaving so fast that I couldn't form a coherent insult.

"Bastard!" Cailis seethed. "I should—"

"You should do nothing." Drachu's canines flashed. "If you're wise, you'll accept this quietly and go about your way. If you come after me . . ." Malice flashed in his expression. "I shall do as I see fit to ensure the power of my kingdom."

I stared up at him as hair flew in my eyes. My attention snapped to his necklace. Was that how he'd also known of the power I carried and how he'd known when I arrived on his shores? Did he have endless magic with that necklace? Perhaps that pendant gave him the ability to see what magic lay in others or allowed him to see the future. And if he'd tricked others as he'd tricked me—other fae with powerful gifts—it was possible that Drachu's magic was *limitless*.

Blessed Mother, and I'd just fed his strength.

I rolled back on my shoulders, my new wings bending

easily to accommodate the movement, then bent my elbows, placing my hands by my ears, and pushed off with my arms and kicked up to a stand as my warrior affinity throbbed within me.

Drachu's eyebrows rose. "Impressive."

I bared my teeth as my blood boiled. It was such a contradicting feeling since that strange need to be near the Lochen king still flowed through my veins. "Give me back what's mine."

He laughed. "I think not."

I eyed his necklace. If I could reach it and snap it from his neck, perhaps his control of my affinities would break.

A scowl darkened his face. "Don't even consider it. Do you really think you'd be the first fairy to try and steal this from me?" He placed a hand protectively over the pendant.

Hope surged through me. So the necklace was the full source of his channeled power. I needed to take it from him if I didn't want to be tethered to him for the rest of my life.

I was about to attempt another attack, his warning be damned, but a tearing feeling in my stomach doubled me over, and then a huge whip of air magic knocked me off my feet. *My* air magic that the king had just stolen again.

Pain ricocheted up my spine I landed so hard.

"Don't, Ilara," the king warned. "You won't win."

I hissed in agony, clutching my belly as I pushed to a stand, but a rumble of power shook the mountain beneath us, stopping my advance. Magic flashed through the air, and then my mate, Sandus, Ryder, Haxil, and Nish stood before us.

I blinked, then blinked again.

All five of them still stood there.

Oh dear gods, I'm truly losing it. I'm hallucinating that my mate is here.

"Ilara?" the prince growled. In two steps he was in front of me, his expression turning to shock as he assessed my white wings.

I was dreaming. I had to be.

Mother Below, I'd lost my damned mind.

"Ilara . . ." His voice turned to that of wonder as he lifted a finger and trailed it across one of my white feathers.

A shiver shot all the way to my toes, and *Blessed Mother* . . . that sensation felt amazing.

"How?" he said, confusion painting his features.

I shook myself and tentatively felt his chest. Warmth and firm muscle greeted me. "It's really you?"

His jaw locked, and he gave a single nod. "I'm here."

I flung my arms around him, and in the same beat, he crushed me to his chest.

"Truly?" Cailis asked, spinning toward the crown prince's guards.

"It's us, love," Sandus replied.

"I feared I'd never see you again." I pulled back and cradled Norivun's cheeks between my palms as the impossibility that he was here pounded into me.

"I got your note." He smirked, his lips curving up as his four guards spread out around the Lochen king, their hands on their swords, their expressions filled with intent.

Drachu and Tylen took a step back and watched them warily.

Understanding hit me. "You found it?"

"Yes, my love. It was clever of you to hide that letter where you did."

"Norivun." I hugged him again and breathed in his scent of cedar and snow. Something within me calmed and for the first time since I'd learned of what Drachu had done, fear wasn't consuming me.

My mate's hands settled on my hips. His pounding aura threatened to consume me. Wings snapping out around us, he shielded me from view.

"How?" he said again on a low growl as he began pressing urgent kisses along my neck. Possessive kisses. Desperate kisses. "How do you have wings?" Blazing sapphire eyes stared down at me when he lifted his head. His face swirled in darkness as he skimmed over my features, his expression oscillating between one of fury, fear, desperation, and love.

"God Zorifel."

His eyes widened. "Did you—" He glanced toward the top of the temple.

I nodded. "The God of Power gave me my affinities back, along with two more." I nodded toward my wings, then said, "Turns out I did have a warrior affinity slumbering within me as well as whatever gave me these." I flapped my wings.

Something flashed in the prince's eyes. Pain or perhaps fear. I couldn't tell. He swore softly beneath his breath. "Are you okay?"

Tears welled in my eyes anew because I wanted to say that yes, I was fine, but I wasn't. I was anything but okay.

I shook my head as a tear spilled onto my cheek.

The prince's jaw locked, the muscle bulging like a marble. His power rose like an avenging demon. Wings snapping in tight, he released me from his caged shield, as he shot a glare to the Lochen king. A brush of his death affinity caressed my soul as it stirred around him.

"What did you do to her?" Norivun demanded.

Drachu glowered. "Nothing that will hurt her, so put that lethal force of yours back where it belongs."

"Did he hurt you?" Norivun asked me.

My nostrils flared because this battle was mine to fight with Drachu, but I also knew that Norivun wouldn't relent.

"He says I'm tethered to him now."

"Fuck!" Norivun's eyes squeezed shut just as a huge burst of power erupted from his pores.

"I'm sorry," I cried as the mountain rumbled beneath me. "I didn't know."

"It's not your fault. I knew Drachu would try something like this if given the opportunity." Norivun's expression set into that unrelenting mask he wore just before he ended someone. He swirled toward the Lochen king, murder in his gaze. Before I could say anything further, his death affinity shot out of him.

Genoova screamed, then fled from the impending bloodshed as the strength of the prince's affinity flew across the mountain's peak.

Fear twisted Drachu's expression a second before

Norivun's malice reached him, and then I barreled over, screaming in pain. It felt as though my life-giving affinity was being ripped from my body.

Drachu's terror-filled expression morphed into savage victory as Norivun's affinity and mine collided in an explosion between the Lochen king and my mate. The force of it sent a shockwave through the air. Everyone was blown from their feet, all of us flying through the air to land dozens of yards away.

"Father!" Tylen called.

"Stop him!" Drachu growled as we all pushed to a stand.

Rage dripped from the crown prince as his affinity and mine tangled in the air. I'd never seen Norivun look this murderous before, not even when he'd been intent on killing Vorl.

My mate's roar pierced the late afternoon sky as his affinity rose even higher. The Lochen king backpedaled. Sweat dripped from Drachu's brow as his face became a mask of concentration.

The prince leapt the distance to Drachu, and as his death affinity continued to blaze through the air, his hand curled around the king's throat.

Drachu hissed, his canines flashing as another wrench of my life-giving affinity tore from me.

"Norivun!" I screamed as I doubled over again.

But as had happened before, the second the prince's death affinity touched Drachu's soul, the king manipulated even more of my life-giving affinity to Shield himself.

I barreled over again, clutching my stomach as I fell to the ground.

Sweat beaded on Drachu's face as his muscles rippled with exertion.

Norivun didn't let go of the king, but Drachu didn't fall before my mate.

Tylen, mouth gaping, stood frozen beside my sister.

I curled into a ball as Drachu channeled my warrior affinity, and then chaos unleashed.

The king and prince turned into a blur of dueling fists, punches, and blazing magic. They were moving so fast that I couldn't keep track of who was who as affinities swirled and slashed around them.

I frantically looked to his guards, but Haxil shook his head from his readied pose. "It's too dangerous when he's dueling this close. We can't intervene, Ilara."

The guards fanned out around their prince, each on the balls of their feet while their hands stayed on their swords, just waiting for an opportunity to strike.

I managed to get to a kneeling position, but the pain from Drachu's control of my affinities didn't allow me to rise.

"Tylen!" Drachu roared when Norivun kicked the Lochen king's feet out from under him and sent him sprawling.

The crown prince whipped his sword from his sheath in a blurred move, then flipped it in his grip into the perfect striking position.

A savage snarl tore from Norivun's throat just as his

sword cleaved through the air, but then Tylen was there, leaping the few feet to my mate from where he stood.

Drachu smiled maliciously when his son's hand brushed along Norivun's shoulders. All four of the prince's guards lunged toward Drachu's son, but Tylen's contact was so fleeting that the young Lochen prince was already several feet away from my mate.

Norivun's sword stopped midair, his eyes widening in disbelief as he shot a wild look at Tylen. Haxil had a knife to Tylen's throat, and Nish had one at his belly. But even though Tylen could no longer reach the prince, Norivun still stared at him with horror.

Another tug came from my gut, and then a ring of fire erupted around Drachu. Ryder and Sandus both jumped back a second before they got burned.

"Tylen," Drachu bit out.

I felt another rip on my affinities, and Haxil and Nish were slammed out of the way with a gust of wind, allowing Tylen to reach Drachu's side. Groaning in pain from the vicious use of my powers, I cradled my stomach and rocked forward.

Norivun's hand opened, and he dropped his sword as he continued to stare at Tylen with an emotion I'd never seen him wear around anyone—fear.

"What in all the realm is happening?" my sister cried, her chest heaving.

I looked to Norivun, then Drachu, then Tylen before Drachu grinned. "Tylen is a null."

Norivun's chest rose rapidly, and it suddenly struck me that I no longer felt his commanding aura.

"What happened?" I rasped, still rocking, but before Norivun could respond, the Lochen king gave my mate a triumphant smile.

"You shall never command me again, Solis prince. I now control the magic of your mate. Should you come to my shores again and demand that we stop our raids, you'll be met with a far different outcome than you did last time."

A portal key appeared in Drachu's grip, and the fae king smirked in my direction. I wanted him and hated him simultaneously with such intensity. I'd never despised someone like this before, not even Vorl, and the way Drachu had just used me . . .

All of it made me sick.

The Lochen king winked, and then he whispered the words to activate the portal key. In a flash of power, Drachu and Tylen disappeared, taking the diamond that contained my channeled affinities with them.

CHAPTER 12 - NORIVUN

"Ilara?" I flew to her side, my arms going around her as I helped my mate to her feet even though rage was still making my entire body shake.

Groaning, she stood, still clutching her stomach.

"Are you all right?" I carefully assessed her, but she had no outward wounds.

"I'll be okay. Now that he's stopped pulling on my magic, it's getting better."

"I'm going to *fucking kill him*." My chest heaved as Ilara trembled in my arms. Her white-feathered wings fluttered in the breeze, and if so much hadn't happened in the past few minutes, I would still be marveling that my mate *had wings*.

But now was not the time for celebration. Drachu was gone. His power-nulling son had disappeared with him, and my mate would forever be in the Lochen king's clutches unless we found a way to free her.

It was my biggest fear come true.

The salty ocean wind whipped around us as my guards' feral expressions grew. Cailis looked ready to vomit.

"I knew he might have something up his sleeve, but I didn't think it would be this bad," Ilara breathed. Shivers continued to wrack her frame.

"We'll find a way to undo it."

She gave a small nod, but worry still rolled across her features as she peered up at me. "Are you all right?"

"I'm fine." I tentatively called upon my death affinity, but it still refused to respond. I cut off the snarl that wanted to work up my throat as Haxil assessed me with a frown.

"Is your magic coming back?" my guard asked.

I shook my head. "No, not yet. He was a powerful null." So powerful that all it took was a fleeting brush of contact to lock down my affinities so tightly it was as though a steel door had slammed shut on them.

"A null?" Cailis said, her gaze whipping between me and my guards. "What in the realm is a *null*?" Her chest still heaved, as did Ilara's, but my only concern was for my mate.

I placed a hand on Ilara's lower back, drawing her closer in hopes of soothing her frayed nerves. Addressing Cailis, I said, "A null is a Lochen fairy that has the ability to cut off fae from their own magic, or in a Solis's case, from their affinities."

"You mean . . ." Cailis's eyes widened. "When Tylen touched you, he stopped you from accessing any of your magic?"

As much as it pained me to admit how vulnerable I was, I nodded. "Yes, but it's more than that. He stripped me of them. In that moment, and even now, I'm as magicless as a child. My speed and strength, which I'm able to amplify with magic, were also cut off. It's why I didn't kill Drachu. I couldn't."

Ilara's arms wrapped around me, and she buried her face in my chest.

Something in me instantly calmed, and I forgot about Cailis, Drachu, his son, and my guards.

I gathered Ilara to me and wrapped my arms and wings around her. Breathing in her scent brought the first stirring of peace within me since the final test of the Rising Queen Trial despite the predicament we currently found ourselves in.

She squeezed me in return, and any concerns over what Tylen had done or what the fucking Lochen king had master-planned fell to the back of my mind.

Because even though Ilara's affinities had been grossly compromised, something otherworldly had happened to her in this temple. She now had wings, and given how I saw her move, she was right. She'd finally manifested that warrior affinity that Sandus and Matron Olsander had suspected she harbored.

My mate was strong now, despite what Drachu had done, and she was alive and safe. And by the gods, I would make sure that nothing further was done to her if my life depended on it.

I bent down, and my lips grazed her ear. "Are you ready to get out of here?" I whispered.

"More than anything, but I have nowhere to go." Her voice sounded so small, so broken, that it nearly undid me.

"I'm taking you home."

Her head lifted as worry filled her eyes. Before she could voice her concern, I silenced her with a finger to her lips. "I'm going to take your sister to the Cliffs of Sarum. Cailis can stay with your parents and brother so no harm comes to her, then I'm taking you back to my chambers in the castle, where you will stay until we can sort this mess out."

The relief I'd expected to see in her eyes didn't come. Instead, her jaw dropped. "You want to make me a prisoner again?"

I growled, the bond inside me twitching at the anger that suddenly wafted in her scent. "No, not at all, but in my bedroom chambers, I can protect you." I hoped she understood my intentions. Even my father couldn't enter my chambers without me knowing. If my father hadn't sent guards to the Exorbiant Chamber so quickly following the Rising Queen Trial, I could have offered her that reprieve.

Granted, keeping her in my chambers would have taken some planning and scheming to make happen since Ilara would have been under my father's ever-watchful eye, but I would have figured out a way.

But Ilara shook her head, doubt evident in her tone when she said, "What if they search your bedroom chambers? Surely, that's not a safe place for me to stay."

"True, the day may come when my father decides to do a raid, but my illusion magic is strong enough to fool him. I could cloak you. He would never know you were there." I knew it wasn't ideal. I knew Ilara detested being locked behind walls, but I didn't know what else to do to keep her safe. My father was hunting her, yet I *would* keep her safe.

"No."

Her single word took me so much by surprise that I nearly growled. Somehow, I managed to suppress it. "What do you mean, *no?*"

"I won't be a prisoner ever again, and you can't make me. Our bargain forbids it."

"Blessed Mother." I sighed heavily because even though I ached for my mate with a fierceness I'd never experienced before, the female also knew how to drive me absolutely fucking mad. Ilara had a stubborn streak a millee wide, and it was showing gloriously right now.

Taking another deep breath, I reminded myself that my mate didn't like to be commanded. I still remembered what she'd told me when she'd had her date with Lord Waterline. She would rather I spoke with her and take her feelings into account. I needed to compromise. Not demand. I grumbled within. *Fucking compromises.* Life was so much easier when I could just command things of her.

But when she gazed up at me, as she was now, with that fighting spirit shining in her eyes . . . *Damn.* I couldn't do it. I wanted to make her happy, so I asked in as patient of a tone as I could muster, "What would you suggest as an alternative plan?"

Her face softened, and a small smile parted her lips, and seeing that my question brought her joy made my irritation fade and for the first time I really understood what living with my mate would be like. It wasn't all about me anymore.

Ilara placed her hand on my arm. "I propose that you take Cailis to the Cliffs of Sarum *if* she's willing. I agree that's a good idea, but I'm not going back to the castle, and I'm not going to be a prisoner in your room. I need to figure out what's causing the *orem* in our land to die. I can't do that by hiding in your bed chambers."

My lips kicked up. Even after what had just been done to her in this temple, she was still fighting. "And how do you propose we figure out what's killing the *orem*?"

Her brows drew together as those feather-soft wings continued to ripple in the breeze on the mountaintop. My guards and Cailis listened raptly around us, not interrupting, as my mate and I figured out our lives.

"When I was with God Zorifel, he said something very curious. He said that the veil smothering my affinities wasn't of this universe. And remember whatever suppressed my magic came directly from the Isalee field, which means whatever's killing the *orem* also isn't of our universe."

My eyes narrowed. "Not of this universe?"

She nodded. "Isn't that strange?"

"But if it's not of this universe, then where did it come from?" Cailis asked as she pulled her bottom lip into her mouth.

"Could it be from the gods after all?" Haxil asked.

Ilara shook her head. "The gods and goddesses still exist within our universe."

"Meaning, it's from *another* universe?" I thought out loud.

Ilara's chest rose in a breath, drawing my attention to her

delectable breasts. She still wore the same clothes she'd been in during the final test of that ridiculous Rising Queen Trial. My mate filled out her green tunic in a way that made it hard to look away, even if the back was ruined when her wings had shredded through the material.

Nish snickered behind me, and I knew he'd detected the arousal in my scent. I shot him a glare as Ilara started picking at her fingers.

"Do you suppose it could be from that . . ." She made a face. "*Other* universe? The one you purchased your whiskey from?"

I arched an eyebrow. "But we don't deal with that realm, not like the Nolus do. How do you suppose it would be from there?" But then my thoughts tumbled toward my father, to what Lord Crimsonale had overheard. Perhaps whoever my father had conspired with was from the *other* realm . . .

Ilara shrugged. "I don't know, but considering it's the only *other* universe that our realm currently has access to, isn't it fair to say it could be from there?"

Cailis scoffed. "But they aren't even magical there."

"That's not entirely true," Haxil corrected. "There are species that exist in that realm that wield magic. I've read about it."

Ilara smiled. "You shall have to tell me what book that was."

"Indeed." Haxil grinned.

My nostrils flared as I cut my guard a look, telling him to back the fuck off so I didn't lose my control to the irrational jealousy scorching through me.

Haxil inclined his head and retreated a step.

Ryder stroked his defined jaw. "I've heard that some of their magic-wielders are quite powerful."

"Powerful enough to create magic that would suppress an entire continent's *orem*?" Ilara asked.

My thoughts again returned to what Michas had told me as I ran a hand up Ilara's hip, then back down. Gods, I just needed to touch her. "It could be possible. To be honest, I don't know much of their kind, but I've heard rumblings similar to what Haxil and Ryder said."

My mate's breathing increased as I continued to stroke her hip, and a musky tint entered her scent. I grinned wickedly, and not just because my sensory affinity was beginning to fully respond.

"Oh gods, they're at it again." Nish rolled his eyes.

"Not to be too familiar, but can you just bed her already and get it over with?" Sandus asked.

Ilara gasped, which got a laugh from Ryder as Haxil muffled a chuckle.

Cailis also appeared to be smothering a smile as Ilara cleared her throat.

"We're getting off track," Ilara said as a blush stained her cheeks.

My lips hooked up. I loved that color on her, especially when I was the reason behind it. But knowing as she was still embarrassed at how easily I aroused her, I diverted the conversation back to the matter at hand. I had so much to tell her. She needed to know what Michas had revealed, but that was a long conversation to be had later. We had things to sort out first.

"Perhaps we should secure your sister in the Cliffs of Sarum and figure out a suitable place for us to stay in the interim." I ran my hand lightly along her skin again. "I agree that discussing this more may lead to some answers, but first things first, right?" I gazed down at her as I assessed her bright eyes, pert nose, and those alluring lips.

She relaxed under my grip, and some of the bright color in her cheeks faded. "Okay, I agree that makes sense. Does that sound okay to you, Cailis? Would you like to stay with Mother, Father, and Tormesh while Norivun and I continue working on a solution?"

Her sister gave a little jump in happiness. "I would love nothing more than to see our family again."

Since Ilara's affinities were back and even stronger than before, she insisted on mistphasing all of us to the Cliffs of Sarum. I didn't argue. My affinities were slowly beginning to respond, and considering I would need a large amount of magic to open the veil hiding that village, I knew I needed to conserve what power I could call upon.

We reappeared in a whiteout, just outside of the hidden city I'd built within the enchanted cliffs. Ilara's wings blended into the snowy background, and Cailis peered anxiously around, searching for a rip in my illusion affinity.

Cold wind bit viciously into my cheeks, but I didn't call upon my air affinity to Shield it.

Taking a deep breath, I had to dive deep into my power to summon the amount of magic it would take to slice through my illusion, allow Cailis entry, and then to once again hide it from any onlookers. My illusion here was so thick that it felt as though I had to cut through stone with a knitting needle every time I did this.

But despite the toll it took on me given what Tylen had done, seeing Ilara's reaction to her sister dissolving into tears when Cailis was finally reunited with their family made the aching fatigue worth it. And seeing Ilara's family marvel over her new wings made pride surge through me.

I didn't rush any of them. I gave Ilara time with her family too, knowing how much she loved them and cherished their support. So I waited and stood tall despite the pain slicing through my limbs at how depleted I was.

My guards all stayed behind me, shuffling their feet, and they looked downright uncomfortable when the Seary family also pulled them into hugs. They all allowed it, though, even Nish, which told me that my guards had fiercely accepted Ilara as a female they would give their lives for.

"We shall make a meal for all of you. Come inside." Ilara's mother beckoned us to join them, and my mate nodded eagerly.

We spent the next hour being pampered by her mother while I ate as much food as was put in front of me. Some of the black hole inside me began to fill. Each bite helped slightly, but it would take until tomorrow for me to fully recharge. Worry pulsed through me at how easily Tylen had rendered me useless even though his nulling magic had finally, fully worn off.

When we finished eating, her mother eyed the couch. "Would you all like to sit? Or perhaps go for a walk? This time of the day, the sunlight through the ice is quite beautiful."

Ilara squeezed her mother's hand. "We can't, not at this time." Ilara eyed me, her brow furrowing, and I knew she was thinking about everything we needed to do. "Soon, though, I promise."

Cailis and Tormesh were in a deep discussion over what they'd been doing for the past year, not even listening to us, but they stood when we said we were leaving.

After tearful goodbyes and more hugs—all of which made Nish look slightly ill—we slipped through my illusion, and I had just enough magic left to fully stitch it back together.

Once done, my knees sagged, and I braced myself on them as I took deep breaths. *Fuck.*

A soft hand settled on my back as Ilara's roses and dew scent drifted around me.

"Where can we go that's not the castle?" she asked quietly. "I'll mistphase all of us so you can rest."

A part of me wanted to argue and tell her that I was strong enough to do it myself, but one look at her unrelenting expression, and I accepted it for what it was. After an entire day of mistphasing myself and my four guards repeatedly around the continent, the huge physical and magical blowout I'd had with Drachu, Tylen's nulling magic depleting me, and then having to tear through my illusion at the Cliffs of Sarum before repairing it . . . all with no rest and hardly any food in between had nearly run me dry.

"There's a village on the southern tip of Mervalee, near the border with the Nolus continent," I told her. "The village has an inn that I've frequented from time to time. The owners have always been discreet. They won't tell a soul that I'm there or that I've brought a black-haired, white-winged female with me."

She gave a nod, and her face morphed into one of concentration as I told her exactly where the village lay.

Fierce wind continued to howl around us as my mate's magic took hold of me and all of my guards. I just thanked the Mother that I'd found her and she was safe, even though in the back of my mind, it still hit me that Drachu had his clutches in her—possibly permanently—and right now, there was nothing I could do about it.

CHAPTER 13 - ILARA

The village Norivun requested we venture to sat at the base of the Elixias Mountains. We appeared just outside of the tiny town in a field filled with short grass and nightill flowers. Their little buds of purple and black were some of my favorite wildflowers, but we didn't often see them near my village, only during the years when we were blessed with slightly warmer temperatures. But here, at the southernmost edge of our continent, they bloomed abundantly.

Fragrant scents from the blossoms permeated the air. Ahead, the small village waited. It didn't appear much larger than my home village, given its single lane and two dozen buildings making up the entirety of the village's center. It held the usual outposts from the looks of it: a school, a council building, a few eating establishments, a salopas, a market for trading goods, a few shops, and an inn.

Fiddle music strummed through the air from one of the

eating establishments as the sun hung low in the sky, beginning to disappear behind the steep mountains that rose ominously and divided our continent from the Nolus fae. Snow-tipped peaks swirled in the clouds, and the tree leaves in the forest surrounding the mountain's base shone silver in the dying light.

I took a deep breath and couldn't believe that strong magic still rumbled inside me after mistphasing all of us at once for a second time, but even mistphasing six of us across a vast distance hadn't depleted much of my power.

"Ock, you all right, Ilara?" Nish asked. "That's quite the feat to mistphase so many fae at once so far."

"I was just thinking that." I probed my magic within my gut again as that strange sensation brushed against my back when my wings lifted involuntarily.

I still wasn't used to the weight or feel of my brand-new wings. Truth be told, I hadn't given them much thought yet or considered what an affinity that gave me feathered wings even meant. I also didn't know the first thing about flying, but learning and understanding all of that was for another day. Right now, I needed to help my mate restore his magic.

"You're all right?" Norivun's hand settled on my lower back, right beneath my white feathers.

I nodded. "I'm fine. Truly."

And amazingly, I was. Whatever God Zorifel had done this morning had truly unlocked everything within me. I felt strong. Powerful. And for the first time in my entire life, I felt *free*. I just hoped that I would be able to master my two new affinities without Matron Olsander's help. Who knew if I would ever be able to seek her training again.

"I'll get us checked in," Haxil offered when Norivun didn't make a move to venture into the small village. "No need for all of us to show our faces."

Norivun grunted, and since none of us were covered in illusion masks, I knew his magic was weaker than he wanted to admit.

A strum of worry billowed through me, and as though he scented it despite his depleted state, Norivun leaned down and pressed a soft kiss to my neck.

"You're amazing," he whispered. "So strong. I knew you always had it within you."

A shiver ran through me as the scent and feel of him pulled at something deep inside me.

I curled my fingers around his upper arms. A thrum of heat billowed through my limbs, making me want to mold my lips to his and forget everything that had gone wrong in the past few days. I knew my mate could provide that. Being close to him, getting lost in his scent and feel . . . it made the realm around us disappear. The magnitude of what we faced didn't diminish the instincts surfacing within me that wanted to taste, caress, and stroke every inch of his skin. It would be so easy to get lost in our bond.

Nish snickered while Sandus and Ryder simply crossed their arms and fell a respectful distance away.

Norivun gave Nish a side-eye before snapping his wings out to hide us from their view. "Do you sense Drachu at all?"

he asked quietly as he continued to do those embarrassingly pleasurable kisses along my throat.

"No." And thankfully, not only did I not sense him, but I no longer felt the urge to go to the fae king and be near him. Perhaps it was only in Drachu's immediate presence that I craved those things.

"Good." A low growl rumbled through his chest. "We'll figure out a way to release you from him. You won't stay tethered to him forever."

I nodded and had to suppress a moan when he pressed more kisses against my skin and ran his tongue near my ear.

"But right now, I want to take you to my bed."

My entire body shivered at that possessive declaration, and as if on cue, Haxil sauntered up to the group and held out keys. "Three rooms secured, two to a room. Food shall be delivered shortly. Nori, we'll take turns standing watch so you and Ilara can rest easy."

"Thank you." Norivun inclined his head before the six of us ventured into the inn, using the back door so as not to draw attention to ourselves.

The rooms were all on the second floor, and we had to climb narrow, creaky steps to get to them. Similar to Liss Lodge, the main floor of the small inn held a dining area, and given the hum of voices and boisterous laughs that carried through the walls, I guessed it served alcohol as well.

"Who stays here?" I asked. It didn't seem like a likely place to establish an inn given the village's tiny size.

"Mostly fae crossing the border for illegal trade," Norivun replied as Haxil waved us to the end of the hall.

The guards hung back to decide who would be taking which shifts during the night. "It's a convenient area for Nolus and Solis fae to meet without the Nolus having to venture that far into our territory or vice versa. It's like Elsfairdasvee—on the Nolus side—in that aspect. There's also an inn in Elsfairdasvee for Solis who find themselves on that side of the mountain range."

I arched an eyebrow as curiosity billowed through me. "The illegal trade doesn't bother you?"

He shrugged. "It's only illegal because my father doesn't like us having anything to do with other fae. The actual trading of goods isn't hurting anyone."

My lips thinned, and my curiosity fled as something darker took its place. "And, if it were up to your father, Elsfairdasvee would belong to the Solis along with this mountain range and the entirety of the Derian Forest."

"And all the way down to the Nolus capital and Adriastic Sea, possibly even farther." Norivun placed the key in the lock, then opened the door.

Unlike Liss Lodge, no protection ward hummed against my skin when we crossed the threshold, and the lodging wasn't nearly as luxurious. Dim light from the setting sun dipped the room into shadows. Neither of us bothered to find a fairy light.

Norivun closed the door behind us, and then cupped the back of his neck. "You deserve better. I'm sorry that I couldn't think of another option."

I circled my arms around his waist and rested my chin against his chest. "This is far nicer than anything I stayed in during my childhood. We never traveled much when I was young. Only twice, and never farther than Coolisbar. Trust me, this is perfect."

And it was. To me, this room felt quaint and cozy even though the bed was barely big enough for two adult fae, the fireplace was small, and the chest of drawers was so narrow it was a far cry from palace life, but I was with my mate. Nothing could be better.

"You're sure?" he asked gruffly.

"More than sure."

Warmth immediately bloomed around me, soaking into my skin from his hard form. He was always so warm even though he didn't carry a fire elemental affinity. I wondered if his inner dragon had anything to do with that.

"Besides," I whispered. "Nobody knows we're here, and we're alone. How many times has that happened?"

The crown prince pulled me tighter against him until my entire focus became his chest and scent.

The bond hummed inside me, unfurling along my limbs until sheer contentment washed through me. Having him hold me was like coming home, to a home I'd never known I'd lost and had no idea I'd been searching for.

"What is it?" he asked softly and pushed back a lock of my hair when I shuddered against him.

"I was just thinking about how right this feels, and how all of these months, I hadn't even realized that you were all I needed."

His arms tightened, and I could have sworn his breath hitched. Then his lips found mine, and my hands were tangling in his hair as I was swept out to sea in the powerful tide that was my mate's presence.

Both of us were breathing hard, our bodies taut with unquenched tension when a knock came at the door.

"Youdy-who!" a female called from the hall. "Sup's gonna get cold if ya leave it out here. Best bring it into ya room."

A low growl came from Norivun, but the fatigue lining his eyes and lack of pounding aura told me he needed nourishment more than he needed me.

"Do you have enough in your reserves to mask my appearance for a few minutes?" I nodded toward my black hair and white wings.

His eyebrows drew together, and then the feeling of a light mist drifted over me before it extinguished.

Before my eyes, my hair turned silver, and my white wings, visible in my peripheral vision, took on a black leathery form.

I gave his hand a squeeze of thanks, then opened the door to see Sandus standing watch and a middle-aged female—similar in age to King Novakin—holding out a full tray of simple food. "T'was told to pack enough food for ten, ya? 'Twill be enough, ya think?"

Her uncertain look and lack of fancy fare told me the food scarcity had drifted this far south, and the simple sustenance presented to me, consisting of hot broth, salted meat, pickled beetroot, and dense bread dotted with forest berries—something commoners typically foraged in forests and added to their baked products when wheat ran low—told me their selection was as sparse as what Cailis and I had been used to.

I took the tray, giving her a grateful smile. "This is perfect. Many thanks."

She dipped her head, her uneasy smile disappearing before she sauntered down the hall.

"Have you eaten?" I asked Sandus.

He shook his head. "The boys are saving me my share once my watch is done, love."

"Would you like some of this now to tide you over?"

Sandus held his hands up. "No, of course not. The prince needs that more than me."

My expression softened. Sandus hadn't hesitated, not even for a moment, before he'd given his reply. "Thank you for everything you do for Nori."

A warm light entered the guard's eyes before he said gruffly, "It's my honor to serve him."

And maybe it was because so much had been asked of the prince by his tyrant father, or maybe it was because much of the continent feared and hated my mate, but seeing that unwavering devotion in his guard—his guard who truly *knew* who Norivun was—made tears form in my eyes.

Sandus chuckled and gave my shoulder a squeeze. "None of that, love. Warriors don't cry."

I rolled my eyes and blinked back the tears. "I'm fairly certain I saw a tear in your eye when you were looking at your niece in a looking glass last week."

A soft laugh came from the room, telling me Norivun had heard that comment, but Sandus merely shrugged. "I probably had something in my eye. It happens often when Harpelin's telling me something in her baby gibberish."

I pressed my lips together, holding back a smile. "Whatever you say, Sandus."

The guard gave me a knowing wink before I closed the door.

Alone with Norivun in the room, I set the tray on the bed. "You need to eat."

He prowled toward me from across the room, and even though his aura wasn't filling every inch of space around us, it didn't detract from his overwhelming presence.

"I can think of something I'd like to eat a lot more than what's on that tray."

His husky words lapped at my insides, and my lower belly tightened. "But your magic—"

"Will be replenished by tomorrow after that tray is consumed and I've had a full night's rest. But right now . . ."

The prince's illusion cracked around me. My true hair color and wings appeared again, and then the prince was there, his arms going around my waist as his mouth found mine in a hungry kiss.

Before I could breathe another word of protest, my back was to the wall, my new wings involuntarily spreading wide as he hooked my legs around his waist.

Heat instantly flooded me as the prince's chest pressed to mine, and he nestled himself between my thighs.

Our tongues danced, and his hands gripped my hips, before he settled my core right on his cock. His length strained against his trousers, and my pulse leaped as that aching sense of wanting him, *needing* him, began to overwhelm me.

For so long I'd craved this male. I'd ached to have him inside me. He was mine. I was his. And I'd always known that on some level long before I ever fully recognized the mating bond.

"Ilara," he growled and kissed down my neck, his tongue tasting as he nipped and bit at my skin. "When, Ilara? *When?*"

He strained in my arms, his muscles bulging as his cock grew even harder when I released a low moan. And in that moment, I knew it was foolish to wait. There was never going to be the perfect moment. A time when neither of us had a Trial looming over our heads, an arranged marriage threatening to break our commitment, or a king determined to destroy all we loved.

That moment might never come, but Prince Norivun was my mate, and I was going to claim him here and now as fiercely as he'd always wanted to claim me—the king be damned.

"Make me yours," I said, then moaned again when his hips tilted, and he scraped against the most sensitive part of my flesh. "Now."

A low snarl of satisfaction rumbled in his chest. And then the food tray was on the floor by the fire, and my clothes were being pulled off by demanding large hands as I worked the crown prince free of his attire just as fast.

Skin to skin, he lifted me in his arms and swept back the sheets. We fell in a tangle of limbs.

On the bed, our movements grew frantic. Raw. I gripped at him, clawed him, bit, kissed . . . our need for one another turned animalistic and instinctual, as something as old as time commanded that I join my body with his.

"I've wanted you for so long," he said when I wrapped my arms around his neck, and he positioned himself at my entrance.

I strained against him, lifting my hips while my air affinity trailed down his back and along his wings in that way that I knew drove him mad.

His entire body shuddered as the broad head of his shaft prodded against me.

My breath sucked in as our eyes locked together. The shadows dipped his face into a portrait of savage victory. Veins swelled in his neck as he gripped my hips and tilted me up more, and then he pushed into me, his shaft so thick that my breath sucked in.

"Take it in, my mate." His breath hissed as he pushed in more until he was filling me bit by bit, my body stretching and expanding to accommodate his thick girth. "All of it. Take all of my cock until I've filled every inch of you."

I clamped a hold of his shoulder, my teeth biting into him as the most delicious feeling of stretching and expanding threatened to drive me feral.

"Fuck, yes," he breathed, and then he drove in completely until he was buried inside me to the hilt.

A scream of pleasure parted my lips.

"I like that sound," he growled.

I moaned deeply even though he didn't move as he kissed along my neck and settled his weight between my thighs. Fully seated, he just stayed there, his cock filling me completely as his muscles quivered every time I squeezed and marveled at the expanse with which he consumed me. Gods, he filled me up so much.

"You're so tight. So hot," he whispered.

His grip on my hip tightened as his gaze once again locked onto mine. His position awarded me the perfect view of his face, his eyes, his intense expression as he slowly withdrew and then pumped into me again.

I cradled his cheeks in my palms and leaned up to kiss him softly. My lips brushed against his reverently at first but then our tongues tangled and our kiss turned raw and frantic.

A low growl tore from his throat when he thrust again.

My head tilted back while my body arched. With each pump, my body sang. He fit inside me perfectly, and I knew I'd been made for him and him for me.

"You're everything to me, Ilara." The muscle in his jaw tightened as his thrusts increased.

I kissed him once more. "As you are to me."

His movements grew faster, and each pump became harder and more demanding as he owned me, dominated me. Claimed me.

I didn't know where he ended and I began. All I knew was that something deep inside me heated and warmed with each thrust of his cock, like an unfurling rose was blooming within my soul and coming to life before the sun after a lifetime in darkness.

I clung to him, and as every aching moment passed, that blooming feeling inside me unfurled more, as though a secret was being unveiled—a secret that had always been there but had merely needed the right key to be opened and unlocked.

Our mate bond fully heated and welded together. My heart expanded as my mind connected with his. My entire being wrapped around the male who was plundering my core, until my sensations became nothing but the male laying claim to me as every part of my essence wrapped around him.

Mine.

My mate.

Forever.

"Norivun!" His name tore from my lips when the final part of the bond locked into place. My climax ripped through my body as every part of me was intertwined with his essence, his power, his commanding presence. Wave after wave of intense, mind-numbing pleasure reverberated through me.

His own release came at the peak of mine, and Norivun's roar of triumph as his hips bucked and his seed spilled into me while I clung tightly to his frame was magic and rapture. Perfection and bliss. I'd never felt so complete. So loved. So right as I did at that very moment.

Because Prince Norivun Deema Melustral Achul, first son of the king, Bringer of Darkness, Death Master of the continent, son of Prinavee Territory, and crown prince and heir to the Winter Court's throne was mine. Forever he would be my mate, and I, Ilara Seary, daughter of Mervalee Territory, Giver of Life, Faithful Restorer of *Orem*, and rightful Rising Queen to the Solis Continent was laying claim to the male before me.

Fire flashed through my soul as a deep, demanding instinct awoke and pounded through me. Fierceness made my lips peel back, and I bit Norivun's shoulder just as he did the same to me.

Mating marks swirled underneath our skin as a smattering of stars appeared along our shoulders in faint ink that forever marked us as one another's.

This male was my mate. *Mine.*

And I would fight whoever tried to take him from me.

CHAPTER 14 - NORIVUN

Ilara lay on the bed beside me, nibbling on salted meat and sipping broth. Her unbound hair fell in waves around her shoulders, and her new beautiful white wings draped down her back. We'd finally lit the fairy lights. The soft light flickered off her snowy feathers, and every time the light flashed on her mating mark a swell of immense satisfaction coursed through me.

My mate. *Mine.*

And she was. I'd claimed her completely, and she was now bound to me, carrying my mark and a hint of my scent. Any male would know she was a claimed female once they scented her, which firmly put her off limits to any male searching for a mate.

Pride and a sense of victory fired through me. I knew once we were fully bonded that I would feel this way. Every mated male fairy I'd ever encountered said the final act of tying the female to you was undoubtedly the most satisfying experience of their lives.

I had to agree. My lips curled up when I ran a finger along my own mating mark. Three small stars were inked under my skin at my shoulder, the same gracing Ilara's skin. She was now my female. My queen.

Gods, the possessiveness I felt toward her was nearly unhinged.

She gave me a side-eye when she picked up another slice of berried bread. "You keep watching me."

I growled as my smile broadened. "I can't help it."

Her lips curved, and I knew she liked that I was entirely obsessed with her. The contented feeling flowing through her strummed into me on our newly sealed mate bond.

She arched an eyebrow. "Will you be staring from now on?"

"Possibly. It's hard to look away when the most gorgeous creature I've ever encountered is right in front of me."

Her cheeks pinked, and I had to suppress a smirk. Her embarrassment was one of the traits I found most enduring in her. Despite claiming her three times in the past hour, while she begged me each time to go harder and deeper, she still blushed like a virginal fairy who'd never done such brazen acts before.

A stirring rumbled through me, and I made my thoughts turn away from any male fae she'd been with prior. Murder made my gaze shine red at just the thought of another male touching her.

She popped another bite of bread into her mouth. "We'll

have to be careful, if we're going to be doing this often. I could become with child."

My smile grew. The thought of seeing her belly swollen with my child made feral pride surge through me. But alas, the timing was not right for that. "You don't need to worry. I've taken precautions."

Her eyebrows shot up. "You have?"

I tore off another bite of meat and swallowed before saying, "The second I knew you were my mate I began taking a monthly potion to prevent conception."

"You mean . . ." Her surprised look increased. "You've been taking that potion for months?"

"Indeed. I knew when this time came that I didn't want to worry about planting my seed inside you. I knew when the time was right for us that we could begin trying for such a blessing, until then I'll take the potion."

Her lips parted, her expression softening. "You want to one day make a family with me?"

"Of course, I do. You're my mate. One day, if you're willing, you shall bear my children."

She laughed lightly and took a sip of the broth, long cold but still delicious. "I never thought I would bear children to any male since I'd always been a defective. I never thought anyone would permanently want me."

I grumbled. "No male shall give you children but me."

She blushed. "I'd only want children with you."

I leaned closer to kiss her, and she ran a finger softly along my mating mark.

Arousal heated inside me, but I made myself pull back

and keep eating. We'd already consumed half of the food, and my magic was returning. By the morning, I still wouldn't be a hundred percent—not after all that had happened—but at the rate my affinities were growing I would be close to it by tomorrow night.

But more than that gave me pause. My mate needed a break from my cock. While her body was made for mine, her pussy was incredibly tight, and I'd plundered her so many times that I knew she was growing sore, so I suppressed the desire to take her again, and instead brought up a subject that needed to be addressed. Even though I was loathed to discuss this following such a sacred act as sealing a mate bond, I also knew that until the king's plans were stopped, he would forever be a threat to Ilara.

"There's something you need to know." I chewed on another piece of meat. "I think my father is behind everything that's going wrong with our home."

She dropped the piece of bread she was holding, her jaw dropping. "What? What are you talking about?"

So I told her about my encounters with Michas and what he'd revealed.

Her eyebrows shot up. "*That's* what he was going to tell me on our date?" She grabbed my arm. "And Michas said his father smelled rot too? That's exactly what I scented the night I'd been nearly attacked following my date with Lord Waterline."

I nodded. "Which leads me to believe that whoever my father met nearly a full season ago, is also the one behind the missing fae."

Her eyebrows scrunched together. "But why would your father do that? Why would he order the abduction of his own fae?"

I explained how the diminished *orem* had created support for war. How almost everyone on the king's council was ready to march on the Nolus fae and take their land. How all of these talks only united our continent with one clear goal—to save our race—and with the king being the most against it, he appeared the most innocent of wanting war at all. He'd maneuvered an entire population to do his bidding, kidnapping our fae in the process and stirring rumors of *me* being the culprit, all to make himself look innocent of any wrongdoing.

"Starvation is a powerful weapon. Survival instincts have ignited, and fae are turning feral as you saw in Pentlebim's market. Only a master manipulator could have made it play out as my father has. It all makes sense now."

"And you're certain it's not actually the Crimsonale's? That they haven't planted this seed in your mind that it's your father, tricking you into thinking it's him, when in actuality it's them?"

I cocked my head. The same concern had played through my mind briefly, but Ilara didn't know the Crimsonale's as I did. I'd known them my entire life, just as I had my father. Of the two, I knew which one would betray their nation. "I understand your concern, and you make a good point. You're right that the Crimsonale's are power hungry, but they're loyal to the Solis. They would never stoop so low as to plot against their own kind. I'm certain of that."

She gave a nod, then sneered. "In that case, no wonder your father loves Georgyanna. She's just like him."

My nostrils flared thinking about my arranged fiancée. That witch made my skin crawl, and my dragon roared with desire for her head.

My mate picked up her bread again. "So do you think Wormiful or Crimsonale have anything to do with the suppressed *orem*?"

"I don't, not any longer."

She picked at a fingernail as worry strummed through our bond. Gods, I could feel her so viscerally now. "How close is the council to acting on invasion?"

"They're not there quite yet, but I have no doubt they will be soon if my father isn't stopped."

"How long do you think we have?"

"A few months at least, a full season at best. The food stores will be gone by then."

"And you truly think this is all because he wants more power?"

I shrugged. "He's already been king for hundreds of winters. He's united the territories. The Solis continent is firmly under his control. I'm not surprised that he's now set his sights further. His thirst for power has always been his driving force."

She nodded. "It makes sense." A soft scoff left her. "Mother Below, he's clever. So he's devised a way to suppress the *orem*, making it look like a natural occurrence, and he did it all to create concern over the state of our crops. And then as support grows for invasion, once fae firmly believe our crops are dying, he pretends that everyone's overreacting, which in reality only made the council members more enamored with invasion since the king has been blowing them off." She leaned back on the pillows, her expression stunned. "It's the perfect plan. They'll love him for it even more when he finally acquiesces and invades. He'll look like the savior in the end."

I popped another bite of salted meat into my mouth. "Exactly. There's no better way to drum up support for a war than having an entire continent on the brink of starvation."

"Does anyone else suspect him?"

I scratched my chin. "Honestly, besides the Crimsonales, I don't know."

She nibbled on her lip. "So figuring out *how* the king created the veil and removing it is of utmost importance."

"There's more."

Her eyebrows arched. "More? Do I need to round up some leminai?"

I tried to smirk but fell short. "My father has demanded that I find you and return you to the court within the month. He wants you present at my wedding to Georgyanna, and he still wants you married off to Lord Woodsbury."

Her breathing picked up as anger strummed along the bond. "He doesn't want me dead for defying his command?"

"No, he feels you're too valuable to dispose of."

"I won't marry that pedophile." Her jaw ground together, and that stubborn streak I admired in her so much made an appearance.

"No, you won't, because you'll be marrying me."

Amusement sparkled in her eyes. "I will be?"

"If you'll have me." A smile curved my lips. "If we return to the court married, there's little my father can do about it other than torture my mother in punishment, something he's already threatened if you don't come back."

"But, Norivun . . ." An ache formed in her tone. "Queen Lissandra should not bear the brunt of our misdeeds."

I worked my jaw, warring emotions oscillating inside me. "No, but she would sooner have me marry you and deal with my father's wrath than allow either of us a lifetime of misery."

She picked at her fingernails again, her movements growing more agitated. "I couldn't bear to see her hurt."

"Me neither."

"Which means we need to expose your father for who he really is. If everyone knows what he's done and what he continually does to your mother, maybe it will stop."

"Even if the continent knew, he's still the king. He would still rule even if he was hated."

"Unless he was overthrown."

She said it so casually, and a wide smile streaked across my face. "Did you really just speak of overthrowing the king that easily?"

"I did. Before, I simply wanted our arranged marriages stopped, but now . . ." She shook her head. "If he's done what he has, he can't be king. He no longer deserves that title, and who else could overthrow him but you?"

"I do love when you speak of violence."

She laughed. "I wondered when I'd see your dark side again."

"It's always there, my love, just waiting to come out."

She snorted and rearranged how she was sitting on the bed. "So we need to stop the *orem* from being suppressed, that's of utmost importance, and then we need to find a way to expose your father all while keeping your mother safe from his hands."

"Proving his involvement is more necessary than exposure. Unless we have proof, the council won't believe us, and we would need the council on our side. It's the only way to peacefully remove him from power. If the council votes unanimously to have my father dethroned, Solis law demands his abdication."

"So we'll find proof of what he's done."

"We still need to get married, and you're forgetting one other thing that's equally important—releasing you from Drachu's hold." Anger rumbled in my gut at just the thought of my mate's tie to the Lochen king.

Ilara frowned, then leaned forward to grab another piece of bread. I pulled her closer, needing to feel her lips on mine.

She fell into me, squealing, but I used the opportunity to kiss her thoroughly. A grumble of pride raced through me when her toes curled against my calves, and my pride only increased when arousal entered her scent just as fast.

When she inched back, she licked her plump lips and eyed me playfully. Damn, that look made me harden instantly.

I pulled her in for another kiss, and the fairy lights

flashed on her irises. For the briefest moment, I halted, then I forced myself to lean back. "Are your eyes a different color?"

She blinked. "What?"

I peered closer at her, studying her eyes. "Blessed Mother, they are. It's subtle, but your irises have a purplish tint now, almost like a violet color."

A flash of a memory brushed my thoughts. When we'd sealed our mating bond, we'd been eye to eye as I'd fucked her, but the dim lights then hadn't revealed the change.

"Really?" She rose from the bed and went to the mirror by the chest of drawers. Her mouth dropped when she studied her irises. "They are a slightly different shade."

For a moment, she stayed there, her frown increasing as she gazed at her reflection, before she returned to the bed.

I forced my ardor to cool even though her curved backside and perfect breasts made me ache to draw her near again.

"Why do you suppose that is?"

I shook my head as I racked my brain. "I don't know."

"Do you think it has something to do with the Adrall Temple? I don't think my eye color was different before I met God Zorifel."

"Perhaps? Did that priestess or Drachu mention anything like that happening when they conducted that séance?"

Her frown increased. "No, but it's not like Drachu was honest about everything." A hint of bitterness crept into her tone. "I doubt he would have told me even if he knew meeting a god could create a change in me like that. Do you think they'll always be this way?"

"No idea."

"So I not only have white wings but violet eyes. Wait, let me try something." She closed her eyes, her brow furrowing. Not even a second passed before a swell of magic pulsed from her skin, and her wings disappeared. Taking a deep breath, she opened her eyes. "What color are they now?"

I leaned closer and cocked my head in surprise. "They're blue again, just like they always were."

She closed her eyes again, and once more called forth her wings. The speed with which she did it and the immense magic pulsing around her was impressive.

"And now?" She opened her eyes again.

I smirked. "Violet. Very clever, Ilara. You've figured out the cause of it. So your violet eyes are tied to whatever animal affinity created your feathered wings."

"But what animal has violet eyes and white wings?"

I scratched my chin. "That's a good question. Maybe Haxil will know."

"Or maybe God Zorifel would. Maybe he's the one who gave me this affinity when we met."

"Doubtful. Every time he's interacted with our kind, it's been to release the powers we were born with or to amplify them. He probably just speeded up the process of your affinities being born. But these wings of yours were always there. They just hadn't appeared yet."

"Perhaps, but I guess we'll never know since that bastard Drachu disappeared before truthfully explaining what that séance had done, including how he'd tethered me to him." She seethed softly.

I placed a hand over hers, and her soft skin met mine. "We'll release you from him. I promise you that."

"Do you think we can?"

A growl rumbled in my chest. "I'll find a way if it's the last thing I do. I'm not sharing any part of you with him."

"That would require finding him."

"True."

"Which could prove tricky," she added. "He knew I was coming to his shores the night that I did, and now that I know what his necklace can do, a part of me wonders if he has psychic abilities, either naturally or *borrowed* from another fairy who he stole from. If we try to find him, he may know we're coming and flee."

Even more magic rumbled in my gut. My power was definitely returning. "We'll still find a way."

Her wings ruffled slightly when she reached for the last piece of beetroot. She munched on it, her expression lost in thought as worry scoured her features.

I hated seeing that worry on her face. I hated *feeling* it pulse through our bond since it meant I wasn't properly caring for her.

I ran a finger along one of her white feathers when it brushed the pillow. A shiver ran through her, and a tint of lust entered her scent.

My lips curved. *That's better.*

I inhaled the delicious musky fragrance and touched her again, this time to a feather closer to her spine.

A moan released from her, and some of the worry I'd

detected through our bond faded as something else took its place.

My cock instantly hardened.

"What affinity do you suppose created these?" I asked, my voice slightly husky. Her wings were unusual. I'd never seen feathered wings on any fairy before. "A bird affinity perhaps?"

She glanced over her shoulder at her new appendages and shifted herself slightly to extend the one near the edge of the bed.

"Maybe?" she replied. "It's so strange, though. To finally have wings. I can feel them, and I understand a new limb has been added to my body, yet it's so *strange*." She cocked her head, and I ran my finger along a third feather.

"So this is why you never grew wings. All along, this affinity was waiting to be born, and it needed your back to stay bare to accommodate them. These are your Solis wings. Wings of snow. They're beautiful, Ilara, as beautiful as you." I ran a finger along another feather.

Her legs squeezed together, and I inhaled deeply. My sensory affinity was back to full capacity. It was usually the affinity that returned fastest when I was depleted, and at the moment, I'd never felt more thankful.

"You're not too sore?" I asked softly when I began to stroke her.

"Not for that. Not for you."

I growled as the muskiness in my mate's scent grew more potent, so I let my finger trail along a fifth feather.

Her breathing increased as she let her outer wing relax,

and another low growl rumbled in my chest when the sheet drifted down to reveal one of her round breasts. Her nipple was peaked, begging me to suck it.

"It seems your wings are as sensitive as mine." I set the tray on the floor beside me, then shifted along the mattress until my erection pressed against her thigh. Her eyes fluttered closed when I kissed her shoulder and licked her mating mark. I trailed my lips down her chest until I found that delectable nipple.

Another moan vibrated her throat when my hand dipped between her thighs to gently prod at her clit. She was wet again. Always wet for me. A vicious snarl of victory rumbled in my chest. *Mine.*

"Do you suppose you would enjoy it if I fingered your feathers while taking you from behind?" I stroked her more, and her thighs parted as her head tilted back. The worry in her scent and along the bond was completely gone now. *Much better.*

Her hand curled around my shaft and began to pump me in long, hard strokes. My breath sucked in when she gave a quick nod.

"Tell me," I growled. "Tell me that you want it."

"Yes," she breathed when I swirled my finger around her clit more. She swelled in my hand, and the muskiness in her scent was so strong that I could taste it.

Fuck, I could eat that scent up all day.

"Yes, what?" I demanded.

"I want you to take me from behind while fingering my wings."

My cock grew so hard it throbbed. "If you insist."

Before she could respond, I flipped her over on the bed. Her round rump rose, her womanly lips swollen and glistening with her essence. The dragon within me snarled with possessive fury, and in a blink, I was crouched between her legs from behind as her wings flared out.

Her pussy was so ready now she was dripping. I lifted her more and brought her wet entrance to my mouth, licking her clit first before lapping at her.

She gripped the sheets, her fingers curling so tightly into them her knuckles turned white as she pushed her pussy even more into my face.

My length throbbed, and I licked her again until I turned into a beast behind her, devouring her until she was moaning and writhing against my face.

Straightening, I shifted into a kneeling position. Her white wings were still spread out as her limbs trembled. I knew she was close to coming again.

"Do you want my cock?" I pushed the head of my shaft into her entrance. I hissed. Gods, she felt so hot. So ready.

"Yes. *Please,*" she moaned.

Leaning forward, I fingered one of her wings as I slowly pushed into her, grunting under the strain of how tight she was.

Her walls clamped around me, making my muscles tremble with the need to fuck her hard. Unable to hold back, I thrust into her completely, groaning at the absolute bliss.

Her body was made for me. She accommodated my thick girth perfectly, holding me tight and gripping me so beautifully that I was on the verge of coming just from the feel of one thrust.

I grabbed her hip with one hand to anchor her to me, and with the other I stroked her wings again as I began to pump into her with deep, long thrusts, my release building.

I fingered her feathers more, stroking them up and down in time with my pumps. Her entire body shuddered as she pressed her ass more into me.

"Do you like that?" I hissed.

Her response was guttural. Words absent. My mate was a writhing creature, so consumed by my cock and what I was doing to her feathers that language didn't come.

I grunted and began pounding her in earnest.

She screamed, not even a second later, and her walls clamped hard around me when her orgasm hit.

A final run of my finger along a feather, and she came entirely undone, her spasming pussy coming all over me as her wetness coated my cock.

I released her wing and gripped her hips in both hands.

I let her ride the waves, keeping my shaft buried deep inside her with small movements that hit that perfect spot to heighten her pleasure.

It was torture, though, not being able to thrust as I wanted to, but I waited until her pleasure was complete, and then I gripped her tightly and pumped hard and fast. My release was upon me in seconds. With a final thrust, I roared my climax and emptied myself into her, loving how she clamped onto me so hard that I saw stars.

The shudders went on and on, and when they finally

subsided, I collapsed on top of her, then gathered her in my arms.

"You're perfect," I whispered into her ear.

She yawned and snuggled into me as the fire crackled in the hearth.

Satisfaction rolled through me that the only emotion my mate was feeling now was happiness. The worry I'd felt in her only moments ago was long gone.

Her eyes closed just as mine grew heavy.

And even though we still had so many challenges ahead of us, for the first time since I took her from her village all of those months ago, something in me fully calmed. Settled. She was my mate, the only female I would ever want or crave, and I would burn the entire realm if I needed to in order to keep her safe.

A swell of magic rippled along my limbs as Ilara's contentment pulsed through me. Securing my arms more around her, she nestled onto my shoulder as we both fell fast asleep.

WE AWOKE the next morning to a fresh layer of snow on the ground. Even though I knew we shouldn't stay here long, I couldn't stop myself from claiming my mate two more times before sunrise.

Her skin was so soft, her lips delectably plump, and her pussy . . . Blessed Mother, I could die with her pussy wrapped around me, and I'd be an elated fairy perfectly fine with venturing to the afterlife.

"*Damn,*" I groaned when I slipped out of her. My heart was pounding from how hard she'd made me come.

She gave a sleepy smile as she flopped back onto the bed. "You made me see stars." She leaned over and kissed me softly, her tongue trailing along my lower lip.

I nipped at her, growling, and she laughed before playfully swatting me away.

When we finally got out of bed for the day, imbued magic heated under my skin. My affinities rumbled, and my Outlets opened involuntarily. Already my magic had greatly returned, which meant our reprieve had to end, as much as I didn't want it to.

Nish was in the hall when we went in search of my guards, and the grin on his face that he wasn't even trying to hide made Ilara blush furiously but got a smirk from me.

My guard clapped me on the back. "About time, my prince."

A chuckle escaped me as Ilara's blush migrated all the way to the tips of her ears, which got another sharp laugh from Nish.

"No reason to be embarrassed, Lara. Mating is a perfectly natural occurrence." His cheeky quip only made her scurry down the hall as he laughed again.

I punched him lightly in the shoulder, only because I knew Ilara would appreciate it. "No more sex jokes today. My mate doesn't like them."

Nish brought a hand to his chest in mock sternness. "As you wish, my prince."

I smirked again as we strolled down the hall. Clanging pots and the sound of someone singing came from the kitchen beneath us as the scent of fried bread drifted through the air.

"So, since you two are fully joined now, have your mating instincts finally calmed?" he asked, the joking from his voice gone.

"Yes, rest easy. I won't be leveling any cities today."

He grinned and nudged me. "Just between you and me, I couldn't help but hear some of your performance in there. Impressive, I have to say. I had no idea of the stamina the mate bond infused in a male." He scratched his chin. "It almost makes me want to find my mate."

My eyebrows shot up. Nish banged females as often as my other guards did, but he'd never shown any interest in a commitment. "Did I just hear you say that you would like to find your mate?"

He scowled. "Keep your voice down."

I somehow smothered a laugh. "Right. My lips are sealed."

Still, as we jogged down the stairs to join Haxil, Ryder, Sandus, and Ilara, I couldn't help but grin.

Nish wanted a mate.

The realm had truly turned upside-down.

CHAPTER 15 - ILARA

Outside, an inch of fresh snow covered the vast field filled with nightill flowers. The six of us stood with crossed arms as we discussed how we should begin tackling our problems. Since I'd cast a silencing Shield around us, and Norivun had woven an illusion affinity to cover our appearance, none of the local villagers knew we were there.

"So there are two issues now," I said with a sigh. "Uncovering how the king has suppressed the *orem* and . . ." I was loathed to bring it up. I felt like such an idiot for ever going to the Lochen king. "Somehow finding a way to retrieve that diamond or the entire pendant from Drachu and cutting my tie to him."

Norivun stood with his arms crossed, his pecs visible through his tunic. He screamed *male perfection* with his thick silver hair, deep-set eyes, strong nose, and powerful build.

But instead of his lust constantly pulsing toward me on

our bond—a new perk of our sealed mating—another emotion traveled to me. Blessed Mother, I could *feel* his rage so viscerally at what Drachu had done. It was like a dark cloud of malice coated his insides.

The prince's aura strengthened around him as his nostrils flared. His aura was potent enough to carve the field in deep slashes, and a twinge of relief filled me that his magic had mostly returned.

"Which one do you suppose we should tackle first?" Ryder asked.

"The *orem*, most definitely," I replied. "Our continent comes before me."

Norivun growled and gave me a side-eye.

I arched an eyebrow. "It does. The *orem* first."

Haxil settled his hands on his hips. His usual round-cheeked smile was absent as a shrewder expression took its place. "All right, the *orem* it is."

"We'll have to work fast. We only have weeks to figure this out." Sandus frowned as his eyebrows drew sharply together. "The king has demanded that Norivun find you within the month and bring you back to the castle. If Norivun doesn't, I'm afraid the queen—"

"I know." I cut him off as I paled. To know the queen would bear punishment for *my* misdeeds . . . It made me sick. "Norivun told me last night."

"Lara, none of that." My mate stepped closer to me, and a brush of his air affinity wrapped around me in stroking soft waves. "As unlikely as it seems, you made the right choice by going to Drachu."

"I did?" A pleasant shiver struck me when a kiss of his air trailed along my neck. Nobody had ever told me how incredibly intimate it would feel to be mated to someone. Still, I had a hard time believing him even though I didn't detect any deceit through our bond. "How was that the right choice?"

His affinity stroked me more, and *Blessed Mother*, I was growing aroused again. "Because if you hadn't gone to Drachu, there is not only a chance that my father's hunting fae would have found you, but you also could still be dealing with your affinities being suppressed. And you're forgetting that your encounter with God Zorifel revealed a clue that could possibly be the most important piece of information we've found. God Zorifel revealed that the veil suppressing the *orem* isn't of our universe." My mate placed his hands on my hips, and it took visible effort not to become breathless. "As much as I hate that Drachu's tethered you to him, a few good things did come from you fleeing to the Glassen Barrier Islands."

"Like learning that we now have to deal with the *other* realm." Nish sneered, getting a sigh from the prince.

"As much as I don't want to interact with them either," the crown prince said, "we have no choice, especially if my father has hired someone or manufactured something from that *other* realm to kill the *orem*."

Norivun's aura clouded around me, and I nodded and licked my lips.

"Does this mean we're going to the *other* realm?" Ryder's expression turned shrewd.

The prince shrugged. "Unless we can find a way to avoid it while also getting answers."

I shuddered at just the thought of leaving the fae lands. I could only ever remember encountering one portal that led to the *other* realm. A green shimmery outline of a billowy door was in the forest outside of Coolisbar. I'd seen it once on a trip my family and I had made to that village. It was a popular attraction in a way, but it had been otherworldly enough to make me not want to go anywhere near it.

A wall had been built around it, and the barrier was warded with magic. A fairy could still see the door through the ward, but nobody ever went inside the wall, and if anyone from that *other* realm ever happened to stumble into our realm, they quickly found the wall and ward to be a tough barrier to cross. My guess was that normally if anyone had tried to venture to the Solis continent, they'd quickly reversed course and returned to wherever they'd come from.

Another shudder ran through me. To think that whoever Lord Crimsonale had overheard speaking with the king had perhaps gotten through one of the portal doors and crossed the warded barrier to work with the king with the intention to mess with our *orem* . . .

That didn't bode well for who we were up against. I thought again of the rotting smell I'd detected the night I'd nearly been attacked. I had no idea what kind of supernatural creature created that kind of stench, because if they came from the *other* realm, it was unlikely they were fae.

"How many natural portal doors are there on our continent that lead to the *other* realm?" I asked my mate.

Norivun placed his hands on his hips. "Six total. Two in Mervalee, one in Harrivee, two in Prinavee, and one in Osaravee. But the court has built walls around all of them with domed wards. Even though those portal doors were created by nature, we've never wanted *other* visitors stumbling onto our land. We have an entire staff of fae with constructo affinities dedicated to ensuring those walls and wards never fail. Nobody has ever entered the Solis continent from one of those naturally occurring portal doors. I'm sure of it."

"Could another one have formed?" I asked. "Perhaps one we don't know about?"

"Doubtful." Norivun tapped his chin. "The last time that happened was nearly eighty winters ago, and the rip in the realm it created produced enough energy for it to be felt hundreds of millees away."

"Then how did whatever's suppressing the *orem* get here?" Sandus asked as he stroked his beard. "If something is in our land that originates from that *other* realm, then the king's accomplice must have traveled from the *other* realm to deliver it. How else would their magic, or whatever it is that caused that veil, have arrived here otherwise?"

"Perhaps my father helped his accomplice enter," Norivun replied.

I cocked my head. "Could your father have disassembled the wall and wards temporarily to allow someone entry?"

Norivun frowned. "Unlikely. It would have had to be a different way. Too many fae would have been aware of that to keep it quiet."

My lips parted as I remembered something else from my

near attack in the castle. "I think I know how someone could have come to our continent undetected. Remember how it seemed as though he disappeared from the realm, right before he was going to attack me following that date with Lord Waterline? Well, what if he used a portal key, like the one Drachu used? What if those portal keys allow one to transfer between realms? Drachu did say they were created in the *other* realm, so it seems possible creatures from the *other* realm use them regularly."

"You're probably right, and that would explain how he got away from me," Norivun said. "It also explains why he disappeared without a trace since those keys work like mist-phasing." A vibration of his anger strummed to me on the mate bond. I looked up at my mate, expecting to see a scowl, but his face was blank.

I smiled smugly.

"What?" he said.

"I'm afraid your blank expressions are no longer indecipherable to me."

A sly smile tugged at his lips. "Are you saying you can tell what I'm thinking now?"

"Not quite, but I can certainly *feel* it, and the fury you feel over someone entering our continent to cause us harm is quite potent."

Nish threw back his head and laughed. "Oh, how I wish Prince Nuwin was here right now. He would get the biggest kick out of knowing that you've finally met your match."

Norivun arched an eyebrow. "I suppose it's a good thing I no longer feel the need to hide how I feel from her then."

A huge rush of lust shot through the bond, hitting me so suddenly that my entire body heated, and my core throbbed. *Mother Below!*

I gasped. "Is that how much you—" But then I realized we had an audience. All four of the prince's guards were watching us raptly.

An answering stroke of air slid from the prince to me. "Yes, Princess," he said on a low growl. "That's how much I want you."

Nish smacked a hand to his forehead. "Ock, and we all thought once he claimed her, their lusty scents would lessen."

Haxil sighed. "Perhaps you two should return to your chambers and leave the rest of us in peace." He rearranged himself in his pants and gave Norivun a shrug of apology when a growl tore loose from him. "Sorry, my prince, but a male can only handle so much before it affects him too."

My cheeks were heating in earnest when the prince scooped me up in his arms and mistphased us back to our chambers at the inn. He threw me on the bed, causing me to bounce and my wings to involuntarily flex.

"Norivun, this is beyond embarrassing. All of your guards know that we're going to . . . you know . . ."

"I know." He stripped his clothes and prowled toward me. "Don't keep reminding me. I want to rip off their heads for not only hearing us last night but for being able to scent your arousal and feel the heat between us. They all need to go get laid while I bed you one last time before we depart."

I spread my thighs, and he crawled onto the bed and positioned himself over me. Mortification burned through me that all of them knew how much my mate and I wanted one another, but it didn't stop me from welcoming him inside me.

"Oh gods, that's so good." My head tilted back when his length sank all the way in. "Will this ever fade?" I gasped as he began to pump in long strokes. Gods, he filled me so completely. "Will I ever not crave you like this?"

He kissed the side of my neck as he groaned in pleasure when my nails dug into his rear, pulling him even deeper inside me. "I've heard it . . . dims after a few months, that this part of a newly formed mate bond is most intense at the beginning, but—" He hissed when he plunged into me again. "But no, it never goes away." He grinned, his smile full of swagger. "You're always going to want me, Princess."

I laughed, which turned into a moan when he rubbed himself deep in my core. "You sound quite pleased about that."

"I am, and I always will be. You're mine, Ilara Seary, from now until the end of time."

I closed my eyes and let myself get lost in the magical feel of the prince, but it didn't stop an inkling of reality to sprinkle into my thoughts. The crown prince was still engaged to Georgyanna. The king was behind our land's dying *orem*, and Drachu still had me tethered to him.

But for now, for this one aching moment, I allowed myself to be swept away by the crown prince.

❋

An hour later, we were fully checked out from the inn and standing in the field.

A brand-new tunic swathed my upper body in warm wool, the green one I'd worn previously burned in the fireplace. When my wings had first emerged, they'd ripped through my tunic, so Norivun had insisted that I buy a new top from the local seamstress. It was soft yellow, and for the first time in my life, I wore clothes made for an adult with wing slits. It made me feel ridiculously proud.

Smoothing the new fabric over my hips, I asked, "So, if somebody from the *other* realm was able to bring something to our continent that suppressed our *orem*, where do we even start looking for answers? We know nothing about supernaturals from that realm."

Ryder shook his head. "That's a very good question, Ilara."

Norivun's brow furrowed. "Haxil, do you remember that meeting we had a few winters back with the Nolus king's nephew . . . what was his name, Baver—" He shook his head. "No, Bavar, I think? Didn't he mention something about having close contacts in the *other* realm?"

Haxil nodded, a contemplative look forming on his face. "Yes, I believe you're right. Bavar Fieldrock or Fieldstone, something like that. He mentioned that he worked for an organization in that *other* realm that commonly dealt with supernatural problems."

I raised my eyebrows. "All of this meaning . . . what?"

"That perhaps he would be a good first contact," Norivun replied. "Apparently, the king's nephew spends quite a bit of time in the *other* realm, and he's very familiar with relations between our realm and theirs. Perhaps we could start with him and see if he has any ideas about where we begin looking."

Hope surged through me. "So are we venturing to the Nolus capital then?"

"Indeed." My mate grinned wickedly.

"Best consult a map first." Sandus reached into his pocket to extract a map of the realm. "I haven't been to the Nolus capital in ages. I'd probably end up in the Adriastic Sea without a clear mistphasing landing point."

"You and me both," I agreed.

"There's a gate surrounding the entire city," Norivun added. "Sentries guard it. We'll have to mistphase outside of it. I'm unsure if the capital's wards will allow us entry since we're not using a naturally occurring portal."

I peered over the guard's shoulder as the others did the same and studied where the capital was on the map. It was much farther south than I'd realized, in an area of the Nolus continent that was undoubtedly warm and flourishing with natural plant life.

Norivun clasped my hand. "Ready?"

I shrugged as my heart began to beat a million times per minute. "As I'll ever be."

CHAPTER 16 - NORIVUN

We landed in a field outside the Nolus capital's wall as a warm breeze brushed around us. Ahead, the massive city sprawled across a large hilly mound that swelled and stretched upward like a mountain. Houses and shops lined the rising landscape, thousands of stone and thatch buildings stretching along zigzagging streets. At the top of the large hill stood the palace. The golden-walled castle shot up from the tip of the mountain, its spires thin and numerous.

At the mound's base, a tall wall encircled the entire city with several gated entry points on golden walkways. Two sentries stood ready and waiting at each gate. In their hands, they held long spears, with sharp points visible in the bright sun.

"Wow, it's so . . . big," Ilara breathed. "And not one trace of snow, frost, or ice." She rolled up her sleeves, then tipped her chin toward the pale-green cloudless sky. "And it's warm."

Nish sneered. "Too warm. These fae would probably wilt and die in our climate."

"Now, now, Nishy," Haxil said, patting his shoulder. "Best to remember we're guests here."

Nish's lip only curled more as Sandus and Ryder laughed.

My ears pricked toward the other fae heading toward the capital, but my eyes narrowed as I studied them. They weren't fae.

Ryder quirked an eyebrow. "So those are who come from the *other* realm?"

Ilara's eyes widened when she spotted them. They were currently stopped at the closest gate and being monitored by the sentries. All of them were males.

One was a Nolus fairy with bright-purple hair and slightly glowing skin. Another was one of those completely foreign species. His rounded ears gave him away, a trait that screamed he inhabited the *other* realm. He could have been one of many of the unusual species found there. I inhaled, trying to detect what he was.

A faint hint of sulfur drifted toward me. *Ah, so a full-blooded demon cloaked in that species' form.*

The third was a male with skin as white as snow, and when his lips peeled back, canines lengthened in his mouth as the sentry assessed him.

Ilara's eyes bulged.

"I believe they're called vampires in that *other* realm," I whispered to her.

"And that one?" She subtly pointed to the male beside him who was as large as me. A powerful aura rippled around him.

I inhaled. The male carried a woodsy scent.

"That's a . . ." I elbowed Haxil. Of my four guards, he was the most well-read. "What do they call them?"

"Werewolf, I think?" Haxil stroked his chin. "They appear like the species of the *other* realm when they're unshifted—as you can see from his rounded ears—but they can turn into wolves, like Solis can with animal affinities."

My mate's eyes widened even more, and my lips tugged up. I'd ventured to the Nolus continent a few times, so had seen most of this before, but to Ilara . . . I knew it was all new.

"And the last one?" she asked, still keeping her voice down.

"He smells of sulfur, so he's likely a demon cloaked as a . . . what's the word, Haxil?"

"Human, I believe," Haxil replied.

"Ah, yes. A demon traipsing as a human."

"And *humans* are the species in the *other* realm?" Ilara's lips curved into a true smile. Delighted curiosity strummed from her into me on the bond.

"Yes, they're entirely unmagical," Haxil explained. "But there are some that appear human but aren't, and a whole host of species live there: vampires, werewolves, witches, sorcerers, half-demons, psychics, and so on . . ." He shrugged.

"Some of them visit the Nolus continent regularly, usually the capital, so you find them in abundance here."

"Why do you suppose we never see their kind on our continent?" she asked, her eyes wide.

I frowned, suddenly wondering when it was we decided we wanted nothing to do with that realm. "'Tis just how it's always been. We don't allow their entry. Never have." I gestured toward the group. "From what Bavar told me, if I remember right from when he visited us, some in that *other* realm don't even know anything about us. They think the fae lands only consist of the Nolus continent, and they think our realm is much smaller than it truly is. It's not only us who's ignorant of them."

"Fascinating." She grinned, and Haxil chuckled. Once again, I felt the mutual interest the two shared in learning. A rumble of jealousy stirred in me, and she gave me an apprehensive look.

I slung an arm over her shoulder and nuzzled her neck. "I can't help it. I don't like it when any male appeals to you."

She pinched my side playfully. "He's just my friend."

I kissed her temple. "I know, which is why I'll have to learn to live with it."

She squeezed me in return, then released me when we reached the capital's outer wall.

Large golden gates rose at least fifteen feet high. The sentries flanking them stood alert, having watched us approach for the past few minutes. Their large builds were like ours, but they were entirely golden and *different*. I wasn't sure what species they were, but they stood taller than even me.

Dark irises, so dark they were nearly black, made them look otherworldly. They stared down at us from their imposing heights. Both had heavily muscled and exposed chests. Leather strap-like clothing covered their lower halves and part of their shoulders. Golden helmets adorned both of their heads.

"Quite the ensemble," Nish said under his breath.

"'Tis what all sentries wear who guard the capital." Haxil ran a hand through his hair, his voice low, but I could have sworn the sentries still heard them.

When we stood only a few yards away, the sentries widened their stances and extended their spears toward the center of the gates, creating an X.

When their spears touched, a loud *clang* reverberated through me. A push of strong magic barreled from the spears, and it felt as if we'd hit an invisible wall.

"State your reason for visiting the capital," the sentry on the right said.

I lifted my chin. "I'm the crown prince of the Solis continent. I'm here to find Bavar Fieldstone, nephew to the Nolus king, if he's in residence."

"And the fae with you?" the one on the left said, his voice so deep it didn't sound natural.

"My four guards and my mate," I replied.

The sentry's gaze shifted to each and every one of us. Their dark irises whirled as they assessed us, turning to shimmery silver before becoming inky black once again. Another rush of magic stole over me, making my affinities stir in response.

With a swift move, the sentries pulled their spears back to their sides. "Proceed."

The golden gates opened soundlessly behind them, and the five of us ventured forward. Each of my guards had a hand near their sword, their postures appearing relaxed, but I'd been with them long enough to know they would have those swords in their grips before I could blink.

Music carried faintly on the breeze, and the curiosity strumming from my mate increased even more.

Ilara twirled around, her face a mask of wonder as she soaked it all in.

Behind the giant gates, the capital lay in an endless sprawl of gardens, colorful houses, and a bustling city. Nolus males, females, and children scattered about, along with various species from the *other* realm.

A few glanced our way, their gazes raking over our silver hair and leathery wings, but when they spotted Ilara, more than one visibly gawked.

With her black hair and white feathery wings, Ilara truly was a sight to behold. Nobody in the entire realm looked like her, and she was so incredibly beautiful that several males took notice.

A Nolus male with apple-green hair elbowed his friend, another male with hair the color of fire. Both appraised Ilara with appreciation, then wide smiles.

A snarl tore from me, and their attention snapped in my

direction. When my aura hit them, they both flinched and stepped back.

Ryder patted my shoulder. "Tame that expression of yours, Nori. You look about to kill someone."

Another growl rumbled in my chest as my death affinity undulated out of me of its own accord to the two males. When it wrapped around their souls, I gave a tight squeeze and bared my teeth.

One of them squeaked, the sour stench of fear rising from him, as the other slacked in my grip, his hands rising in surrender.

"Nori," Haxil said in a patient tone. "They mean her no harm. They're simply admiring the view."

My jaw worked. "I don't like other males desiring her." My dragon snarled within.

"We've all noticed," Ryder replied dryly.

A soft hand caressed my forearm, and my affinity began to relax as a strong push of love came through the bond. The red coating my gaze finally dissipated when I glanced down at my mate.

"Leave them be." She leaned up and kissed me on the cheek. "We're not here for them."

Slowly, the intense desire to shred their souls abated. Once I fully released them, the two Nolus males pulled out a portal key and disappeared. The others who'd witnessed what had transpired began to whisper.

A few words drifted toward me.

"Have you seen the Solis fae before?" one hissed.

"Not in these parts in quite some time," their friend replied, "although I did see a few up in Culasberee last year."

"He's a big one," another said, nodding toward me. "I wonder what his magic is. The Solis have strange magic, don't they?"

"I think so," the female beside him replied. "To be honest, I don't know much about them. They always keep to themselves."

My guards flanked my and Ilara's sides as we followed the golden walkway, which had widened into a street and continued up the winding hill to the palace.

Off to the right lay a small park. It was bursting with jungle gym equipment, miniature castles, bridges, and play houses. Dozens of small Nolus children darted about. Each of them had a head of brightly colored hair.

"So idyllic," Ilara said quietly. "This is nothing like my village."

"'Tis the warmer climate they have." Sandus shrugged. "They don't have the hardships here that we face. Life is easier for the Nolus."

Her forehead furrowed. "I can see why King Novakin covets this land. It's beautiful, but it's not home. As much as this is captivating, I venture to say I would grow weary of the constant warmth and sunshine."

Haxil nodded approvingly. "Spoken like a true Solis. And that right there, Ilara, is why *you* should be queen, not that appalling Georgyanna."

My mate sneered at the mention of the Kroravee witch.

"How is Georgyanna, anyway?" she asked me, an edge to her tone.

"Probably still picking out wedding dress material while driving Daiseeum mad."

Her breath sucked in. "Daiseeum is her lady's servant?"

I growled when her expression grew hurt. "My father insisted that Georgyanna be put in the Exorbiant Chamber, which is the chamber that Daiseeum services, otherwise she'd be nowhere near it."

Ilara's frown grew, and everything in me wanted to smooth that expression and tell her I'd toss the witch out the second we set foot back on castle grounds, but before I could open my mouth, Ilara abruptly pitched forward and came to a careening halt.

My mate grabbed her stomach, bending over as a mewling sound parted her lips. "Oh gods!"

"Lara?" Pain thrust toward me on the bond. I snapped my wings around her. "Ilara, what's wrong?"

All four of my guards leapt into a protective circle around us, their blades already in hand as their warrior magic reared.

"Ilara?" A snarl of fury tore from my throat as I frantically searched her belly for a wound or puncture or whatever had caused her to stagger and pitch forward. "What is it? Did something hit you?"

More mewling sounds came from her.

"Ilara!" But no matter how hard I looked I didn't see anything protruding from her skin or a weapon that had pierced her clothes.

I straightened and stretched my senses more, my eyes

wild as I sought out the threat. Every Nolus fairy walking near us halted and backed up. Some even ran.

My breaths sped up. "There's no one on the roofs. Do you sense anyone or anything?" I asked my guards.

"No, there's no one," Ryder called.

Haxil raised his sword higher. "Check the alleyways."

"Protect your queen!" I roared.

Ilara grabbed my hand. I crouched toward her, fury making my moves frantic and blurred. Pain contorted her features. I would destroy the realm. I would destroy *every fucking creature* that made her look this anguished.

"What's happened, my love. Tell me. Where are you hurt?"

"It's not . . . anyone . . . here," she panted. "Drachu. It's *Drachu*. He's sucking my affinities."

CHAPTER 17 - ILARA

Pain. Pain. Oh gods, the *pain*.

I doubled over again, groaning and clutching at my stomach. Drachu was yanking on my affinities so viciously that I could barely see.

No. No! Too much. He's taking too much too fast.

Ripping agony tore through me again as though someone was cleaving my belly open with a hot knife. The Lochen king was pulling so much, so quickly. My stomach was tearing apart.

Panting breaths escaped me.

My vision blurred.

Power undulated from my mate as his four guards surrounded me in fighting positions. Their swords were still in their hands, yet those weapons were entirely useless.

"My love," Norivun said. Terror twisted his features. "Tell me what to do."

All of the Nolus fae around us had fled completely, leaving the street empty.

Clutching my stomach, I shook my head. "I don't know."

Norivun's eyes flashed wide as another wrench on my affinities had me falling.

He snarled in fury and caught me just before I hit the cobblestones.

I curled into a ball in his arms and bit my tongue to keep from screaming.

"Ilara? Fuck . . . *Ilara?*" He cradled me to his chest. "Can you fight it? Push him off somehow?"

"No. Don't . . . know . . . how." I panted as another moan vibrated from my throat, then everything around me became a blur.

Can't take it. Can't take it.

Too much.

I'm going to die.

Magic flew out of me. It was entirely unnatural. Too destructive. Drachu was draining me. Killing me. I was being ripped apart.

He's taking my very essence.

My eyes drooped.

My heart slowed.

Oh gods.

"Dammit, he's taking *everything* from her," the prince snarled.

My eyes closed more. *Sleep. Go to sleep. Yes, sleep will make it go away.*

In a wink, my wings disappeared.

Someone gasped.

"Her wings—" Sandus said just as Norivun lifted me.

"Her wings are an affinity," Norivun bit out. "If Drachu's draining her, her body can't sustain it. Fuck! She's shutting down."

"We need a healer!" Haxil said frantically.

Norivun's grip tightened around me more as everything inside me began shrinking, shrinking, shrinking . . .

And then . . . blackness.

A COOL CLOTH slid across my forehead, and a pounding aura filled the air around me.

"My oh my, she was quite depleted. Dangerously so, and in a way that was entirely unnatural," a female said. "But have no fear. I gave her a hefty dose of the potion we often use to treat fae lands withdrawal. I have a feeling that given enough time, she'll recover."

Awareness of my surroundings grew. Someone was holding my hand. A male from the feel of it. Rough callouses rubbed against my palm. Entwining his fingers around me, he grunted. "Fae lands withdrawals?"

Norivun. That's who's holding my hand.

"It's something we can see in powerful adult fae who travel to Earth for the first time."

Earth?

"But she doesn't have withdrawals," Norivun replied. "She's not in that *other* realm. That bastard Drachu depleted her magic and almost killed her in the process. All of which occurred in *this* realm."

The woman *tsked*. "It may not have been actual withdrawals, Prince Norivun, but the effects on the body are similar enough that the potion we use to treat such withdrawals should work in a case like this. It reverses the course of magically induced effects."

Another grumbling sound came from him before a terse, "Very well. You have my thanks, and I'm in your debt."

The female laughed softly. "Nonsense. I came at the request of Major Fieldstone. I'm merely doing my job. No debts are needed, Prince Norivun."

My eyes fluttered open to see the female on one side of me and my mate on the other.

Norivun's aura swelled like a tidal wave around him, constantly pounding and crashing, only to rise again. The second he realized my eyes were open, he leaned over me as his fear strummed along the bond. "Ilara?"

"Hi," I croaked.

The prince gathered me close, pulling me into an embrace.

I hugged him in return even though my arms felt weak.

His four guards stood behind him, and another male I didn't recognize—a Nolus fairy with bright-orange hair—stood on my other side with his hands clasped behind his back.

The orange-haired male beamed. "Ah, look who's decided to join us!" He grinned, awarding me a clear view of his sharp teeth, before he angled his body to Norivun, who didn't seem to have any intention of letting me go. The light caught on a dagger tucked into the male's belt, and it shone like a mirror. "I told you Cora would know what to do. Much obliged indeed, dear Cora."

The female stood and dipped her head. "She'll continue to recover, but it's best you carry one of these at all times." She slipped a small vial into Norivun's hand. "Administer it immediately if such an event occurs again."

The female eyed me, her expression sympathetic, and with a start I realized she wasn't fae. Rounded ears stuck out from her head, clear as day since her hair was swept back. A long robe covered her frame, so I couldn't see the rest of her, but everything else about her looked like me. Except for the ears.

My surprise increased when she turned to the orange-haired Nolus. "This is a most curious case indeed. I heard once that the Lochen fae can be tricky, but we know so little of them, and I've never seen such magic before." The female then turned to Norivun, who finally relaxed his grip enough for me to lay back on the table. "Did you know you're the first Solis fairy I've ever met? It's been a most enlightening morning."

"Indeed. For all of us," the orange-haired fairy agreed.

The female smiled. "I'll diligently catalogue what she suffered from, Major Fieldstone, so the SF is aware that this potion is effective in cases such as hers."

"The SF?" I croaked. "What's the SF?"

"That would be the Supernatural Forces, my dear," the

orange-haired fairy, Major Fieldstone, replied. "They're an organization on Earth."

There was that strange, foreign word again. "Earth?"

"It's the *other* realm, as I believe you Solis fae like to call it." Major Fieldstone inclined his head to the woman who'd been healing me. "Excellent plan to convey what we've learned today to the SF. I'm sure Douglas and Farrah will be very intrigued."

The female healer laughed. "That's the understatement of the year."

"Year?" I shook my head, my brow furrowing.

Haxil leaned over and said, "I believe a *year* means a full season."

"Oh," I replied as fatigue swelled in me. "I see."

The healer gave me another warm smile. "Since you're recovering, I better return to the healing center."

Major Fieldstone's dagger caught the light again when he rounded the table I lay on. "Of course, you have my gratitude, dear Cora." The Nolus fairy walked her to the door, talking quietly with the healer as Norivun kneeled at my side.

"How are you feeling?" Worry lines pinched the corners of his mouth as his gaze flew over me.

"Okay, I guess." My entire body felt sore, as though I'd run for millees after digging in the fields all day, but other than that . . .

I assessed myself internally. Magic rumbled in my gut, but it felt diminished, as though I'd depleted myself entirely, and I was still recharging. Shifting, I lay a hand over my stomach, and with a start realized my back felt bare since no wings had moved beneath me.

I glanced over my shoulder, and my breath caught. "Where did my wings go?"

The prince's hand curled around mine, and the feel of his unyielding strength flowed through that simple contact. "Your wings disappeared when Drachu drained you." His jaw tightened. "It just proves even more that your wings are an affinity. They can come and go, similar to when I choose to shift into my dragon form."

Some of the panic in me eased as I felt for that strange power between my shoulder blades. A glimpse of it stirred when I focused on that area, but it felt weak. "I don't think I could call them forth now."

Norivun growled. "I'm not surprised. Drachu nearly killed you by what he did. I just thank the Mother that we were able to find help so fast."

A flutter of fear ran through me when I recalled how abruptly the Lochen king had sucked my powers. It'd come from out of nowhere. Drachu had grabbed a hold of all of my affinities—my life-giving, fire, air, wings, warrior—all of them. It was similar to what he'd done at the temple when he'd been battling Norivun, but the second time was so much worse. The Lochen king had done it faster and with greater ease, as though he'd learned following the temple how to better manipulate his control on me.

I gripped the prince's hand harder. "What do you suppose happened that made Drachu do that?"

Norivun's lip curled. "I don't know."

The door closed in the corner of the room, startling me back to our strange surroundings, just as the orange-haired fairy traipsed back to us.

"That's the Nolus king's nephew, Bavar Fieldstone," Norivun said under his breath. "He's who we came looking for."

My eyes widened as I took in the Nolus fairy's toned frame and bright eyes.

"You're quite lucky, Ilara, that Bavar was in residence when we arrived at the palace's doors," Sandus said gruffly. The guard's hands were on his hips, his wings tight to his back. "Your pulse was growing weaker with every minute that passed, love."

"We're at the palace?" I asked, my voice rising.

Ryder nodded. "The Nolus palace."

"The Nolus palace indeed!" Bavar said with gusto when he reached our sides. "I have to say, this has been one of the most interesting days I've had in a while. When one of the palace sentries alerted me to not one, but *six* Solis fae at our doorstep demanding entrance so they might speak to me . . . Well, I was most curious, especially when I learned it was none other than the crown prince of the Solis continent and his new mate." Bavar's smile stretched as he clasped his hands behind his back and gave a deep bow in my direction. "A pleasure to make your acquaintance on this side of consciousness, Ilara. Although perhaps if we meet again, it will be under better circumstances."

I tried to sit up to properly introduce myself but winced when my stomach muscles screamed in protest.

In a flash, Norivun's arms were around me, and he lifted me up. He held me aloft in his arms.

The prince's voice became stiff when he said, "If you have a chaise or chair for Ilara, I would be in your debt."

Bavar clapped his hands. "Of course! How rude of me not to offer sooner. Now that your mate is no longer at death's door, I would bet to say that she's famished as well as fatigued. Come, I shall have the staff bring refreshments while we discuss what it is that brings you to our great capital on this fine day."

Bavar led us out of the room into a large hall as Norivun continued to carry me. Just to the right were two huge ornate golden-rimmed doors carved with mystical engravings. Sentries stood by the doors, and their pitch-black eyes assessed us when we strode past. Similar to the sentries at the capital's exterior wall, deadly-looking spears were clenched in their grasps, and their golden-hued skin had an otherworldly glow to it.

"Where are we?" I asked under my breath.

"This is the palace's main foyer." Bavar waved to the golden-rimmed doors. "Those lead out to the capital. I'm afraid that since you all came in such a rush, that I brought you to the nearest room." He waved to the chambers we'd just exited. "I apologize for the informality. That receiving room is usually used for admitting service fae, but seeing as you're here to press upon me urgent matters, it seems only fitting that we move into a more comfortable space in order to discuss such issues while allowing you to rest."

Bavar strode ahead of us, his orange hair shining like my

acorlis vines at sunset. He led us down endless halls and past spiraling staircases until we reached a large sitting area with an open balcony.

Bright sunlight streamed into the sitting room. Rich, plush carpet covered the floor, and dozens of plump sofas and chaise lounges filled the space. Tapestries hung from the walls. Some depicted various battle scenes, others more like artwork of country estates.

Everywhere I looked was vibrant and filled with color. This entire area of the realm seemed so alive and warm.

"Hopefully this will suffice?" Bavar waved toward a chaise lounge near a cold fireplace. The mint-green pillows decoratively displayed on the dark-blue lounge reminded me of my former lady servant's affinity. Daiseeum could make anything look beautiful. She would have thrived if hired to decorate this room.

A frown downturned my lips when I pictured Daiseeum assisting Georgyanna now.

"Thank you." Norivun set me on the chaise, and I gratefully leaned against the supporting pillows.

"I'm usually not like this," I said, blushing under Bavar's concerned appraisal.

"Now, now, none of that." He waved his finger at me. "Every fairy who's suffered what you have would be in a state such as this. Nothing to apologize for." He clasped his hands behind his back again and dipped forward on the balls of his feet. "Would you care for some refreshments?" He beckoned a staff member who stood near the door.

The young male bustled over and deposited a tray filled

with cakes, crumpets, pies, cookies, and every other sweet imaginable.

Bavar's eyes lit up with delight. "I do so love the kitchen's sweets. Please, take whatever your heart desires."

I leaned over and helped myself to several of the miniature fruit pies. My stomach growled in appreciation of the sugary fragrances.

Everyone took part in the delectable sweets, even Nish. Once everyone had a plate and was seated, Bavar addressed the crown prince.

"Prince Norivun, as lovely as it is to see you again, I must say that I'm dreadfully curious what brings you today. I can't recall the last time a royal Solis set foot in our capital."

Norivun adjusted how he was sitting at my side, and through the bond, a hint of his embarrassment flowed into me.

He cleared his throat. "We are in need of your . . . assistance." The last word felt forced, as though he was loathed to ask for help at all, especially from our southerly neighbors.

Bavar's eyebrows rose clear to his hairline. "Oh? Do continue."

"Something is amiss on our continent and has been for some time." In a begrudging tone, the prince told Bavar about the suppressed *orem*, our dying crops, and what'd happened to me in the Isalee field that had affected my affinities. He further told him about my visit to the Adrall Temple and how God Zorifel had insisted whatever magic we felt on our continent originated in the *other* realm. Following that, he told him how we suspected an individual from the *other* realm was behind the veil in our soil.

The crown prince divulged enough information for me to realize that he was bordering on desperation. With only weeks until his wedding to Georgyanna and the Solis king's council becoming more and more supportive of marching upon the Nolus continent, time truly was of the essence.

The only thing Norivun didn't share was that he suspected his father was ultimately behind it all and that we believed King Novakin was working with the supernatural from the *other* realm. But we had no proof that the king was the culprit, so I wasn't surprised he withheld that detail.

When Norivun finally finished, Bavar tapped his chin, then shot to standing and began to pace in front of the cold fireplace. "So the God of Power actually came to you?" He looked at me, his smile widening. "Fascinating, indeed. It's been years since I've heard of the gods willingly interacting with us. You must have made quite an impression." He winked, then continued in a more serious tone. "And God Zorifel said that the substance in your land that is suppressing your magical *orem* and also had suppressed Ilara's affinities wasn't of our universe, and you think that substance may stem from a supernatural individual. Hmm, most curious indeed."

He turned swiftly on his heel and began to pace back in front of us. "How very baffling, although, to think that such a dire state could lead to your kingdom marching on ours . . ." He shook his head. "That I find quite troubling, obviously."

Bavar stopped at the refreshment tray and picked up a

cookie. I'd lost count of how many he'd consumed. While munching on it, he placed his free hand on his hip and faced Norivun. "What can I do to be of assistance?"

The prince and I shared a look before I said, "We're hoping that perhaps you would know somebody from that *other* realm who could help us. We need to figure out what's suppressing our land and how to stop it."

He laughed lightly. "Ah, yes. Indeed, I have many contacts on that planet. As a commander in the Supernatural Forces, I deal regularly with troubling occurrences on Earth, but you have to understand, the SF's jurisdiction stops at the *other* realm. They have no authority in the fae lands."

I swallowed the ball in my throat. This entire conversation made me feel nauseous, and given Prince Norivun's barely contained scowl, I garnered he felt the same.

My entire life, I'd been taught that the Solis relied on the Solis only, and while traveling to this continent had indeed been eye-opening and entertaining prior to Drachu's attack on me, it didn't mean that my pride had disappeared. We currently appeared weak and unable to handle our issues on our own. But since so much was at stake, I was willing to admit our faults and ask for help.

Even if that help came from *Earth*.

"Is there anything you can do?" the prince asked, his voice gruff.

"Oh, of course!" Bavar dusted off his fingers after finishing his cookie, and a swell of magic cleansed his hands. "There are many things I can do. I was simply saying that the SF may not be the best resource since I would need to obtain permission from my uncle to allow a squad entry, but that doesn't mean we need a squad to investigate this field in your territory."

He tapped his chin. "Let me have a think about this. Do you plan to stay in the capital for long? I'm hoping to have some ideas for you within the week on the best way to pursue answers."

A surge of rage pulsed into me from Norivun's end of the bond. My eyebrows drew together as I gazed at him questioningly.

"We won't be staying here for the week, but we'll be back." The prince stood, and since the food had recharged my strength enough for me to stand unassisted, I joined him.

Ryder, Sandus, Nish, and Haxil crowded around us, all of them looking to their prince.

"Very well." Bavar nodded. "I shall see you in a week's time then, hopefully with some ideas on how to tackle this unfortunate event."

"Thank you." I brought my fist to my chest and bowed, while continuing to wonder what had made Norivun so angry. "We appreciate anything you can do for us."

Bavar bowed as well, then showed us to the door. "It is my pleasure, and I must say I'm hopeful our shared alliance will only lead to further friendly relations in the coming years, or as you Solis say *full seasons*."

The king's nephew led us back through the labyrinth of halls and stairwells until we reached the tall doors lined by two sentries.

Once outside, I gazed up at my mate. "Why are you so angry? And where are we going if we're not staying here?"

Norivun's expression turned glacial. "We're finding Drachu and putting a stop to his control on you. After seeing what he's capable of, his tether to you ends now."

CHAPTER 18 - NORIVUN

Once outside of the palace and back on the capital's streets, thatched-roofed houses, gleaming walkways, and shops filled the view.

Ilara peered up at me with anxious eyes as she shielded her gaze from the bright sun. "How will we find Drachu? If he truly knows when we're coming, like he did when I mist-phased to the Glassen Barrier Islands, he'll be impossible to find. Won't he? Since he'll always know our movements in advance and be able to flee?"

I ushered her carefully forward, mindful of her steps since she still appeared weakened from Drachu's attack. "We'll have to scry for him and hope he's distracted enough by whatever caused him to steal your powers. With any luck, he won't see us coming."

Her brow furrowed. "Scrying? What does that entail?"

"Magic, blood, and an item belonging to the fairy you're trying to find."

Her eyebrows shot up. "Do you know how to scry?"

"I do, and I'm pretty good at it. I know I'll be able to locate that bastard, but we need to act quickly and hope he's still distracted."

"But how will that work? Do you have anything of Drachu's?"

I smiled wickedly. "Of course. I make a point to keep an item that belongs to all of my enemies." I withdrew a purple shell from my pocket.

She stared at it blankly, then her eyes widened. "Is that a shell from Drachu's house in Vockalin?"

"Indeed."

"But . . . how did you get it?"

"I took it when we went there searching for you. I knew if I wasn't able to find you, then my only option would be to scry for the king and hope that he knew where you were."

Her eyes widened. "Is this something you do often?"

"Take items from random homes? Not usually, but when it comes to my enemies, yes, I always keep an eye out for the opportunity. This isn't the first time I've swiped something from Drachu. It's always best to be prepared."

Her lips curved at my wry words, and some of the worry in me eased. She was alive and recovering, and I had a potion in my possession that would help her should Drachu try to take all of her magic again. Still, my affinities rumbled inside me, threatening to rise and swell. The Lochen king had hurt my mate. *Retribution is coming for you, Drachu.*

Taking a deep breath, I encircled Ilara's waist with one arm to support her weight more. "Come, we need to find an inn or somewhere quiet and private for you to rest and me to scry. It's imperative that I'm not interrupted." I led Ilara through the cobblestone streets, my guards following us. It was a downhill walk since the palace was at the highest point in the city.

Nolus fae were everywhere, along with the occasional *other* species. It felt so strange to be in a land like this, where so many mixed supernaturals mingled and lived in harmony. In a way, it made me question again why our continent was so reclusive.

Shoving that thought aside, I gestured toward a building down the lane. It rose two stories from street level and had a small, vibrant garden filled with blooming flowers gracing its front lawn. Its thatched roof shone in the sun, and its wooden siding was a bright, cheerful yellow. Hanging suspended over the main door was a sign reading *Crystal Inn*.

I smirked. *How fitting.*

I led Ilara up the walkway to the main door, and it wasn't lost on me that even here, in the diversified Nolus capital, we still garnered a few stares. I had a feeling most of the fae here had never seen our kind.

When we reached the inn's threshold, I had to duck to avoid my wings scraping against the rim. Inside, the inn's height wasn't much better. The ceiling was so low that it brushed the tips of my talons, and given the screeching sound that followed, I figured I'd inadvertently left a few unintended scrapes on the plaster.

A breeze came through an open window from down the hall.

"It's so warm in here," Ilara commented as she fanned herself.

It was indeed too hot for comfort. Despite the open window, the day's heat made the room unfamiliarly sweltering.

Nish grunted. "I prefer a chilled breeze myself and a bit of snow on the ground compared to this."

My mate rolled her eyes and elbowed him playfully, getting a chuckle out of my surliest guard.

"May I help you?" the fairy working at the counter asked us with raised eyebrows.

I kept my expression bland as I approached him. The inn employee stood no taller than four feet. Horns sprouted from the top of his head, curling like a ram's, and hooves peeked out of the bottom of his plaid trousers.

I inadvertently studied him. I hadn't seen a Silten fairy in many winters. Inhaling, I assessed his damp, earthy scent. Tails, hooves, scales, and horns were the common features of Silten fae.

"We'd like a room," I replied as I dug a few rulibs from my pocket.

The innkeeper ran a gnarled finger down his open ledger. "Do you have a reservation?"

"We don't. Do you have any available rooms?"

"I do on the ground floor if that suits you?"

"It's fine."

"Very well. Place your hand here." He waved at an opaque sphere at the end of the counter that looked like a glass ball.

Frowning, I did as he requested. Magic immediately enveloped my palm, its glittering bands holding me in place. I scowled as the sphere glowed brightly. A second passed, and the magic released me just as luminescent words erupted across the innkeeper's ledger, as if being written out of thin air.

My name and place of residence appeared in ink across the page.

Crown Prince Norivun Deema Melustral Achul. King's castle, Solisarium, Prinavee Territory, Solis continent.

The innkeeper's eyes grew as round as saucers. "Oh my. Oh dear." He bowed deeply. "A thousand apologies, Your Highness. I did not realize that you're of royal blood. I had no idea you were the crown prince of the Solis continent."

"No need for apologies."

"Just the key then." Nish held his hand out.

"Nish," Ilara hissed. "Manners . . ."

Haxil snorted but Nish only shrugged and replied, "We're in a hurry."

The innkeeper's hand shook when he grabbed the key from under the counter. "Of course. Here you go. Let me show you the way—"

"No need for that either," Nish interrupted. "We'll find it."

My guard gave the innkeeper his back, his ample wings on full display. He ushered Ilara forward as Ryder gave the inn employee a polite nod.

"Thank you," I added even though I didn't particularly care for that magical sphere.

The innkeeper inclined his head. "If there's anything you need, please let me know!"

Sandus waved over his shoulder as Nish propelled Ilara down the hall.

"Ock, I was just doing what was best for you, Ilara. You need your rest," Nish grumbled. "If that innkeeper hadn't been blabbering on—"

"He wasn't blabbering, Nish." She gave him an exasperated yet amused look. "He was just doing his job."

I placed my palm on Ilara's lower back when Nish found the room, then led her inside. "Nish is right. You need to continue recovering. You're still not fully well."

"What about you?" Her eyebrows pinched together. "You were so depleted yesterday."

My stores were still only half full, but I wasn't about to let her worry. "I'm fine, more than fine." I signaled my guard over her head. "Sandus, do you want to find us some food?"

Sandus nodded and did a one-eighty out of the room as Nish, Haxil, and Ryder did an interior perimeter sweep. I highly doubted that anything was a threat here, but my guards were the best on the continent and never took my safety for granted.

"Do you need your supplies to scry?" Ryder asked.

I gave a curt nod. "I do. A knife and my crystals. The knife will be easy to come by, but I'll have to mistphase back to Solisarium to get my crystals. Will you guard Ilara?"

"With my life," Ryder, Haxil, and Nish replied in unison.

Immense satisfaction bloomed through me when I took in their savage expressions. I wasn't sure when it'd happened, but sometime in the past few weeks, my guards had gone from protecting Ilara because I commanded it, to doing so because they loved her as fiercely as I did.

I APPEARED in my bedroom chambers in the Solisarium castle in a flash of mistphasing magic. The second I fully reassembled, I strode straight for my wardrobe. Within a secret safe, tucked behind my royal capes, were my most valuable items. My crystals, letters from my mother, a lock of Ilara's hair, a looking glass, a portrait of me and Nuwin when we were young, among other things.

After whispering the spell to unlock it and allowing the safe to prick a drop of my fresh blood in identification, the safe opened. I grabbed the small yellow crystals off to the right. They tingled within my palm, and I tucked them into my pocket. Some Solis preferred ancient bones to scry, but I'd always connected more with the magical crystals harvested from the mines in Harrivee's floating meadows. They channeled my power with more precision than bones ever had.

Before closing the safe, I slipped my hand into my tunic and pulled out Ilara's letters—the one she'd written to me on the night she'd fled as well as the one I'd found on the beach near Vockalin. To others they were invisible, but my illusions were never disguised from me.

Crinkled papers sounded between my fingers. I read her first letter again as my gaze traveled over her hurried scrawl. The night of the Rising Queen Trial's final test, my mate had promised to fight my father's commands once she found a way back to her powers.

A small smile curved my lips. I was truly enjoying the more assertive sides of her that had emerged, especially when they were directed toward the king.

I tucked her letters into the safe, then resealed it. Now that I had my mate back at my side and she was fully bonded to me, the need to keep her letters close faded.

Striding from the closet, I allowed my magic to rise so I could mistphase back to Ilara and my guards, but before I could, my bedroom chambers door flew open.

"Oh, my prince, oh dear. Thank the Mother you're back!" My personal servant, Balbus, careened toward me as his thin hair flew about his head while his large belly jiggled. His shirt was partly untucked, and perspiration beaded upon his upper lip. Panting, he stopped before me in a sudden jolt. "I'm so very grateful that you've finally returned. I keep coming in here, hoping to see you, but you're never present."

His hurried tone birthed my scowl. The only prior times that Balbus had acted this flustered had been when my father had done something entirely wicked. "What's wrong?"

The portly servant took gulping breaths, his chest heaving. "It's Lady Endalaver! She has Daiseeum in one of her manipulation thralls. The poor lady's servant has been like this for hours and is ready to claw her eyes out!"

"*What*?" I roared. "Are you telling me that my *fiancée* is using her affinity against a servant?"

Balbus's jowls vibrated he nodded so fast. "Yes, my prince, that exactly."

"Fucking female," I hissed under my breath. "Where is she?"

"In the Exorbiant Chamber. Please, help Daiseeum, my prince. *Please.*"

Knowing I needed to conserve my magic for what was to come with Drachu, I didn't mistphase. I strode out the door and down the hall to the Exorbiant Chamber.

The guard outside the room straightened as I neared, but I didn't let his greeting slow me.

I barreled into Ilara's former chambers to see Daiseeum wailing, clutching her ears, and frantically pacing about the room while Georgyanna lay sprawled on the couch reading a book.

"Make it stop! Make it stop!" Daiseeum collided with the bedpost, then cried in pain as she clutched her head more. "Oh please, my lady, make it stop!"

"What is the fucking meaning of this?" I seethed.

In a flash, Georgyanna was sitting up on the couch, her eyes wide. "What are you doing here? I thought you were gone."

My lip curled as I prowled toward my wretched fiancée. "Are you torturing your lady's servant?"

Darkness gathered around my shoulders, but instead of cowering in my presence when I let it rise—a typical reaction in most Solis—Georgyanna closed her book and raised a haughty chin.

"She disobeyed me. She deserves to be punished."

"Disobeyed you how?" I snapped.

"I told her I wanted the rose elixir added to my bath, and

she put the peteesium elixir in, instead." She stared at me pointedly, as if that justified her behavior.

Rose elixir? Is she trying to smell like my mate?

My dragon roared within me, and I locked him down to keep smoke from coming out of my nose. "That's hardly disobeying you, Georgyanna. That sounds like a genuine mistake and by no means warrants this kind of punishment." I nodded toward Daiseeum, who didn't seem to be able to hear me from whatever Georgyanna had done to her. The poor servant was still wailing and pacing. "This is *not* how we treat servants."

Georgyanna sniffed as Daiseeum continued to cry in agony. "Well, maybe you should. If you did, your staff would be better behaved."

"Choosing the wrong elixir does not warrant *this*!" I flung my arm out toward the poor servant, who was now banging her head against the wall.

Georgyanna snorted. "Pathetic, isn't it? All I'm doing is making her believe a vise is around her head. She's not actually being hurt. She just thinks she is."

My nostrils flared, and before the witch could blink, I traveled to her on a gust of air and had my hand curled around her throat. "Release her. *Now.*"

Georgyanna's eyes bulged when I exerted pressure, then she clawed at my hand when I didn't let go.

I arched an eyebrow. "It's not very enjoyable to be hurt by someone who's more powerful than you, now is it?"

An oily sheen filled the air and coated my Shield. When that didn't work, the tang of her constructo affinity came next, then the heat of her fire as she tried to stab and burn past my magic, in attempts to force me to stop.

Her affinities were laughable. I smirked. "And to think my father truly believes you're stronger than Ilara. How wrong he is. Ilara can punch right through my Shield." My mate had done so the night I'd tried to kill Vorl at the Betrothed Ball, allowing that bastard archon to live.

Gurgling, Georgyanna clawed at my hand more, then gasped, "Fine! I'll stop hurting Daiseeum. I'll stop!"

But it wasn't until Daiseeum's wails ceased and the servant gazed around in confused wonder that I finally released the Kroravee witch.

Georgyanna fell to the floor, coughing and sputtering.

"Thank you, my prince!" Daiseeum wailed right before she fled from the Exorbiant Chamber.

Georgyanna heaved in deep breaths. "You . . . you . . ." She glared up at me with spiteful eyes.

I propped my foot on the coffee table and rested an elbow on it as I gazed down at her. "You're not to touch any of the servants again, not with your hands or your affinities. Understood?"

Georgyanna bared her teeth, then lunged upward, her hands turning into claws as she tried to attack me.

A solid wall of air blocked her. She collided with it full force and was knocked back on her arse again, which only got another enraged howl from her.

Darkness gathered around my shoulders, and I let my dragon rise just enough for my teeth to elongate into fangs and my eyes to morph into reptilian slits.

She gasped, her face turning white as I let the full power of my affinities grip hold of her and the air around her. She tried to fight back. Tried to use her affinities against me again, but it was as easy as swatting an annoying fly away.

"Do you understand?" My voice sounded more demon than fae in my partly-morphed dragon form. Georgyanna tried to scramble back along the floor, but another wall of air that I'd erected behind her back stopped her. "I'm not asking again. Do you *understand*?"

"Yeeee . . ." Her throat bobbed in a swallow, her eyes glistening with unshed tears. "Yeees, my prince. I understand."

"Good. Because if I hear that you've hurt Daiseeum or any servant again, you'll be answering directly to me, and I don't take kindly to fae disobeying my orders."

I abruptly released her and suppressed my dragon affinity until my appearance returned to normal.

Georgyanna gulped in air. Fear shone from her eyes, and for the first time she looked at me with apprehension. Gone were her playful swats on my arm or teasing fingers trailing down my stomach. I'd allowed her flirtatious antics previously only out of good manners, but now . . . good manners be damned.

From now on, she would only see the Death Master. Especially if this was the kind of crap she pulled when I wasn't in residence.

I did a one-eighty, then stalked toward the door, intent on tracking down Balbus before I left to see what other misgivings Georgyanna had been up to in my absence. If she'd hurt others, I wanted to know so I could do right by their families.

I couldn't directly do anything, of course. My father never allowed it since it didn't portray me as the monster he'd so carefully crafted in the public's image, but I'd found ways around that.

Daiseeum wouldn't be the first servant in this castle to stumble upon a box of rulibs in her home or baskets of fresh food and produce on their kitchen counter. I had to do all of those acts discreetly and anonymously, but Balbus knew that and assisted me each time.

With Daiseeum, it would be no different. I would find a way to provide something for her too. It wouldn't in any way detract from the horrors she experienced today, but perhaps, it would ease some of the burden she felt—that most Solis felt —in the harsh state of our continent's failing crops.

I was at the door, my hand turning the doorknob, when Georgyanna abruptly spat from behind me, "You're a monster! Truly, you are! You're as despicable as everyone says you are!"

I faced her as I swung the door open, then showed my teeth again even though they were back to normal fae form.

I smirked. "You're the one who wanted to marry me."

She picked up her book and threw it at me.

A gust of my air affinity knocked it off course before it was even halfway across the room. She shrieked in outrage, then stomped her foot and stormed to the bathing chamber before slamming the door behind her.

Smiling darkly, I walked into the hall and closed the door behind me, intent on finding Balbus before I left.

❈

I found Balbus and quickly confirmed that Daiseeum wasn't the first servant to suffer under Georgyanna's hand. Consequently, I made a list of what I needed Balbus to do for the families she'd affected.

Once finished, he bowed deeply. "It will be done, my prince."

He held his chin higher, a righteous gleam in his eye. I knew he would help right all of the wrongs my witch fiancée had enacted.

"Is there anything else I need to be aware of that's happened while I've been gone?"

Balbus frowned. "There is one other thing, Your Highness. Another servant has gone missing."

I froze. "When?"

"Last night. There's no sign of him, and when he didn't show up for work this morning, we found his supplies in disarray in the domal stables where he labors."

"And nobody saw or heard anything?"

"No, my prince. It's been just like the other times when fae have gone missing."

A sense of foreboding curled around me. "Thank you for the update, Balbus."

He bowed, then swiftly left.

Brooding over the latest disappearance, that my father was most likely behind, I headed to my mother's tower in a hurry. If more fae had gone missing, then my father was actively working against us again. I needed to check on my mother even though every second that passed gave Drachu more opportunity to know we were coming.

I crossed the threshold of her warded wing and flew up the hundred steps to the top of her tower.

I found the queen of the Solis continent sitting in her favorite chair, near the balcony. I slipped into her chambers, completely silent, yet I knew she detected me before I was halfway across the room.

The magic that caged her affinities sequestered her from much of her abilities, but it would never be able to fully extinguish them. She was too strong. Too powerful. Yet, here and now, she was a shell of the fairy she'd once been.

"Mother? Are you well?" I asked, coming up behind her.

She abruptly stood and walked outside to the balcony before placing her hands on the railing.

"I'm fine, Norivun," she called, still staring straight ahead. "Thank you for asking. How have your searches been? Have you found Ilara?"

I frowned and followed her out to the balcony. Winter wind bit into my cheeks, and navy clouds swirled in the sky. But as soon as I grew close to her, she turned again, angling her face away from me once more.

Growling, I closed the distance between us and spun her toward me.

My breath sucked in.

Rage clouded my sight, and the wind around the tower began to howl as my air elemental affinity let loose.

"He's been hitting you?" I snarled.

Her chin lifted. Defiance shone in her eyes despite the bruises that covered every inch of her skin.

Some of the bruises were fresh, others were old, letting me know my father's visits to her had been daily. He usually only allowed his abuse to show on her face when he was excessively angry with me. Mostly he kept to her limbs and torso so no one could see her wounds, which meant he was already using my mother as a way to quell his fury over what Ilara had done.

"Fucking tyrant!" My wings snapped out, and I had to turn away from her since the sight of her abuse made me want to level the entire castle.

"It's nothing I can't handle," she replied in a firm tone. "Don't give in to him, Norivun. Do not allow him to control you with me."

I faced her again, anguish in my voice. "How can I stand for this, Mother? How can I let him hurt you like this when I have the power to stop him?"

She took the remaining steps to me before I could blink, and her hands curled around mine, gripping me tightly. "I've had visions. They're so hazy and perhaps more dream than reality since they always come to me at night, but a great change is coming to our continent. I'm sure of it. You *must* stay the course. You must find Ilara and find a way to defeat your father. I'm certain with her at your side you'll be able to, but if she's not . . ."

I gently squeezed her in return as she gazed up at me with a burning intensity in her eyes. My mother was probably the most powerful seer in the entire realm. The ability to see the future was only one of her five affinities, but the fact that she held two psychic affinities—being a seer and being able to read thoughts—meant she was incredibly formidable. Before my father had caged her magic, there had been whisperings that perhaps she should rule the continent. And she was strong enough that she'd seen what I was to become.

I'd told Ilara once about my mother's abilities, even though I hadn't come right out and told her directly what my mother's affinities were. Instead, I'd hinted at one, telling my mate that a powerful seer had predicted my death affinity after I'd been born on the triple lunar eclipse. I hadn't told her, though, that said seer had been my own mother.

And gazing at my mother now, with her fierce determination and unyielding backbone, I knew that her powerful magic wasn't her only strength. The female that had born me had an iron will. It was always me who'd backed down from my father. Lissandra would have borne his punishment, but I had never been able to tolerate it. She had always been my only weakness—until Ilara—and, it was a weakness my father had exploited for dozens of winters.

"Norivun," she said again, her gaze unflinching, and I could have sworn that I saw a glimpse of her fire elemental affinity in her eyes. "You're to marry, Ilara. No one else. Only with her at your side will our continent once again see light."

I nodded even though I knew what that would mean. My mother would rather fall under my father's hand than allow my fate to continue.

And as much as it tore me apart to know what that

meant, perhaps it was time I finally honored her wish despite whatever punishment was to come.

I FOUND Nuwin before I left, needing to see him so I could learn what else had occurred at court during the past few days. And, as much as the bastard drove me crazy, I did miss him when we were parted for long periods of time.

Besides, he always had a way of pulling me out of bad moods, which was my current state after witnessing my mother's recent abuse.

"Ah, brother, I had a feeling you were in residence." Nuwin gave me a cheeky grin when I walked into his private wing. He lay on his couch, one of the court females at his side. Her lips were swollen, and her hair was mussed.

I leaned against the wall and crossed my arms, letting my wings fall slack. "Am I interrupting something?"

"Always." Nuwin sighed and helped the female to a stand. He gave her a sultry smile. "I'll find you later so we can finish what we started." He led her past me to the door.

Blushing, she dipped into a curtsy, her cheeks rosy and a dimple appearing, before she scurried down the hall.

"Another conquest?" I arched an eyebrow after Nuwin closed his door.

"Not yet, but by this evening, I imagine she will be." His lips lifted in a delighted smile. "And since you're back and not looking like Lucifer, I'm guessing you found Ilara?"

I chuckled. Unlike me, my brother didn't hold six affinities, but he did hold three. His weakest was the affinity he'd inherited from my mother, his ability to see. But his seer affinity was so weak that often times it only led to feelings and subtle understandings. It was why he loved to rile fae so much since he was so easily able to detect their reactions. I was guessing it was also how he knew that I'd found my mate.

"Is it that obvious?"

Nuwin shrugged. "To others, no, but to me . . ." He waggled his eyebrows. "Is your cock worn out then?"

I slugged him in the shoulder, which only got a laugh from him.

Holding up his hands, he added, "I couldn't resist. You reek of sex, and I can detect her scent on you, so I figured you finally had your way with her and the bond has been sealed. So, how's she doing? I do miss her."

A low growl vibrated my chest when I thought of Drachu and what he'd done to my mate. "It's a long story." I glanced toward the clock ticking on Nuwin's wall. "I don't have a lot of time, but I wanted to know what's happened. Have Father's hunting fae found any clues to Ilara's whereabouts?"

"Ah! His hunting fae . . ." Nuwin traipsed toward the bar in the corner of his room. "As a matter of fact, they have. It's a pity you don't have time for a drink. I could tell you all about how they've ventured into the wilds of eastern Mervalee, into the Wisareian Forest, in search of dear Ilara and lovely Cailis. One of them had to return after a nasty encounter with a forest sprite, which is the only reason I know the tale."

Nuwin paused from pouring leminai into his glass. "Why are you grinning?"

I smothered my smile. "No reason."

Nuwin's eyes sparkled. "Did you have anything to do with father's fae venturing to that dreadful area of Mervalee?"

I raised my shoulders innocently. "Maybe. Maybe not."

Nuwin's head tipped back with a laugh. "Oh, how magnificent. I shall enjoy hearing more about that when you return, and I imagine Father's fae will have a scar or two from those sprites' nasty bites making their stories just as juicy."

I snorted, a grin splitting my face. "It's good to see you, brother, but I need to go. Check on Mother soon, will you?"

His eyes dimmed. "I've been visiting her daily. Whilst I can't stop Father's hand, I can at least make her laugh while she recovers."

"Thank you." My chest tightened, but before I called upon my magic to mistphase, I added, "And stay out of trouble."

Nuwin winked. "Whatever would I do that for?"

Shaking my head, I nodded farewell as the castle disappeared around me.

I mistphased back to the Crystal Inn, and the second I appeared, my guards and Ilara shot to their feet.

"You're back, finally," Ryder said.

I gave a curt nod, taking in the empty food tray on one bed and a full tray on the other.

"How's your magic?" Ilara asked as she began dishing a plate of food for me. "You'll need the nutrition if you're to scry."

My lips hooked up when her love and concern billowed

to me on our bond. More than anything, I wanted to wrap my arms around her, bury my face in her neck, and breathe in her scent, but she was right.

I needed to replenish my magic if we were to hunt for Drachu. And from the hard edge of my guards' jaws and the determined light in Ilara's eyes—the hunt began tonight.

CHAPTER 19 - ILARA

N orivun consumed all of the food we'd saved for him, then he disappeared into the small bathing chamber attached to our room. He held his small yellow crystals in one hand and the shell from Drachu's house and a wicked-looking knife in the other.

Within minutes of disappearing behind the door, low sounds of rattling and chanting came from the bathing chamber.

Nish stood near the door and Sandus by the window. Haxil sat on the bed opposite Ryder as I paced back and forth in front of them.

The males had been trading off who stood guard where since we'd arrived. They stood calmly. Stoically. Yet I couldn't sit still despite being so depleted only hours before that I'd passed out. My magic was swiftly returning thanks to a nap, all of the food I'd consumed, and whatever potion Cora had given me.

I smoothed my new yellow top over me for what felt like the hundredth time. "How does scrying work?"

Ryder stroked his pointy chin. "Couldn't really tell you. Scrying only works for those with immense magic, hence, why most of us can't do it, but I bet Nori would teach you if you asked."

"Maybe someday I will, when we have time for that sort of thing." More chanting came from the bathing room, and I could have sworn Norivun hissed quietly. A flare of pain came through our bond next, and I couldn't help but wonder if my mate had just cut himself with the knife since he needed blood for whatever he was doing.

I picked at my fingernails as my pacing increased. "How long does this usually take?"

Haxil shrugged. "Depends on how elusive the target is. For someone like Drachu, it could take a while."

I gave a curt nod, and Sandus cocked an eyebrow. "You're going to wear a path into the floor if you keep that up, Ilara. Perhaps you should take all of that nervous energy and use it to practice your new affinities."

I stopped, facing him, and couldn't help but snort. "Are you seriously saying we should practice my warrior training *here*?" I swept my arms out to the small room that felt crowded just from the five of us being present.

His lips tugged up. "I was referring more to the animal affinity you have that gave you those white wings. It would be good if you could learn to call them forth and banish them at will. Even better if you could learn to use them to fly."

Some of the anxiety pooling through my gut abated.

Sandus was right. Perhaps it was best if I used this time to feel out what I could about the strange affinity between my shoulder blades. So much had happened since the Adrall Temple that I hadn't had time to properly assess either of my new forms of magic.

I sat on the bed, and Haxil scooted over to give me room. Norivun's chanting in the bathing chamber and rattling of his crystals continued. I closed my eyes and called upon the training Matron Olsander had instilled in me when I'd first started learning about my affinities.

I probed within myself, marveling anew at how immensely powerful I felt now that I had five affinities. *Mother Below, I have five affinities.* I had as much magic as Queen Lissandra.

That fact slowly sank in as I assessed the magical ball that had birthed my wings. It was still firmly rooted between my shoulder blades, unlike my other affinities that all existed low in my belly.

I stroked the dense ball of light and cold power. Once again, it was the only way I could describe it.

Closing my eyes tighter, I poured all of my concentration into that one area and resorted to the basics—mental imagery. I pictured my wings bursting from my back, their beautiful white feathers as pure as freshly fallen snow when they unfurled.

A jolt of power lashed through my spine, and then the sensation of new limbs appearing along my back came next.

Haxil made a sound before his weight lifted from the mattress, and I opened my eyes to see all four guards standing before me, grinning, as they beheld the huge white wings that had sprouted by my shoulder blades.

I gave Haxil a sheepish look. My right wing had inadvertently extended to where he'd been sitting. I'd probably shoved him from the bed.

"Sorry, Haxil."

The round-cheeked guard winked. "'Tis all right. I moved before you knocked me off."

Thankfully, the new top I wore had wing slits in the back, so I hadn't destroyed another piece of clothing, but that strange sensation of my new wings again overtook me.

I stood from the bed, albeit a bit clumsily, as my brain worked at a frantic pace to make sense of these new appendages.

"Try to extend them." Ryder spread his black wings wide, which were so large they nearly stretched door to window.

I frowned, concentrating on my wings again, and slowly they extended behind me as my warrior affinity heated.

Sandus's grin stretched. "Very good. I knew you would be a natural, love."

My warrior affinity warmed further with each new movement I tried with my wings. Amazingly, I grew faster and faster at closing them, opening them, extending one, then extending the other, lifting them, lowering them, and so forth. A few times I flapped my wings just to see what would happen, even though it was hard in such a small room. Each time, my feet lifted slightly from the floor, the muscles in my wings automatically tensing to accommodate my body's weight.

"Amazing!" I breathed.

Haxil crossed his arms smugly. "'Tis your warrior affinity. It's giving you the ability to master flight at an advanced rate. Most youth struggle to learn the task when their wings first emerge, but since your new warrior affinity gives you an intrinsic understanding of your body and muscles, along with enhanced strength and speed, 'tis no wonder you can already control them."

Sandus nodded, looking as proud as he did when his niece, Harpelin, kicked her chubby little legs. "All of the training we did during the Rising Queen Trial is no doubt helping too. You're a fine-tuned warrior, Ilara, even if that affinity has just emerged."

The crown prince's guards continued watching me, pride evident on their faces.

Warmth bloomed across my cheeks, and I had to force myself not to duck my head. Still, I couldn't help but also feel proud at all that I'd achieved. "Do you think I could go outside and try flying to—"

The door to the bathing chamber burst open, and Norivun emerged. A savage grin stretched across his face, and his aura pounded through the room. Darkness gathered around his shoulders, making him look more demon than fae.

Ryder turned so fast to my mate that his braid whipped between his wings. "Did you find him?"

Norivun's smile stretched. "Indeed. He's in the palace in Vemil Brasea, the Lochen's capital beneath the waves."

My excitement at finding the treacherous Lochen king

came to a careening halt. "But if he's in the ocean, how can we possibly retrieve his necklace?"

"We'll mistphase, and you and I will conjure air bubbles around our faces to allow all of us to breathe underwater. I'll also cloak us under an illusion so nobody can see us."

"Okay," I said hesitantly, then nodded more assuredly when I remembered how I'd done something similar during the second Trial test in the Bay of Nim. I'd used my air affinity to breathe underwater while also propelling me through the waves. It could be done. With Norivun's guards, it would be more difficult, but we could do it.

Norivun's eyes widened when he assessed my wings, his manic energy dimming slightly as he looked at them with wonder. "They're back."

I nodded, and then concentrated on calling my wings back into my body to see if I could make them disappear.

Surprisingly, it was no different than the other movements. In a blink, my wings were gone.

"Incredible," he whispered. "You're quite fast."

I batted my eyelashes. "So I've been told."

Nish snorted a laugh.

"Back to the matter at hand," Ryder crossed his arms. "Tell us exactly what you saw."

Norivun explained what his scrying had allowed him to see about Vemil Brasea. "Drachu's there. I'm sure of it. He's in one of the palace's rooms."

"Are you confident we can get to him?" Haxil asked.

Prince Norivun slipped his yellow crystals into his pocket. "It's hard to say. I have no idea if he's guarded or in a weakened state. Who knows why he pulled on Ilara's powers like he did. We won't know until we get there."

My magic simmered at just the mention of what Drachu had done. He might have helped me by calling upon God Zorifel to restore my powers, but that favor had come at a cost. A cost I'd never agreed to.

"When should we go?" I asked. "Are we strong enough to confront him now?"

More of the manic energy around Norivun faded, and his worry strummed toward me on our bond. "That question is most relevant for you. You're the one who was depleted only a few hours ago. I've had enough time since ripping through my illusion at the Cliffs of Sarum to recover adequately."

"I'm fine." When he raised his eyebrows, I scowled. "I am. Don't baby me. I can handle myself."

His lips curved with pride.

Ryder cocked an eyebrow at the prince. "How likely are you to be able to pinpoint his location again if we don't go after him right at this moment?"

Norivun's lips thinned as he drummed his fingers on his thigh. "I don't know. Every time you use an object to scry, it becomes less effective. Most likely, I would have to return to Vockalin to retrieve something else that Drachu owns."

"Which could potentially alert him to what we're doing." I shook my head. "I've had enough rest and food to be able to do this. We go now, and we put an end to his control on me."

Norivun grinned. "Spoken like a true queen."

CHAPTER 20 - ILARA

We had to find a map of the oceans before we could mistphase to Vemil Brasea. We knew the Lochen capital was in the Adriastic Sea, the ocean just to the east of the Nolus continent that separated it from the Silten continent, but we didn't know its exact location. If we were to mistphase there, we had to know precisely where we were going, lest we end up in some nether region of the ocean.

"What do you remember of Vemil Brasea in your Lochen studies?" Norivun asked Haxil as we strode from the inn back onto the capital's streets.

Haxil ran a hand along his cheek as we headed toward a map shop that the Crystal Inn employee had recommended to us. "It's large, probably the same size as Solisarium, but since it's in the ocean, it's not warded. The Lochen are the commanders of the seas, always have been, and that arrogance has made them feel vastly superior to any other fae in our realm, especially when it comes to the water."

Norivun's lips parted in a malicious smile. "No wards. Excellent."

"Do you have any idea at all where Drachu is in his palace?" I asked as the door to the map shop appeared ahead.

Norivun's wings ruffled, his talons looking like onyx claws in the sunlight. More than a few Nolus fae on the street gave us a wide berth when we strode past them. "No, unfortunately I don't, and as for where exactly or for how long he'll be there, I'm unsure."

We didn't waste any time securing a map once we reached the shop, even though the shopkeeper—a Nolus female with cobalt-blue hair—squealed in fright when we burst through the door.

I couldn't fault her response. Norivun and his four guards, with their massive wings, menacing expressions, and huge builds would have scared the daylights out of any Solis fairy, let alone an unsuspecting Nolus who'd probably never seen our kind in her entire life.

I hurried to smother her fears, and after her blubbering responses, she finally calmed down enough to show us what we needed.

Once we had the map in hand, we returned to the streets to find a quiet area to plan, and we ended up tucking into an alleyway between two shops that smelled faintly of lemons and thyme, making me wonder if an eating establishment was near.

Norivun spread the map wide, allowing us all to study

the beautiful rendition of the Lochen cities within the depths of the Adriastic Sea.

"There's so many," Ryder commented, his eyes narrowing. "How many Lochen are there?"

"Tylen said there's more Lochen than there are Solis," I replied.

Nish scowled. "Ock, Tylen can go fuck his own arse."

Sandus snorted, "I'll be sure to tell him that if we see him again."

"Please do," Nish replied. "Then promptly connect your fist with his face."

Haxil snickered, and even Norivun couldn't suppress a smile. "I didn't see Tylen in my scrying, so with any luck, he's not there. If he is, it's imperative that we avoid him. Our affinities will only mask our arrival and travels if that null doesn't steal them again."

"Not to mention, we'll lose the ability to breathe underwater if your air affinity is stripped away," Ryder commented.

Norivun nodded in agreement. "This needs to be quick and precise. We need to focus on entering the palace and finding Drachu promptly and immediately taking his necklace. Understood?"

We all nodded, and a tingle fluttered in my lower belly at how commanding his tone was. Norivun glanced in my direction, his nostrils flaring as his firm expression turned slightly heated.

Clearing my throat, I did my best to suppress the innate attraction to him that always bloomed through me. As if knowing exactly where my thoughts had turned, the crown prince leaned closer and whispered in my ear, "Tonight, after we've taken that necklace from Drachu, I'm going to fuck you till you scream."

My toes curled, and Ryder elbow-bumped Haxil.

Heat bloomed in my cheeks, but I still pulled him in for a quick kiss before putting more distance between us and forcing my concentration back to our task. "I'll keep air around me, Nish, and Sandus, and you keep air around yourself, Ryder, and Haxil. Got it?"

His lips curved alluringly. "Damn, I do love it when you try to give me orders."

I arched an eyebrow. "Try?"

He chuckled. "You're right. As my queen, you can order anyone in our kingdom."

I suppressed a smirk. "Including you?"

He laughed devilishly. "Depends what the order is. If it's in the bedroom, then—"

"All right, you two," Nish interrupted as he ran a hand over his shorn hair. "Enough of the mating talk. Let's get that bastard. I'm spoiling for a fight."

THE MISTPHASE to Vemil Brasea was more intricate than any I'd ever attempted, which only solidified why the Lochen were so confident in their ability to keep other fae away from their underwater cities. If I found it challenging, a Solis female who now held five affinities and had thoroughly mastered the art of mistphasing, I could only imagine that such a feat was near impossible for other Solis fae.

We moved through the realm in mist and shadows, air and wind, but when we reached the water, everything changed. The magic that allowed me to morph into particles suddenly felt heavy and weighted. It took actual concentration to propel myself and the guards through the water, and it wasn't instantaneous like it was on land.

The force of moving our bodies through the denser material made my magic throb, and the second the mistphase ended, I was so fatigued that I nearly gasped as cold water shocked my system. I stopped just in time when I realized my magic had transported us to the capital, but it hadn't made us reappear with air bubbles around our heads.

Vemil Brasea stretched out around us, but I didn't give myself a moment to study it. Sandus's and Nish's eyes were wide, their cheeks puffed out while they held their breath.

I pulled upon the air affinity in my gut to secure all three of us with a breathing ability. Norivun was in the process of doing the same to Haxil and Ryder, all of their cheeks puffed out too, which made me think that doing the mistphase and enacting our air magic within water simultaneously either wasn't possible or was so difficult that it would take practice to achieve.

Whatever the case, by the time all six of us were treading in the water and able to breathe again, I literally exhaled in relief. We'd done it.

"Can anyone hear us?" I asked Norivun quietly.

He shook his head and began to swim slowly toward the

palace's front gate, being careful to avoid the Lochen fae also swimming within the sea. "We're cloaked completely."

Sighing again in relief, I finally allowed myself a moment to stare at the Lochen's underwater capital as the cold ocean water seeped into my bones.

Vemil Brasea was a magnificent site to behold. Deep within the Adriastic Sea, it was a glimmering oasis of light, color, and sound. Norivun's illusion indeed cloaked us completely, since none of the Lochen swimming past us so much as glanced our way, so I used the moment to soak up every second of this new discovery.

We'd mistphased to right beside the palace, and the ornate structure was made of the same purple shells and stones of Drachu's home in Vockalin, making me wonder if all of his residences were constructed of the same objects. It rose right next to us, soaring from the seafloor with beautiful spires and an intricate design. There were even windows in some of the rooms, many made of stained glass that seemed to glow from within.

"How is there light here?" I asked as the vibrant city shone around us in iridescent colors that seemed to refract off the hundreds of buildings made of sea shells, sand bricks, glass panes, and a smooth cream-colored material marred with darker lines scouring through them. I could only guess it was bone.

"Magic," Haxil replied. "I've read that the Lochen channel the Mother to create such a feat. She provides them with the underwater light while heating their blood." He was gazing around as much as I was, while Nish spent most of his time sneering at any Lochen who came within arm's reach of us even though they were entirely unaware of our presence.

My lips parted when I recalled how Drachu had mentioned magic unique to the Lochen. *Channa* was what he'd called it, saying it heated them from within so they never grew cold in the depths of the sea. I could understand why it was needed. If not for my fire affinity, which I was using to keep me warm in addition to Norivun's illusion—which he'd heated with his magic—we would all be freezing.

As we continued swimming closer to the palace's gates, I beheld the Lochen we swam around. Similar to Solisarium, in which fae flew at varying altitudes through the city, the Lochen fae swam at different depths and speeds within and above Vemil Brasea.

I glanced upward to see hundreds of Lochen swimming in their fish-like forms, their legs gone as a huge single-finned tail took its place. They still had a fae-like body from the waist up, but from the waist down, they were entirely fins and scales. And the colors of their fins reminded me of the Nolus. Some had fins that were only one shade—magenta, brilliant green, pearly white, and light blue were some of the more abundant colors. Others had scales of various shimmering shades that seemed to change in the light. Some only had one fin, and others had multiple fins that seemed to flow behind them, all in various colors, as they swam through the water. It didn't seem any of them were identical, making me think of their custom to also assign each fairy a unique name. In a way, it seemed fitting.

Music drifted around us the closer we got to the gates, as

though a symphony constantly played melodic songs from the heart of the city. It was beautiful, otherworldly, and for a moment I was completely transfixed by it. It stunned me that something such as this could exist without me ever having known it.

I was struck anew by how far I'd come from my small life in Mervalee Territory. It was a life that I'd thought I'd wanted, but now that I'd experienced so many riches of our realm, I didn't know if I would ever be content to go back to an existence that small.

"Fascinating." I swallowed the ball of emotion in my throat just as we swam closer to the palace's front gate, completely unknown to the two guards hovering in the water, one on each side of it.

"So, what did they do with him?" the guard on the left asked the guard on the right. All of us slowed our swimming as we neared them.

"He was fed to the feerily." The right guard shifted the trident spear in his hand. "Two bites, and he was swallowed."

The left guard snickered. "Serves him right. Anyone who comes into the palace and attacks the king deserves nothing less."

I paused and treaded in the water as I eyed Norivun. "So Drachu wrenched my powers from me because someone was attacking him?"

Norivun's brow furrowed as a scowl descended on his face. "Sounds like it."

Nish sneered. "And from the sounds of it, the assassination attempt wasn't successful."

"Obviously," Ryder replied, "or our prince never would have seen Drachu safe and sound in his palace if he was dead."

"Did you see the way Drachu fought?" the right guard boasted, oblivious to our masked conversation. "He used fire underwater within a bubble of air."

The left guard inclined his head while his hair flowed languidly in the water, as though billowing in a slow-motion breeze. "Truly?"

The right guard nodded. "And I've never seen our king move so fast before. That male didn't stand a chance against him."

The other guard laughed. "And now in celebration for thwarting another attempted assassin, our king is celebrating in true fashion."

A loud laugh erupted from the right guard as my nostrils flared within my air bubble. Anger scorched through me. The magic Drachu had used to defeat whoever had attacked him were *my* powers that he had no business stealing.

"Let's end this once and for all," Norivun snarled and propelled himself forward.

The Lochen guards' huge tails stayed motionless beneath them when we swam by. Their boisterous laughs continued, so they were none the wiser by the ripples we created in the water.

When we were halfway through the gate, I couldn't help but glance down, to just below their waists before they were out of sight. It was hard to forget how Drachu had spoken of one of his concubines—Xanimy—the one that he said was even better in bed beneath the waves.

A slight bulge was evident where a fairy's cock would have been in his fae form, and I could only surmise that something was done by the Lochen when they grew aroused. Perhaps they were able to free themselves from over their scales. Maybe magic allowed an appendage to grow, or there was a slit in their scales that I couldn't see that their cock slipped through, or maybe some other magical form was revealed when the Lochen engaged in sexual acts. Perhaps their shape changed entirely into something that didn't resemble what they were now.

A low growl came from Norivun as we drifted past the guards, and I knew it wasn't because of their conversation of Drachu using my affinities.

"I can't help but be curious," I said with a shrug as my curiosity strummed right out of me and into him on our bond.

He inclined his head, but his scowl didn't relent. "Understandable, but you also have to know that I'll never take kindly to you checking out another male's cock."

Nish's eyebrows rose clear to his forehead. "You were just ogling the guards' cocks, Ilara?"

"What?" I glanced toward him, the water making my movement sluggish. "No, I wasn't. I mean, Drachu said something about taking one of his concubines to bed in fish-form, and I was curious and—"

I stopped the moment all five of them began grinning.

Rolling my eyes, I slugged Norivun in the chest when I realized his jealousy had all been for show. "Bastard."

He chuckled. "I apologize, my mate. But your curiosity was so evident I couldn't help but tease. We've all wondered how the Lochen fuck."

Sandus nodded. "It's true, love. We've even had entire evening discussions over it."

I snorted a laugh, just as a huge upward tunnel appeared in front of us. I could only imagine that it led to a higher floor in the castle, similar to what a staircase would have done on land. "Why not just ask the Lochen if you're that curious?"

Sandus laughed. "And admit we have no clue? Never, love."

I was still smiling when we drifted upward in the tunnel, having to move to the side when other Lochen, who I could only assume were servants who worked in this vast castle, swam past us. They were the first servants I'd seen in any of the Lochen king's homes. I wondered if—

My breath sucked in.

A pulsing sensation began in my chest. Thrumming harder, harder, harder . . .

I froze, my heart beating painfully with every throb.

I needed—

No, I wanted—

Drachu.

Find him.

I shot forward. The urge to go to my king, admire him, love him, touch him . . .

I *needed* him.

I swam down a hall, away from Norivun and his guards as all five of them called after me.

Since I'd banished my wings before the mistphase, my sleek form allowed me to move fast, and I followed the call deep within my blood. The call to find Drachu and stay by his side.

Yes, I need him. He's my true king.

I rounded the final turn in the hall, and a vast room opened before me with furniture similar to what I would see on land.

The king of the Lochen lay exposed before me.

Drachu was positioned on a huge bed, two concubines with him, and if I'd had any lingering questions about how the Lochen enjoyed one another.

I didn't anymore.

And Blessed Mother, I wanted to partake.

CHAPTER 21 - NORIVUN

Ilara floated under the doorframe that led into a chamber, and I frantically kicked to catch up. "Ilara!" I called for what felt like the hundredth time.

She didn't stop.

"What in the bloody realm is she doing?" Nish seethed.

I had to stretch my illusion to keep her cloaked. It was difficult in the water, like having to wade through wet sand versus on land, where it was nearly effortless.

Worry punched my gut when wonder, awe, then lust carved through our bond. Just a moment ago, she'd felt happy and hopeful, then reverent and enthralled, but now—

Fuck.

An ominous feeling slid through me.

"It's happening again!" I bit out. "At the Adrall Temple when she was acting strangely around Drachu, the same thing is happening now, only it's—"

I couldn't continue. Jealousy streaked through my insides

like a scorching hot flame as I raced to catch her. I knew she didn't actually want Drachu, that she didn't even like the tricky bastard after what he'd done to her, but it was a response I couldn't stop.

I wanted to kill Drachu. I wanted to murder any male that made my mate's blood heat with desire. I lusted for revenge so potently that I could taste the Lochen king's flesh on my tongue.

Ilara was already halfway across the room when my guards and I finally caught up with her. She was headed right for the king and two females who were—

"Mother Below, am I seeing things?" Ryder asked as Sandus's jaw dropped.

It was only fear for my mate that made me burst forward and grab her, but considering what we were looking at, it was hard to keep my focus.

The Lochen king was currently writhing on a bed, a huge scaled dick standing on end from between his scales as one of his females bounced on top of him in an awkward-looking seated position. A pink slit was evident in her scales that the king's cock disappeared into. The other female sat on the king's face as she moaned and rubbed herself on him while he ate her out.

"I think I need to scrub my eyes," Nish said. "I thought it would be . . . different than that."

I snarled in their direction, even though I was inclined to agree with him. Something about seeing the Lochen in such a state that seemed more animal than fae right now and knowing that my mate desired to join them . . .

Rage fired through me.

Ilara squirmed in my touch, the lust from her ratcheting up through our bond as she tried to go to them.

"No," I growled.

I couldn't allow her to touch the Lochen king, not just because every instinct within me screamed to keep her away, but also because I couldn't hide what they felt. My illusions masked sight and sound but not touch.

My mate fought against me more.

"Fuck," I cursed quietly. "Ilara, stop!"

"No!" Her struggles increased, and the look on her face was so intense, so obsessed with reaching the king. She fought me more, and my grip began to slip.

"Ilara!" I snarled. I shoved a huge burst of frustration toward her on the mate bond, hoping against hope that it would get through to her.

The second my anger reached her, she stilled, then peered up at me as though she'd been asleep and had only just awoken.

Relief hit me hard, but the second her expression cleared, the fog descended anew, and she was once again struggling in my grip, trying to reach Drachu.

Fuck. Fuck. Fuck!

Fury swallowed me. Ilara was too lost in the king's thrall over her. Being this close to him made her entirely vulnerable. And something about being near Drachu in his fish-form seemed to be commanding her even more than he had on land.

"Sandus! Haxil!" I roared. "Hold her!"

But just as my guards reached us, Ilara ripped free and raced the remaining distance to the king using her warrior speed. Before we could stop her, Ilara's hand slid along the king's stomach, touching him with a lover's caress.

Arousal coated my mate's expression, and that response was because of Drachu, not me.

Red coated my vision.

Kill him.

Kill him.

Kill him.

"Oh fuck," Ryder said under his breath. "We're losing them both."

I dove toward Drachu just as the king lifted the female off his face to peer toward his abdomen. His eyes narrowed, and he tossed her to the side, her cry of protest carrying through the water as he sat up.

Ilara's hand wandered up Drachu's stomach, her expression coated with lust as the other female continued bouncing on top of the king, his dick sliding in and out of her.

The Lochen concubine was completely oblivious to what was happening while the look on Drachu's face told me he was growing more aware by the second that something else was at play within his chambers.

My arm whipped out, ensnaring Ilara around the waist, and I wrenched her back. Haxil and Sandus took her, using their warrior strength to keep her from returning to the Lochen king as bloodlust consumed me.

Kill him.

Kill him.

Kill him.

"Norivun!" Nish yelled just as my death affinity burst out of me.

In a heartbeat, Drachu had the female off his cock as his glittering emerald eyes shot daggers our way.

"Can he see us?" Sandus called as he tried to pull me back.

"No, we're still hidden," Ryder replied.

I snarled when my death affinity didn't move faster through the water.

"Ilara," Drachu called in a sing-song voice that immediately sent shivers down my mate's spine. I could practically feel it myself through the bond.

I snarled in fury, and the arousal pounding from Ilara increased just as my affinity reached the king.

I ensnared the foreign king's soul, loving the feel of Drachu's life within my grasp.

His eyes flashed wide open.

The concubine who'd been riding him shrieked, the sound strangely clear through the water, just as Drachu's lips peeled back in a hiss, and the necklace glowed against his chest.

In a swell of power, Ilara screamed then curled over as a huge rush of her life-giving affinity coated the king's entire form. Magic shot out of Drachu, hitting me squarely in the chest and stopping my death affinity in the process.

I flew back in the water, slamming into the wall behind me as my guards descended.

Swords were in Nish's and Ryder's hands as they tried to

tear the necklace from Drachu's throat, but Drachu was too fast, too superior in the water.

The Lochen king whizzed across the room in a blink, his canines lengthening as magic pounded from his form. He still couldn't see us. My illusion affinity was still intact, but he no doubt felt our movements, the water speaking to him in ways it never would to us.

I kicked away from the wall, my hands in front of me as my wings tucked into slits at my back. Ilara continued to thrash against Sandus and Haxil, trying to work her way free just as I swam toward the Lochen king.

"Ilara," Drachu crooned again. "Have you come to join my harem? I do so wish that's the case. I'd love to fuck you beneath the wav—"

I slammed into him, my hands locking around his throat as another rush of Ilara's affinities exploded out of him.

Our affinities collided, the strength of my mate's magic coiling with mine until a ball of dense energy burst between me and Drachu. A shockwave ripped through the water as we fought, his hands on me, mine on him, as our magic's intensity grew.

Walls began to crumble in the room. The two concubines screamed again before diving through a shattered window. Sounds came from down the hall as Drachu shrieked for help from his guards.

All the while, I refused to let go of the king. With that pendant around his neck, he commanded my mate entirely. She would always be susceptible to his reach. Always crave to do his bidding. She would never be free of his greedy power.

Pain continued to thrum from Ilara as I slipped a finger around the tether holding the pendant in place.

Energy sizzled between us as my affinity battled my mate's as the king maliciously pulled her magic from her in unrelenting waves once more.

Her shrieks had ended, and increased pain burst on the bond.

But I didn't stop. I couldn't. If I did, we were doomed. We would never have the element of surprise again. Now that Drachu knew we could reach him within his underwater cities, I had no doubt wards would be installed, and entry into his homes would be near impossible.

"Ryder! Nish!" I yelled. In a heartbeat, they were beside me.

Another rush of magic shot out of Drachu, and in a blink, the bubbles around *all* of my guards disappeared. The Lochen king had ensnared Ilara's air affinity. One glance over my shoulder showed that my mate had also lost her ability to breathe. The bubble around her face was gone.

It was only the strength of my own air element that stopped the king from sucking the bubble from around my head.

Despite being unable to breathe, none of my guards stopped fighting. I shoved against Drachu more, pushing through the pain of my affinity colliding with my mate's, as I wrapped both hands around the back of his neck.

I seized the band holding the pendant and with a huge wrench of power, tore it free.

The second the pendant lifted away from the king's chest, my mate's power disappeared.

Drachu's eyes went wide. Fear painted his features.

He punched through the water, his outstretched hand reaching for the pendant, but I pulled it within my illusion, making it disappear from sight.

Drachu whirled around in a circle just as his guards appeared at the door, trident spears in hand. He yelled to them in a foreign language, and I threw my air affinity around all of my guards and Ilara.

She'd collapsed against Sandus, her body limp, her chest still. *Holy fuck, she's unconscious.*

In a dash of panic, I ensnared my guards and Ilara, then called upon everything I had to mistphase us out of there as my limbs trembled with the effort.

The realm disassembled in a blur of heavy shadows and wet sand just as the guards' trident spears flung toward us.

WE SLAMMED BACK into our room at the inn in the capital. My guards were soaked, their chests heaving as wet hair was plastered to their faces. Drachu's pendant was still entwined between my fingers as I moved at blurred speed toward my mate.

Ilara's face was blue.

Her skin cool.

"She's not breathing!" I screamed.

I slammed my mouth to hers, instinct commanding me to

force life into my mate. I blew a rush of air into her lungs, forcing it with my affinity, but it encountered something wet. Something heavy.

Water. Her lungs are filled with water. She'd sucked in water when Drachu had ripped the bubble from her face.

I blew another stream of air into her, using my magic and strength. "Please, Ilara. Please!"

Another blast of air gusted from my lips while my guards watched silently.

But the feel of Ilara's life dimmed more and more on our bond. *No!*

I held her mouth open wide, then called upon all of my air affinity and spiraled it into her lungs.

She coughed.

Then coughed again and again. I rolled her on her side as a huge gush of seawater spilled from her lips.

Unrelenting coughs shook her frame, then she heaved in shallow breaths. But just as quickly she fell weak again, becoming despondent in my grip.

"What's happening?" Nish yelled.

I frantically wrenched my mate to me, but her lips were turning blue once more, her breathing ragged despite the fact that the water had dispelled from her lungs. "I don't know. She should be—"

And then it hit me.

Drachu had pulled on all of her powers too quickly again while we'd fought underwater. He'd done the same thing to her when we'd entered the Nolus capital. Ilara was once again on the brink of death.

"The potion! Where's the second potion that Cora gave us?" I roared.

Haxil's eyes widened as he dove toward the satchel I'd stored the potion in. Using warrior speed, he was back at my side in less than a second. "Here."

I uncorked the vial and tipped the contents into Ilara's mouth. "Drink, my love. Drink."

It felt like an eternity passed as the potion trickled down her throat.

I held her to me, rocking her as my heart raced so savagely it felt as though it'd escape my chest.

Another second passed, and then Ilara sucked in a breath of air.

She breathed more, the sound ragged, but another second ticked by, and the blueness in her lips vanished.

"Thank the gods," Haxil whispered.

I sagged forward, my throat closing with emotion.

"Blessed Mother," Sandus rasped. "We almost lost her a second time."

All four of my guards wore tortured expressions as I held Ilara to me.

It was probably only minutes, even though it felt like years, before she peered up at me, her black hair wet and sapphire-blue eyes fatigued, but her expression was alert.

Hope, love, sorrow, guilt—every emotion possible streaked across her face in a kaleidoscope of color as it also pushed to me on the bond.

"I'm sorry," she breathed. "I lost control. When I saw Drachu, it was like I disappeared. Only the feel of you and our mate bond pulled me back, but then I was sucked under again, and—"

I brought a finger to her lips, my entire body shaking. "It's all right." I pulled her closer, needing to hold her, feel her, touch her.

I shook so badly I had to clasp my hands together.

She buried her face in my chest, her breath still shuddering as she gulped in lungfuls of air.

"Fuck, that was close." Ryder raked a hand over his face.

"Too close," Sandus agreed.

"Did we even get the bastard's necklace?" Nish asked, lip curling.

"He got it." Ryder pointed to the pendant still threaded through my fingers.

"You did?" Ilara jerked away from me, shock evident on her face.

"I did. Somehow. Amazingly." I held up the necklace as the green stone throbbed in its center.

A moment passed in which she blinked. She shook her head in wonder, then a grin streaked across her face. "You did it."

"*We* did it," I replied.

"And thank fuck for that." Nish sighed as he ran a hand over his shorn hair. "Can we all agree not to go to a Lochen underwater city again anytime soon? As lovely as it was, Drachu's going to be enraged, but without that necklace, I'd wager to say he'll be struggling to hold onto his power."

Ryder snorted. "Wasn't it *you* who was spoiling for a fight and encouraged us to go?"

Laughter burst from Ilara's lips as everyone else grinned.

"Ock, well, the bastard deserved it," Nish growled.

I laughed again as I pulled Ilara close, but my hands still shook. I agreed with my guards. That had been much too close, and if we never ventured to an underwater city again, it was fine by me.

CHAPTER 22 - ILARA

W e spent a few hours at the inn, then decided it was better if Norivun cast illusion masks over all of us before moving to a new location.

With hidden identities, we could all rest easier, in case Drachu attempted to track us down and exact his revenge. Even though none of us feared Drachu outright, especially now that he was without his stolen powers, we also knew that he was undoubtedly furious by what we'd done, even if he deserved it.

So with Norivun's illusion affinity masking our appearances, making us appear Nolus instead of Solis, we reserved three rooms at a new inn, several millees from the capital's palace.

We decided it was best to stay put until we heard from Bavar Fieldstone, so we used the time to rest and replenish our magic. It was also the first time Norivun and I had ever been able to spend days together in bed, doing nothing but soaking up the bliss of our newly sealed bond.

On our fourth day in the capital, I held Drachu's pendant between my fingers and let the light shine through it. It throbbed every time one of us put it near our skin, its power beckoning. Since we'd all seen firsthand what exorbitant power the pendant wielded, none of us had dared put it on. Who knew how it would change us.

"How do you suppose we destroy it?" I asked, as my head lay on Norivun's chest while we dozed naked in bed. My mate had thoroughly pleasured me for the third time that afternoon, and I was blissfully sated.

He ran his hand up and down my back, right between my wings. "Who's to say it can be destroyed? And if we did manage to destroy it, who's to say it wouldn't hurt you in the process."

I nibbled on my lip. "I've thought of that too. But since it contains the diamond that's able to channel my magic, I'm still vulnerable. If this falls into the wrong hands, my affinities would be available to anyone. As long as this necklace exists, I'm at risk."

A low growl rumbled in his chest. "Which is why no one will ever know of it or be able to lay a finger on it."

"Do you suppose someone knows how to extract that diamond and null that gem's hold on my affinities?"

"That's my hope. It's fair to say that priestess would know since the Lochen divine wielders are who invented these pendants."

I propped myself up more on his chest and set the necklace back on the table near the bed. "What do we do with it in the meantime?"

"Keep it hidden. Keep it safe. Once we've destroyed my father, we'll find a way to extract that diamond and return your powers fully to you and you alone. Until then, no one can know about it."

AFTER SIX DAYS in the capital, we received word from Bavar Fieldstone that he wanted to meet with us.

We immediately mistphased to the palace, and the sentries promptly admitted us.

Bavar's orange eyebrows rose clear to his hairline when he joined us in the admitting room. As before, he wore fine clothing, and the same dagger was strapped to his waist. "My oh my, I must say, I expected you to arrive soon but not this quickly."

"Time is of the essence," Norivun replied. "I hope you understand."

Bavar bowed. "Indeed. Come. I'd like you to meet someone."

We followed the Nolus royal to the same room we'd been in previously with the tapestries hanging from the wall, the open balconies, and the beautiful couches and chaise lounges.

The only difference was that another male was present when we entered the chamber.

The newcomer stood near the fireplace, hands in his

pockets, and he wore the most unusual clothes. A black shirt, similar to a tunic but thinner and without a belt, covered his upper half, but his lower half . . . I had no idea what the material was. There were square pockets over his rump, and the material's color was a flecked dark blue. Black boots covered his feet. His footwear was somewhat similar to Norivun's but still different.

With his back to us, it was obvious he was wingless. Broad shoulders stretched his peculiar shirt. His build was tall and powerful, and I would dare to guess his height rivaled my mate's.

The crown prince's nostrils flared as he inhaled, and I almost gasped when the male turned slightly.

The newcomer had rounded ears. He wasn't fae at all, which meant he was *other*.

"Prince Norivun and Lady Seary, Haxil, Ryder, Sandus, and Nish, I would like to introduce you to the Fire Wolf, a dear friend of mine and someone I met through the Supernatural Forces. He's a hunter. He specializes in finding elusive desires, and I believe he may be able to assist you with the troubles of late on your frozen continent." Bavar bowed and made a sweeping motion toward the male.

The Fire Wolf turned to fully face us, and my breath sucked in. The male was striking. And given his pounding aura, chiseled features that wore a ruthless expression, dark hair, and amber-colored eyes—he was also one of the most intimidating males I'd ever encountered. The only other male I'd sensed that kind of power from was my mate.

The Fire Wolf studied us just as intently, his gaze traveling over the males' silver hair and tall black wings. Normally, males of this realm wore a hint of apprehension when confronted with the crown prince and his guards, but this male merely arched an eyebrow. "I'm told you're the crown prince of the Solis continent."

My mate inhaled again. "That's correct. I'm Prince Norivun Deema Melustral Achul, first son of the king, Bringer of Darkness, Death Master of the continent, son of Prinavee Territory, and crown prince and heir to the Winter Court's throne."

The Fire Wolf smirked. "Right. Well, feel free to call me the Fire Wolf. I don't have a title." His lips kicked up in a sardonic smile.

The crown prince inclined his head. "All right, then you may call me . . . Norivun."

"Perfect. I don't particularly care for the title bullshit." The hunter came closer, prowling toward us on silent footsteps. His scent hit me, citrus and cedar. In a way it was similar to Norivun's scent, but without that wintery fragrance my mate always carried, it was less alluring. The energy off the prince increased the closer the Fire Wolf came to us, and I drew myself up to my full height. The hunter's gaze flicked to me briefly, and Norivun stepped closer until his body shielded mine as a low warning growl came from his throat.

The male smirked again. "Relax. I have no interest in your woman."

Woman? The male's forthright comment and casual demeanor made my heart beat even faster as Norivun shared a veiled look with his guards.

"Well, perhaps it's best if we all sit and discuss the matter at hand," Bavar said, jumping back into the conversation. "Please make yourselves comfortable whilst I ring for refreshments."

Bavar traipsed across the chamber as the Fire Wolf took the large chair near the fireplace. I sat on the couch opposite him, and Norivun promptly sat at my side, then placed his hand possessively on my knee.

The Fire Wolf's gaze flickered briefly to that gesture before he eyed the four guards, two on each side of him since Haxil and Sandus had taken the couch to our left and Nish and Ryder the couch on the right.

"You're the guards?" the Fire Wolf asked in that same tone. I couldn't tell if he was bored, or if it took a lot to impress him.

Nish sneered. "We are." He made a point of angling his wing, and his two swords made an appearance.

I almost rolled my eyes at the male dominance that was on full display, but while I could understand the posturing since this male felt powerful, I also knew it wouldn't allow us to work together very smoothly if this continued.

I angled my chin, then asked as conversationally as possible, "May I ask where you hail from, Fire Wolf?"

The hunter's lips twitched, and I could have sworn he suppressed a smile. "North America." My brow furrowed in confusion, so he added, "It's in the realm parallel to yours. Bavar tells me none of you have ever been to Earth before or anywhere in my home universe."

Nish's wings ruffled when he sneered.

Haxil leaned forward in his seat. "You would be correct, and you are a magical being from North America?" the round-cheeked guard asked curiously.

"That's one way of putting it," the Fire Wolf replied.

"Right!" Bavar called, coming up behind us. "Refreshments are on their way. Now"—he sat down on the remaining chair by the hunter and gave us all a wide smile—"The Fire Wolf may be able to help you determine what's causing the magic in your realm to be suppressed. His hunting skills are legendary, *and* he has advanced magical abilities. Also, since he's not a direct employee of the SF, he's free to come and go without my uncle's permission. I figured he would be the perfect candidate for the job. And I do apologize for how long it took to arrange this meeting. The dear Fire Wolf can be hard to find at times."

Norivun stiffened, his hand on my thigh growing warmer. "Do you plan to travel to Isalee with us, Fire Wolf?"

The hunter leaned back in his seat. "I'm assuming I'll need to. Until I can assess the area, I won't be much help."

Norivun nodded curtly, and while his body was still stiff, some of the pounding aura from him relented.

"Now," Bavar said, just as a servant brought a tray of sweets and tea into the room and set it discreetly on the center table before departing just as swiftly, "there is the matter of payment. The Fire Wolf will, of course, be expecting compensation for his time and talents."

"Naturally," Norivun replied dryly. "What's your fee?"

The Fire Wolf inspected his fingernails. "Three thousand rulibs. Half is required before I start."

My eyes popped. *Three thousand rulibs. Mother Below!* That could feed an entire family from my village for a full season.

Norivun cocked an eyebrow. "I suppose that's fair."

I blanched. Of course he did. That sum was probably pittance to him.

"But what if you're unable to provide any insight?" Norivun added. "What if we take you to Isalee, and you're not able to determine anything other than what my mate has already found?"

The Fire Wolf's gaze flicked to me again, and I knew it wasn't lost on him that the crown prince had called me his mate.

"My fee is guaranteed," the Fire Wolf replied easily. "If I can't help, you get your money back, and we part ways."

Money? I figured that was his term for rulibs.

Norivun grunted. "I will ask that we seal this with a bargain, simply to keep each male to his word."

The Fire Wolf inclined his head. "I assumed as much."

The two of them stood, and Bavar continued to munch on a cookie while Norivun and the Fire Wolf declared their terms of the bargain, determined how the rulibs would be transferred, and then sealed it all with magic.

Once they finished, the king's nephew swallowed his last bite and clapped. "Excellent. Prince Norivun, again, it's been a pleasure to see you, but for now, I shall leave you in the Fire Wolf's capable hands. If the Nolus can help in any further way, I do hope to see you again."

Prince Norivun brought his fist to his chest and bowed. "I

won't forget your kindness or willingness to assist us, Major Fieldstone. I am in your debt."

Bavar smiled, revealing pointy teeth. "Of course, and as I said before, I do hope this is the beginning of a friendly alliance. Invasion on anyone's continent is the last thing we need." With that, he brought his fist to his chest and bowed in return.

Once the pleasantries were done, Norivun's cool gaze returned to the Fire Wolf. "I'll mistphase you to the field."

The hunter extracted a portal key from his pocket. "No need. I can provide my own means of travel."

Norivun eyed the key with a smirk. "I'm afraid your traveling keys will likely send you to the wrong location when the field we're going to is so remote and hard to pinpoint. Please. Allow me to mistphase you."

The prince held out his hand, and the Fire Wolf's amber eyes burned with flames.

I swallowed a gasp, but the flames disappeared as the hunter took a slow step forward. "Mistphase?"

"It's how we travel," Nish said with a smirk.

"I'm trusting you," the hunter said on a low growl just before he placed his hand in the crown prince's.

"I know." Norivun's lips curved as he nodded toward me and his guards. "See you there?"

He didn't wait for us to reply. In a wink of magic, the two disappeared.

CHAPTER 23 - NORIVUN

The magical male from the *other* realm reappeared with me in Isalee's field. A blinding snowstorm raged as sharp wind cut into my skin. The Fire Wolf's dark hair blew around him, but despite the skin on his arms being exposed, he didn't shiver. In a blink, Ilara materialized beside me, followed by my guards.

"That was an interesting way to travel." The hunter scratched his jaw, yet his face stayed impassive as he assessed the area. "Do you use anything to channel your magic when you do that?"

I drew my eyebrows together. "No."

"Impressive." The Fire Wolf cocked an eyebrow as he continued looking around.

Regardless of his reluctant respect, I stayed between my mate and the male. While I wanted to believe I could trust him to do the job we'd hired him for, I wasn't a fool. I didn't trust the hunter with my mate, and I didn't trust him to do anything that wouldn't ultimately be in his best interests. The Fire Wolf smelled . . . different. I'd never scented any fae or creature like him, and the power I sensed in him made me cautiously wary.

The mate bond pulsed strongly inside me as Ilara's apprehension and curiosity rumbled along our connection. It seemed I wasn't the only one who'd reached that conclusion.

My mate lifted a hand, fanning it in a circle around her. A ring of fire erupted in a protective barrier about thirty feet in diameter, and my guards positioned themselves defensively near it.

The hunter's eyebrows rose. "Are we expecting company?"

I shrugged. "You never know. We had a previous incident with a snowgum here, and it's not something I care to repeat."

His eyes narrowed. "What's a snowgum?"

"An ice creature who you should hope you never encounter," Ilara replied.

The male smirked. "I'll take your word for it."

A stirring of the protectiveness I felt toward my mate rumbled, causing a low growl to vibrate my chest.

The Fire Wolf took a step farther away from Ilara, not looking at me when he did it, and I immediately quieted the possessive sound. While I didn't know this male at all, something told me that he understood mate bonds, and since he'd just shown a modicum of respect for the fact that I hadn't liked his smirking expression or his close proximity to my mate, I forced the instinct down.

I formed a solid Shield of air around us, halting the snow and wind from hitting us, then hunkered in the snow.

The hunter eyed the Shield briefly, his expression giving away nothing, before he also knelt at my side.

"This is the field where our crops first began to die," I explained. "It was here that Ilara detected that perhaps something is buried deep within the land that is suppressing the natural *orem*."

"What did you detect?" the Fire Wolf asked her.

Ilara frowned. "It's hard to describe. It just felt wrong, and when I tried to push through it, the effects were detrimental. Whatever's down there encased my magic, and it took a god to bring it back. I'd advise you to use caution when assessing it."

"A god?" The Fire Wolf grunted. "Noted." Despite her warning, he still plunged his hand into the snow, much like Ilara did when she was using her affinity, although I didn't feel his aura rise immediately, as though he respected her advice and was practicing caution. "And *orem* is the term that describes the magic that allows plants to grow in this frozen terrain?"

My mate inclined her head. "Correct. Did Major Fieldstone explain that part to you?"

"He did."

My four guards continued to watch the perimeter, not once letting their attention drop, as a rush of magic clouded around the Fire Wolf. I kept my expression impassive, but I watched the male closely to see if I could detect exactly what kind of magic-wielder he was.

A few moments passed, and the impassive expression on the Fire Wolf's face became clouded the more his magic grew. His features grew tight, a scowl forming on his face. A few minutes later, he finally pulled his hand free of the soil and dusted the snow from his palms.

The hunter's shrewd expression didn't abate. "You're correct that there's magic in this land—it's dark magic."

Ilara's brow furrowed. "Dark magic?" She eyed me.

I frowned. There was no *dark magic* on the Solis continent. Truth be told, I didn't even know what the Fire Wolf spoke of.

"It's something I've encountered a time or two," the hunter replied as he stood. Ilara and I joined him. "I believe what you felt, Ilara, is dark magic most likely created by a warlock."

I scowled. "What's a warlock?"

The hunter's lip curled. "The worst kind of magic-wielder from my realm. Warlocks are sorcerers who practice dark magic—*illegal* magic where I come from. And the reason it's illegal is because they need to sacrifice human or supernatural lives to grow their dark power. It's how they produce it."

Ilara paled. "You're saying that a dark sorcerer from your realm had to murder innocent supernaturals or *humans*"—the foreign word rolled awkwardly off her tongue—"or fae in order to create whatever magic is now in this land?"

The Fire Wolf crossed his arms. "That's exactly what I'm saying."

"Fire Wolf, what do warlocks smell like?" she asked.

Worry had etched into her face so deeply, and fear strummed toward me on the bond.

The Fire Wolf merely cocked his head. "Awful, like something decaying. They don't look much better." He went on to describe them, the picture he painted of pale gaunt faces, skeletal features, and sickly-looking bodies sounding worse than their scent. "But don't let their thin forms fool you. They're immensely powerful. Some of the only times I've feared for my life have been during battles with warlocks."

My scowl increased as Ilara grabbed my hands, her grip tight. "That explains the smell I detected when I was about to be attacked in the castle, after that date with Lord Waterline. It was the same smell Lord Crimsonale sensed."

I pressed my lips together in a tight line. "So we were right. The creature my father hired was also the one that was going to attack you."

She nodded vigorously. "Which means that all of the fae who've gone missing have probably been taken by a warlock, perhaps by *the* warlock that's created the veil in this field. Perhaps he's taking them to kill them to infuse his dark magic."

It felt as though I'd been punched in the chest, but my thoughts turned rapid-fire as what she was implying fell into place. "Gods, that means none of them are still alive."

Ilara's eyes dimmed. "And it also means that if your father truly did orchestrate all of this, then he willingly allowed those fae to be murdered. This proves it. If he was meeting with the warlock, and Lord Crimsonale overheard the king giving the warlock directions, it *is* your father that's done this."

Ilara was right. Lord Crimsonale had detected the same scent she had when the warlock had been near.

Ilara's brow furrowed when my anger strummed toward her on our bond. She laid a hand on my arm and squeezed. "I'm sorry. I didn't want it to be him, but you were right."

I clenched my jaw and gave a curt nod. "I'm not surprised. He's vile. He always has been, and this is exactly the type of perverse thing my father would orchestrate." Shaking my head, I added, "It makes sense. Everything is starting to make sense."

"Care to fill me in?" the hunter asked. He'd remained silent while Ilara and I had talked, just as my guards had, but a shrewd expression was again covering the Fire Wolf's face.

"We have reason to believe the king of the Solis continent is behind all of this," I replied.

He arched a dark eyebrow. "I'd gathered that much."

Raking a hand through my hair, I continued, telling him everything, knowing he needed to be aware if we were to work together. "Many lives have been lost to create what's in this land." I told him of the missing fae and how we believed the warlock was using them in sacrifices to fuel his magic. "And this all stems from my father who apparently hired this warlock to create the veil deep within this soil. My father was also selective in his victims. He chose fae that were causing dissent about the dying crops, then blamed their deaths on me. All of this was to make me look like the villain and him the savior. He had me purposefully punishing any fae who voiced concern about the crops, which allowed my father's evil work to continue since it caused our fae to be fearful of speaking up. It's all coming together, knowing what we know now."

"Your father sounds as lovely as my mother." The Fire Wolf smirked, causing a stirring of curiosity to billow through me.

Before I could ask, Ilara squeezed my arm again. "Norivun, I just thought of something else. Do you remember what happened right before we visited this field, on the day of my second test? The veil had felt so strong then, strong enough that I could feel it near the surface. And do you remember what happened the day prior to that? Three fae went missing. *Three.*"

"He was re-strengthening the veil and needed more lives to do so," I said, nodding. "He needed to do it to suppress the life you'd created above his initial veil."

"Yes!" Ilara replied. "If a warlock used three fae to fuel his dark magic and re-create the veil here, it would explain why the crops died overnight and why my affinity hadn't saved them. The warlock had probably used those three lives to create a newer, stronger veil that suppressed everything I'd done to save this field." Her words grew faster. "And if he'd just been here, it would explain why his dark magic was close to the surface before the second test and why it was so easy for me to feel, but when we returned, it'd begun to sink deep within the land, which was why I'd had to dive so far to find it again."

She finally stopped, still panting. Her fingers felt like ice on my skin, her fire element non-existent in her frenzied state.

My insides turned cold. "You're right. That, too, makes sense."

I thought back to all of the fae who'd gone missing in the castle during the past full season. Those disappearances had been spaced out. Some had been supporters of the crop concerns, and others had simply gone missing for no apparent reason. My guess was those had been the first ones to disappear. Perhaps they'd been the initial lives needed to fuel the warlock's dark magic, but the fact that they'd all been taken from the castle further strengthened support that the king was ultimately behind all of this.

My father had the power to allow a warlock to enter the palace, bypassing the wards entirely while allowing the warlock to take unsuspecting fae from within the castle's walls to sacrifice.

It fed into my father's twisted end game to create dissent, march upon the Nolus, enact the Olirum Accords to further strengthen our race so we could hold power over our southern neighbor, and all the while, he appeared completely innocent of any wrongdoing.

My throat rolled when I swallowed.

If the missing fae had been used in sacrifices, it explained why none of their bodies had been found and why none had ever returned.

They were all dead.

A sick feeling swept through me. We were literally standing on a field containing dark magic that was swimming in innocents' blood.

Ilara's jaw clenched. "Your father needs to be removed from power entirely. He's not worthy of sitting on the throne."

"I completely agree, but how are we going to prove that he's behind it?" I narrowed my eyes as an inferno of Ilara's determination strummed from her on the bond. "We have to expose him to the citizens of the Solis continent. We need to turn our fae against him, but nobody will believe us unless we can prove it."

She pressed her lips together, but I was right. Our fae hated me. They loved my father. If it came down to my word against the king's, I already knew who the victor would be.

"We'll have to find a connection between your father and the warlock he hired." Her brow furrowed as she continued. "Rulibs leave a trail. Perhaps we can trace it back through payment, then we can go to the council. If the entire council votes unanimously to remove the king, your father will be forced to abdicate."

"If we want to avoid a civil war, that's the only way to remove him. We need the council on our side."

She nodded. "Let's hope he didn't find a way to hide his payments too."

My grim expression strengthened, because if my father was anything, it was cunning. I highly doubted he would leave a trail like that open, which meant it was possible we'd never be able to prove his involvement, but we had to try.

Right now, though, we had bigger things to deal with. We needed to destroy whatever had been born in this field, and we needed to do it *now*.

"So how do we get rid of this warlock's dark magic?" I bit out. Anger stirred in my gut, rising inside me like an inferno at just the thought of this malicious energy in *my* kingdom and knowing it was something my father had contrived.

The hunter frowned and cocked his head. "Not sure yet. I'll have to consult an acquaintance who knows more about this stuff than me, then I'll come back when I have a better idea of how to tackle this. Most likely it'll be at least a week but probably longer."

I inhaled his scent but didn't detect any deceit. Who knew if my sensory affinity could be trusted with someone such as the Fire Wolf, though. But a bargain did seal us, and those could be trusted to work in any realm, so if the hunter left with my rulibs and didn't return—the bargain's wrath would follow him.

The Fire Wolf pulled a small portal key from his pocket.

"Why don't we plan on meeting in two weeks. I'm confident I'll have a plan by then. Where would you prefer that meeting be?"

Ilara gaped. "You're saying you'll leave, and we'll just . . . wait?"

The hunter nodded. "You have a problem with that?"

"We both do," I replied before Ilara could. "We want to find answers, and we want to help."

The Fire Wolf's brow furrowed as he glanced at the soil. "I understand, but that's not how I work. If you want this veil destroyed, I need to get moving."

"Don't you think it would be better if we joined you?" Ilara rushed toward him before he could leave. "With more of us working on this, we're likely to find answers sooner."

My guards all shifted behind us, listening intently to everything we said. One glance at Haxil revealed that the same interest alighting Ilara's expression was also morphing his.

The hunter's eyes shuttered. "I know you don't want to wait, but I work alone."

"Not on this one," I countered. Ilara nodded, letting me know that neither my mate nor I were willing to leave everything entirely up to him, even if it meant traveling to a realm neither of us had ventured to.

"No," the Fire Wolf growled.

"Yes," I growled back just as deeply.

The hunter's nostrils flared, and a second ticked past in which we studied each other. The hunter finally blew forcefully through his nose. "Fine, but my fee goes up if that's the case."

"How much?"

"A thousand rulibs."

"Done."

Ilara gaped while I merely held eye contact with the hunter.

The Fire Wolf cocked his head, his amber eyes glowing like embers. "All right, but if any of you get in my way or make finishing this job harder, you're returning here and leaving me to work alone, *and* I keep the extra rulibs. Understood?"

I narrowed my eyes as a rush of my power rumbled the land. "I don't take orders from you."

Flames appeared in the hunter's eyes as our attentions locked onto one another. Another second ticked by. My aura rose higher as energy emitting from the hunter heated just as fast.

Behind me, my guards shifted, and out of my peripheral vision I saw them fan out around me.

The hunter's attention flickered to them briefly before he glared at me again.

"Seriously?" Ilara said with a frustrated sigh. "What is it with the male posturing?" She grumbled beneath her breath and pushed herself between the two of us, dispelling whatever dominance display was currently at work.

"We won't get in the way," she said to the Fire Wolf as she pushed me back farther, "but fair enough. If we do, we'll leave, and you can keep the extra rulibs. All right?"

She pressed her back into my chest, forming a full barrier between the hunter and me. Despite barely coming to my collarbones, she wouldn't budge, thanks to her warrior affinity. Still, even if I'd wanted to move her the pleading in her eyes quelled some of my ire. If it were anyone but her, I wouldn't have backed down, but Ilara always had tamed my darker side.

"Deal?" she asked, glancing back at the hunter.

His nostrils flared, but he finally canted his head. "Deal."

"So where to from here?" Ilara asked.

"I had planned to visit an acquaintance of mine who's very knowledgeable about warlocks and dark magic." The Fire Wolf fingered his portal key. "He may be able to help uncover the origin of this spell or a way to neutralize it, but he doesn't live here."

"Your friend is on . . . *Earth?*" The foreign term rolled off Ilara's tongue like silk.

"He is. He lives in Europe."

Ilara and I exchanged a glance. *Europe.* Wherever that was.

Haxil cleared his throat from behind us. "I believe I've heard of that realm."

"It's not a realm, rather a continent in the Earthly realm," the hunter replied.

"Ah, like the Nolus continent or Silten continent?" Ilara's eyes sparkled with interest, and I had the most intense urge to kiss her.

The Fire Wolf inclined his head again. "Yes, exactly like that."

"And we're going there now?" she asked hopefully.

The hunter sighed. "I suppose we are."

THE FIRE WOLF offered to use his portal key to transfer all of us to his Earthly realm. I had no idea if we could mistphase there or not, as I'd never tried it, and since using the portal key meant we all traveled together, I did agree with the hunter that it made the most sense.

Ilara joined hands with him immediately, showing no fear at visiting another universe entirely, but Nish was another story.

His curling lip was sharp enough to cut steel, but by the time he finally accepted Ryder's outstretched palm, it'd relaxed slightly.

Nonetheless, despite my guard's hesitation, all six of us had opted to join the hunter as we ventured to the continent he called Europe.

"This may be a bit jarring," the hunter warned just before whispering the words that activated the key's magic.

A rush of wind surrounded us, then the realm tilted on its axis, and the ground fell out from beneath me.

Sandus's grip on my left hand tightened as Ilara's hold on my right turned just as strong. The feeling of being ripped apart and torn to pieces from the inside out made my teeth clench and my magic swirl in my limbs.

Grunting, I cursed whatever hideous creature had

invented these things, but just as those curses started, the tearing sensations stopped.

I landed hard on something solid, my knees cushioning the abrupt impact.

All of my guards swore as Ilara panted at my side.

"That was even worse than the portal transfer with Drachu," she breathed.

The Fire Wolf smirked. "I tried to warn you. Crossing realms is always rather nauseating."

"Ock, that was nothing like mistphasing." Nish clutched his stomach.

Ryder audibly wheezed before straightening, and Sandus scowled.

I had the most ridiculous urge to vomit, but at least, after one glance at my mate and guards, I knew I wasn't the only one feeling that way.

Haxil clapped Nish on the back as my surliest guard continued to glower. "At least none of us lost our lunch."

Ilara gave a small nod in appreciation.

The Fire Wolf eyed all of us, and I could tell he was trying to hold back a laugh. "I did try to warn you."

I forced my shoulders back, and my stomach calmed as my magic pulsed inside me, but it felt dimmer, as though whatever was in this realm's atmosphere repelled my affinities, or tried to at least.

I called my magic forth despite the new environment. It zoomed along my limbs, much like it did at home, but the air outside of my body was *less* feeling. No magic resided here.

"What is this place?" Ilara asked as she glanced around.

Wherever we were, we'd landed outside. A meadow filled with wildflowers and tall grass surrounded us. Midmorning sunshine shone down from a *blue* sky. Puffy white clouds dotted the atmosphere all the way to the horizon. None of the clouds had colors. *How odd.*

"We're in a country on the European continent. It's called Norway." The hunter eyed all of us. "I take it this is the first time any of you have ventured to my realm?"

"That would be correct." Haxil inclined his head.

"Norway." Nish scoffed. "Strange name." He spat on the ground, his expression still sour. "There's no magic in the air here."

"No," the hunter replied. "Our realm is magicless compared to yours, and the effects of that may cause some problems for you if we stay here long enough since this is your first time traveling here."

"Is that why the air feels weaker?" Ilara frowned. "Because there's no magic?"

"It is, and since you all seem rather powerful, my guess is the effects of my realm are going to take a toll on you eventually. Fae who travel here for the first time, especially adult fae, sometimes feel the effects of fae lands withdrawals."

Ilara's expression lightened. "Ah! Cora told us about that, remember?" She turned delighted eyes on me.

I nodded, a smile tugging at my lips despite knowing we could eventually be affected by this strange atmosphere. "I remember." If not for Drachu nearly killing us in Vemil Brasea, I'd have a potion on hand that would counteract the effects of fae lands withdrawals. "Will we be in need of your realm's potions to stall the effects?"

The Fire Wolf shook his head. "Not if you don't stay here long."

"Fine by me," Nish grumbled.

"Everyone, test your magic," I said to my guards and mate. "I want to know if we're still fully capable here."

I called upon my air affinity, just to see what would happen, as my guards began their warrior warm-ups. Fire appeared around Ilara immediately, and not even a second later, she joined the guards in their movements.

They all moved with liquid grace.

Grunting in relief, I called upon my air element. The wind picked up around me, tingling against my skin, and surprisingly it moved as forcefully as it did back home although it took more concentration. The lesser magic in this atmosphere no doubt the cause. My other affinities responded as well, including my sixth one that Ilara still didn't know about. I smirked.

After all of us had tested our abilities thoroughly, I held up a hand. "So our magic remains just as strong here in Europe."

The Fire Wolf crossed his arms. "It does, just like my magic is also available in your realm, although it always feels slightly different."

I grunted again, not wanting to admit that, but he was right.

"I don't like this. I don't like any of it." Nish crossed his arms.

Ryder punched him lightly on the shoulder. "We still have our magic, Nishy. Nothing to get your feathers in a ruffle about. It's just . . . different and harder to call out, but it's still there."

"Imagine what the humans feel." The Fire Wolf gave a wry smile.

"Humans." Nish rolled his eyes. "Don't tell me we have to meet them."

"Not if we stay in this remote area," the hunter replied. "Hardly anyone lives around here."

"Good," Nish grumbled.

Ryder spun in a slow circle from where he stood. "What a strange realm. A blue sky too, not green."

"And all of the clouds are white. How do you know if a storm's coming?" Haxil cocked his head.

The Fire Wolf arched an eyebrow. "Storms make the clouds turn gray or black, not navy or dark purple like they do where you come from. Now, come on, let's get moving."

We all set out, and the six of us, despite trying to focus on finding the Fire Wolf's friend, continually gazed around. It was hard not to. This place felt *different*. Drab almost and certainly less than our realm.

It didn't detract from its beauty though, but the magicless atmosphere pounded on my senses, making my affinities continually rumble along my limbs, as though they were searching for an outward source to connect with.

"Look, they have mountains," Ilara said to Haxil as she pointed at the steep fjords that rose alongside the meadow farther away.

"It almost looks like the fjords on the Glassen Barrier Islands," he commented.

I grunted. I'd like nothing more than to level the entirety of the Glassen Barrier Islands after what Drachu had done to my mate.

Ilara's dark hair hung down her back as she continually smiled in wonder. She'd banished her animal affinity back in the fae lands, so her wings weren't present, but her wingless back only drew my attention to the delicate curve of her neck and swell of her hips.

I began to harden as I watched her, and Ryder snickered in my direction. I punched him in the arm as the hunter forged ahead.

Budding and sprouting grass brushed against us with every step. All of the grass was green, not like the rainbow of colors one found in the grass of our realm.

"Something to keep in mind," the hunter called over his shoulder. "Sven likes his privacy, so when we reach his house, don't talk and don't touch anything until he gives you permission."

Nish rolled his eyes and did a mock bow.

I gave him a side-eye, and my guard had the decency to look sheepish.

"Why didn't you portal us right to his doorstep?" Ryder asked.

"Let's just say that Sven doesn't do well with surprises," the Fire Wolf replied. "It's better if he feels us coming."

I frowned, wondering how powerful his friend was.

Warmth from the sun shone down on us, and with every step we took, the temperature increased.

"Oh look!" Ilara said in delight when a flock of birds took flight from the meadow. They flew across the sky, their bodies tiny against the strange white clouds.

"What are those?" Haxil asked, his tone equally mesmerized.

"They're called warblers," the hunter replied, his stride never slowing. "They're very common around here."

"Warblers . . ." Ilara repeated, the foreign word sounding slightly different with her accent.

Despite the uneasiness this new magicless realm provoked, I inhaled deeply as my sensory affinity alighted on hundreds of new and interesting fragrances.

"Ilara, look at this." Haxil brushed his hand through the grass, then pulled something from one of the stalks. In a flash, Ilara was at his side.

A growl worked up my throat as a stirring of jealousy rolled through me. I clenched my jaw, forcing myself to endure the torment of her giving attention to another male.

"What is that?" Ilara asked with a grin as she held out her finger.

Something small with spindly legs jumped from Haxil's palm onto her outstretched nail.

The hunter glanced over his shoulder. "That's a grasshopper, and this is why you're paying me a thousand rulibs more."

Ilara and Haxil quickly straightened, guilty expressions on their faces for stalling the Fire Wolf's walk once again.

"We're still moving," I called as I shifted to stand between my mate and guard. My hand automatically went to Ilara's lower back as I propelled her forward.

Haxil arched an eyebrow mockingly but stepped back, and some of the territorial reaction swirling within me lessened.

"Sorry," Ilara said to the hunter. "No more questions. Promise. We'll keep up."

The Fire Wolf did a one-eighty and headed through the meadow again toward what I assumed was a lake or river at the meadow's edge. A fjord rose alongside the body of water.

The hunter walked fast. His giant strides ate up the land, but the six of us easily kept up, even though Ilara and Haxil glanced at everything they could along the way while touching just as much.

The edge of the meadow appeared, and the channel of water twisted along the fjords base. Music sounded ahead, and at the water's edge, not even a quarter millee away, waited a small rustic cabin.

"Is that where we're going?" I asked.

The hunter gave a curt nod. "It is."

Magic abruptly tingled in the air around me, growing with each step we took toward the small abode. Snaps of it prickled my skin and stroked my senses. Whatever this place was, it was warded.

"And this barrier I'm feeling?" I asked the hunter.

He cocked an eyebrow. "You can feel it?"

I gave a curt nod as Ilara chimed in, "So can I."

"Impressive. Most can't detect Sven's perimeter enchantments."

"I take it his enchantments alert him to our arrival?"

"Correct." The Fire Wolf forged ahead. "He's probably already spotted us coming. The wards give him time to prepare for unexpected guests."

"Is he a powerful supernatural amongst your kind?" Haxil asked.

"Very," the Fire Wolf replied. "I haven't met many sorcerers stronger than him. With any luck, by tomorrow, we'll know how to destroy the spell that's killed your land, and then we can return to the fae lands to finish this job."

A twig cracked beneath my boot, and then a blaze of flying magic suddenly rushed through the air, lassoing all six of us in stinging magic.

"Mother Below!" Nish growled as ropes of glowing red light flared around us, pinning our limbs, as though we'd been tangled in ropes.

"What the—" Sandus immediately began to struggle, as did Ilara and my other guards.

I snarled when the rope-like magic tethered my wings in place, but no amount of struggle loosened the imprisoning restraints.

"That's what you get for sneaking onto my property," a male called from behind the cabin before he strolled into my line of sight.

The male, while old, was tall and had blue eyes similar in shade to a Solis fae. Despite his age, his aura glimmered with leashed power.

Another snarl worked up my throat. If the hunter's friend thought this was funny, I sorely disagreed with him.

"Sven, how's it going?" the hunter called, not seeming to care that the rest of us were bound.

Hands on his hips, Sven cocked an eyebrow at the Fire Wolf then nodded toward all of us. "Did you bring me new subjects to conduct my experiments on? Thank you for the gift."

The hunter smiled, then tipped back his head and laughed as the sorcerer gave a wicked grin.

CHAPTER 25 - NORIVUN

"Gift? You're *giving* us to him?" Sandus spat at the Fire Wolf. "We trusted you!"

"You vile loathsome, traitorous . . ." The insults spewed from Nish's mouth.

"No!" Ilara's eyes widened in fear as she struggled in the stinging red magic that continued to contain us. "Not again."

Panic raced through my mate. Her recent trauma with Drachu no doubt feeding her reaction, and feeling her terror through our bond, knowing that I hadn't protected her . . .

An enraged snarl worked up my throat as a primal reaction buried deep inside me unleashed.

Protect my mate.

I zeroed all my attention upon the hunter and his friend as the Fire Wolf stepped toward us and opened his mouth to respond, but savage intent flared within me.

Kill them.

Kill them.

Kill them.

In a flash of magic, I released my dragon.

The world disappeared around me in an explosive cloud of smoke as my reptilian animal affinity transformed me from within.

Magic raced through my limbs as his massive body cut through the stinging red lasso as though it were paper string. The earth shook violently when my dragon's giant feet landed on the soil and cut huge footprints into the land as a ferocious snarl tore from my throat.

Sven's jaw dropped.

The Fire Wolf glowered at him and said something, the hunter's movements agitated and angry, but I didn't hear his words.

I towered twenty feet above their heads and opened my mouth just as Sven's hands swirled through the air. The lasso-magic disappeared from around Ilara and my guards.

They immediately fell into a warrior's crouch, swords in hand, as Ilara's wings burst from her back.

In a blink, she hovered in the air beside me as balls of fire erupted from her hands.

"Prince Norivun!" the hunter called, a glacial scowl descending upon his face. "Calm down and let me explain!"

Kill them.

Kill them.

Kill them.

I opened my mouth and rained dragon fire upon them. Ilara screamed with equal fury as her elemental fire spewed down on the Earthly traitors. Streams of our joined magic erupted the land into flames.

Not even a second passed before black scorched soil appeared in a fifteen-foot circumference where the hunter and his friend had stood.

We'd fried them to death within seconds.

Panting heavily, Ilara withdrew her affinity just as my dragon stopped his murderous rage.

"Fucking traitors!" Ryder yelled.

Smoke billowed around where the hunter and his friend had stood, opaque as a thick fog. A slight breeze blew around us, and I shifted back to my fae form as my heartbeat finally calmed.

My clothes were in tatters, but I cast an illusion over myself, creating clothes to hide my naked body just as the smoke cleared.

"No way." Nish breathed, his eyes widening.

My eyebrows shot up when the Fire Wolf and his sorcerer friend stood before us, entirely unscathed. Something shimmered around them, a barrier or perhaps a spell of protective magic. Whatever the case, it was nearly translucent, and from the expression on the hunter's face, he looked ready to rip our heads off.

I stiffened, about to call upon my dragon again, but the hunter whispered a few words, and the barrier disappeared.

"This isn't what you think it is." Fury glowed in the Fire Wolf's eyes, making his amber irises alight with crimson fire. "Sven wasn't trying to hurt you or kill you. He simply didn't know that we were coming, so he did what he always does to newcomers when they arrive. He detains them until he knows if they're friend or foe. I tried to warn you of that," he added on a low growl.

I relaxed my dragon affinity more, and Ilara's eyes flashed to mine. That faint violet hue filled her irises again as her wings flapped. Her feet touched down until she stood beside me, and her beautiful white wings folded behind her.

"But, your *friend* said he was going to do experiments on us," Ilara said firmly.

"It was a joke." Sven held up his hands and gave a rueful laugh. "I apologize. My humor is a bit . . . unusual. Or so I've been told."

"Is this a laughing matter to you?" Ilara's teeth clenched, the sound audible when her jaw snapped closed.

"No one's laughing." The Fire Wolf's nostrils flared as he gave Sven a nudge. The sorcerer's grin disappeared. "Those red restraints were merely a precaution Sven takes. I would have explained that and would have asked him to call off his blaze-bands if you'd given me a minute, but you all assumed the worst and immediately went on the offensive."

"Something I would do again in a heartbeat if my mate was threatened." My lip curled.

"Sven *did* ask if we were to be his experiments." Nish reminded the hunter with a glower. "You can hardly blame my prince's reaction."

Sven gave another laugh, and I couldn't help but wonder if his mind was stable. "It's an instinctual reaction anytime my wards tell me strangers are in my midst. And the Fire Wolf and I go way back. The experiment joke is from . . ." The sorcerer shook his head. "Never mind, but sorry about that." Sven chuckled again, then dipped his head. A bald spot appeared on the crown of his scalp. The male also had deep wrinkles around his eyes and a slight bend of his spine. Sven was incredibly old. But powerful nonetheless.

Fire still rolled in the hunter's eyes. "Are we good then? Can we carry on now without any of you trying to kill us?"

I glared at him. "We've only just met, yet you act like we should trust you."

"A mistake I won't make again," the hunter snapped.

Haxil put his hands on his hips. "I have to ask, since nobody else has pointed this out. How did you two survive dragon fire? Nobody survives dragon fire."

The hunter glanced skyward and took a deep breath. "None of your business."

"Will there be any more jokes we can expect?" Ilara crossed her arms, and her magnificent white wings glittered in the sunlight.

"No," the hunter bit out, then gave the sorcerer a pointed look.

"No, no," Sven agreed hastily. "No more jokes. Promise."

Nish snorted. "As if that means anything," he said under his breath.

Sven sighed. "I apologize, but you do have my word. I won't do anything like that again." His attention drifted to Ilara, curiosity alighting his eyes.

A growl rumbled in my chest when the old sorcerer continued to look at my mate with fascination. "Something you'd care to share? Or do you always stare at mated females like this?" I snarled.

Sven shook himself. "Oh, excuse me, you'll have to pardon my reaction. I just . . ." He stepped closer to Ilara, and she bristled, but he held up his hands in a non-threatening manner. "I haven't seen an angel in centuries." His watery old eyes grew even more alive with interest. "Do you herald from Emunda?"

Ilara's brow furrowed, and she and I both said simultaneously. "Emunda?"

"Yes." Sven nodded eagerly. "The land of lost angels."

"We're Solis fae from the fae lands." I again wondered if this strange sorcerer had gone senile. "My mate doesn't herald from any realm by the name of Emunda, nor is she a lost angel. She's *fae*."

Sven cocked his head. "How curious." His interest turned to me. "So you wield power from the underworld in your dragon form, and your mate wields power from the divine realm in her angel body." He gave the hunter a delighted grin. "How intriguing, opposite yet equally strong powers. Today is getting more interesting by the second."

The Fire Wolf arched an eyebrow, his expression turning exasperated as my brow furrowed even more.

Divine realm? Angel form? Ilara and I shared another baffled glance as the sorcerer's words sank in. Sven was implying that Ilara's affinity was the equal of mine, and that she wasn't channeling bird wings but *angel* wings.

My brow furrowed more as I contemplated her first affinity. Ilara's strongest affinity, the ability to create life, was the opposite of my strongest affinity—my ability to inflict death. And now, her new winged affinity, according to Sven, was from a divine realm, the exact place my dragon affinity heralded from, but in the opposite direction.

"Sven, we're getting off track." The Fire Wolf pinched the bridge of his nose and muttered something under his breath. "We're here to learn what you know of warlock dark magic, specifically a spell that could plague and spread throughout an entire continent and kill all of its crops. Should we get to it?" The Fire Wolf gestured toward Sven's cabin.

"Oh, zippity do, such a fascinating day, indeed. Very well." Sven nodded in agreement, but he still studied me and Ilara. "Most curious, most curious indeed. If we have more time, I would give my left nut to learn more about your strange powers, but until then—" He shrugged and turned on his heel, moving surprisingly agilely for a male his age, especially a male who'd just rather eloquently agreed to give us a testicle.

Ilara continued to gape as the old sorcerer shuffled back to his cabin while I glowered.

"Angel?" Haxil cocked his head and studied Ilara's wings again.

"Yeah, angel," the Fire Wolf called over his shoulder as he followed his friend to the door. "The only beings who have purple eyes like that and feathery wings that white are angels." He raised his eyebrows. "Did you not know?"

All of us shook our heads.

I had limited understanding of angels, similar to my

knowledge of demons, not because I was disinterested, but because neither divine being was something we ever saw on the Solis continent. Demons that came to our realm seemed to favor the Nolus continent, probably due to the warmer climate, and I'd never heard of angels in the fae lands, at least, not in recent history.

"I've never seen an angel," I finally conceded.

"Most haven't," the Fire Wolf replied at the door's threshold. "You Solis fae are truly enigmas, but let's get on with this. By the time we get back to your realm, with how much time we're wasting, a full week will have passed. You do know about the time difference between our universes, right?"

My nostrils flared. "We're not entirely ignorant."

"Good, then move it." The Fire Wolf ducked into the cabin, mumbling again about how a thousand rulibs wasn't enough payment for the extra time we were taking from him, but none of us heeded his call just yet.

The six of us stared at one another in confusion and awe.

"So, you're not a bird after all, love," Sandus said affectionately to Ilara.

She ducked her head, her cheeks turning rosy. "I guess not."

"I always knew you were special, and this just proves it even more," I said as I pulled her to me. My mate's final affinity wasn't an animal affinity. It was that of an angel—a divine creature just as my dragon was. "The gods truly did make us for one another."

"They did, didn't they?" she replied, a small smile

forming on our face. "Opposites in so many ways, yet we fit together perfectly."

"A SPELL that can bury itself deep in the land, move undetected, suppress magic created by the gods, and kill all plants above it." Sven flipped through another large text as he propped his elbow on his wooden table. "Fascinating. Truly fascinating. Definitely the work of a powerful warlock."

All of us sat around Sven's rickety wooden table that felt as old as the sorcerer seated beside us as we flipped through page after page of books from Sven's extensive personal library.

A fire glowed in the small hearth as a nighttime sky shone outside. The supper we'd consumed a few hours ago still hadn't been washed up. Sven insisted he'd use a cleaning charm once we all left, so none of us had bothered.

I massaged the back of my neck as I hunched forward. Since my clothes had been ruined when I'd shifted into my dragon, and only my illusion had covered my naked form, the Fire Wolf had gotten me a change of clothes that he stored at Sven's home. I'd had to tear the back to accommodate my wings, but other than that, the strange clothing fit well since the hunter and I were of similar size. He even said I could keep them as a memento of my trip to Europe.

Dust rose from a scroll when I unraveled it, and swirls of ink stared back at me. I scanned the document.

Scabs from a warthog's nose. Pig heads. A human fetus's

right hand. I read the list of ingredients. They grew more gruesome with each line. Every single text I'd read from Sven's personal library had some form of human, supernatural, or fae body part. The Fire Wolf hadn't been kidding when he said warlocks regularly committed live sacrifices to grow their powers.

I flipped the scroll closed with a disgusted glare when it finally revealed that such magic could be used to create a demon dog with two heads. Apparently, such a dog had to eat small children to sustain itself, but one bite from its poisonous canines could incapacitate any supernatural, regardless of their strength or power, for up to an hour.

And who knew what a warlock would do to that supernatural during that time.

"Gross," Ilara muttered as she came to the end of her text, then grabbed another off Sven's shelf.

We'd been at this all day, looking through old texts and searching for answers that would explain how a warlock had poisoned our land, yet we'd only just reached the halfway mark on Sven's vast collection.

"I'm curious," Haxil said as he thumbed through a page in the tome he was reading, "why such a fascination with warlocks?"

"He didn't tell you?" Sven looked up, his eyes appearing bigger through the spectacles perched on his nose, as he nodded toward the hunter.

"Not my information to share," the Fire Wolf grunted in reply as he sat in a chair by the fire.

Haxil cocked his head. "Tell us what?"

"My father was a warlock," Sven replied.

All of us looked up from our readings.

"Come again?" Haxil replied.

Sven shrugged. "He wasn't always. He didn't turn until I was around eight years old, but it left a . . ." He tapped his chin, his expression dimming, "a lasting impression. That was when my interest in warlocks started."

Ilara gazed at the old sorcerer sympathetically. "Did he ever hurt you?"

"What?" Sven quickly shook his head. "Oh no, nothing like that. My mother took me away immediately after my father turned, and hid us until her death. I was sixty years old by then and more than capable of looking after myself, but she feared him so much she refused to let me leave, afraid my father would come after me." That pensive look overtook his face again. "Warlocks often use people of their own flesh and blood when conducting rituals to increase their powers. While they can grow strength from the death of any human, fairy, or other supernatural creature they sacrifice, they grow their strongest powers from their kin."

Ryder's eyebrow shot clear to his hairline. "Warlocks sacrifice their own children?"

"Oh yes," Sven replied matter-of-factly. "It's their most preferred source of power, hence, why my mother refused to let me leave."

"So . . ." Ilara bit her lower lip. "Did your father ever come after you?"

Sven smiled and patted her hand. "The crotchety beast certainly tried. After my mother passed, I returned to the normal world, out of our warded abode, as I refused to hide any longer. I knew such a choice would mean he'd eventually track me down. Not surprisingly, he did, but at that point, I was ready for him." Sven tapped on the books in the middle of the table. "I'd dedicated my life to learning everything I could about warlocks. I knew how to kill them even if I wasn't the strongest sorcerer in our land."

Ilara's eyes widened.

"So when my father finally caught up with me, probably thinking I would be an easy kill, he had another thing coming." Sven laughed, the sound a maniacal cackle that sounded slightly unhinged, and got a jump from my mate.

"Sven, you're scaring our guests," the Fire Wolf said with a sigh.

Sven snorted, then pounded the table. "Sorry about that. I get a bit excitable when I talk of him."

"As I can see," Ilara replied as her throat bobbed in a swallow.

Sandus nodded in approval, not seeming to mind Sven's eccentric nature. "Good for you. It takes balls to kill someone you're related to."

Sven nodded. "I can assure you I have very large balls."

Nish blew the tea he was drinking through his nose, and Ryder muffled a laugh behind his cough.

"Sven," the hunter called from his chair. "We've talked about this . . ."

Sven didn't even blink. "Ah yes, my apologies. I forget that speaking of one's genitalia is often frowned upon."

Ilara's cheeks flushed, and I had to suppress a smile since blatant embarrassment was projecting from her on our bond.

"Anyway, where were we?" Sven reached for another book. "I know there's an answer here somewhere. I could have sworn I read something during my studies about a spell that could do such a thing."

I watched my mate as everyone returned to scanning their texts.

She glanced at me briefly, probably detecting the resolve that had just settled in my gut. Sven, while a bit *off*, did seem like a decent male. Yet, he'd killed his father. Knowing there were others with fathers equally as evil as mine, others who'd done what was needed in the end and didn't bat an eye over it, only fed my growing belief that my own father needed to die, not just be removed from power.

Ilara threaded her fingers through mine beneath the table and squeezed. I returned the gesture even though her worry was for naught.

Like Sven, I wouldn't feel an ounce of guilt when the Solis king's soul was shredded beneath my affinity.

CHAPTER 26 - ILARA

"Ock, nothing's here," Nish grumbled an hour later as he finished looking through his eighth tome.

"Oh, it'll be here, somewhere," Sven replied with a grin. "I have more documents than any sorcerer on Earth when it comes to warlocks and dark magic, well, except for the Bulgarian libraries, but my dear hunter friend made the right choice by coming here. I can assure you that your answer lies somewhere within my books."

I turned the page on a dusty text I was reading, suppressing a cough when the nauseating scent of potent thyme drifted up from it. "How can you be so sure?"

"Because I've been studying warlocks and collecting information on them since I was a young boy. Everything there is to know about warlocks is right here."

I raised my eyebrows as Haxil asked curiously, "May I ask how old you are?"

"Two hundred and eighty-four years." Sven grinned. "I take a preserving elixir daily. My own special concoction."

"Most humans can't live as long as Sven, sorcerer or not," the Fire Wolf said dryly as he leaned back in his chair. The wood groaned under his weight.

That spark of curiosity ran through me again as I soaked up everything Sven had revealed. Living hundreds of full seasons, or years, as those in this realm called it, was nothing compared to our kind. Solis fae who were three hundred winters hadn't even reached their prime. They were still considered young.

I arched an eyebrow. "I take it most sorcerers can't live that long either?"

"No, they can't," the hunter replied, then stood, prowling to the bookshelf to grab another text.

We'd gone through about seventy percent of Sven's tomes, books, scrolls, and mystical markings. The mess we'd left was scattered around. Books piled everywhere. Scrolls stacked against the walls. Tomes that were too big to be held in one's lap rested by the door. Everywhere one looked lay books, books, and more books. I could see why the Fire Wolf had chosen to start searching for a counter spell with this old sorcerer. Since all Sven seemed to read about was warlocks, he did seem a tad obsessed with understanding their power.

Sighing, I thumbed another page in the book I was halfway through. A new chapter heading appeared: *How to Create and Counteract a Veil of Death.*

Brow furrowing, I scanned the text beneath.

. . . bury a veil within soil, rock, water . . .

. . . suppresses any magic created by supernaturals or otherwise . . .

. . . regular sacrifice needed to maintain its strength if it's a large area . . .

I shot to standing, my chair toppling over behind me. "Mother Below, look at this." I pointed at the spell and the paragraphs highlighting what it did and how it was created. "See what it says here. It talks about creating a veil that can be buried and will dampen any magic beneath it. And it says that sacrificial lives are needed to maintain it."

Sven pushed his spectacles up his nose as my mate and his guards all crowded around me. Even the Fire Wolf joined us from his reclusive chair by the hearth.

"Ah, yes. There it is." Sven nodded as his gnarled finger scanned the text. "I knew it was around here somewhere."

"Where's the counter spell?" the hunter asked as Haxil leaned forward and tried to turn the page.

"Should be at the end of the chapter." Sven flipped the book to the front cover. The black leather binding was blank, no text on it anywhere, as was common among all of Sven's homemade books. "I really should consider labeling all of these," he said, almost as an afterthought.

Nish rolled his eyes. "You think?"

Norivun drummed his fingers on the table. "Sven, could we perhaps flip back to that chapter and learn what counter spell is needed to reverse such a veil."

The Fire Wolf grumbled, "Please do."

"Griminy witches titties, you're all a grumbling bunch!" Sven sighed and flipped the pages in his book again until he returned to the chapter I'd found. "Ah yes, the counter spell. Here it is."

An entire page of foreign words appeared in a language I didn't understand.

The hunter blew forcefully through his nose. "Latin. Why is it always in Latin?"

"It's the language of choice for our magical ancestors," Sven replied without missing a beat.

"I know," the hunter replied as he rubbed at the back of his neck. "It's just a pain in the ass. My pronunciation isn't the greatest."

Sven patted his shoulder. "You've always managed before. I'm sure this will be no different. Now, let's see if any special ingredients are needed. Ah, look here." He pointed to the sole line. "Perfect, only one!"

I leaned closer, my heart plummeting when I saw what it was. "Lava rock from the Isle of Malician in the underworld."

Sven nodded as though such a thing were trivial. "Typical. Warlocks do love their dark objects."

I glanced at the crown prince and his guards. Dismay was written on all of their features. "But we're not divine creatures," I replied. "We can't go to the underworld."

Sven gazed at me through his spectacles, which made his eyes look twice the size of normal. "One would question if that were true given the magic I saw in both of you when we first met."

But any hope I felt dimmed even more when the crown prince shook his head.

"I won't risk it," Norivun replied. "To venture to the underworld could result in our deaths if you're wrong."

"But you'll never know unless you try." Sven grinned.

The Fire Wolf pulled out an object from his pocket, a slim metallic device that was a rectangular shape. He tapped something on the surface, and it began to glow as square-like objects appeared on it. Holding it over the book, he tapped the rectangle, and a sound emitted.

"What are you doing?" the prince asked, his question guarded.

"Snapping a picture of the spell," the Fire Wolf replied, then showed us the replica on his slim object.

A perfect image of the spell and Sven's book appeared.

Nish backed up, eyeing the hunter's apparatus. "What is this sorcery?"

"It's like a looking glass!" Haxil elbow bumped me. "How fascinating."

The hunter snickered but didn't enlighten us. "I'll get the rock needed from the Isle of Malician."

I frowned. "How?"

The Fire Wolf smirked. "I have my ways." He put the rectangular apparatus in his pocket again, then raised his eyebrows. "Since you can't go to the underworld without testing your mortality, I'll plan on getting the lava rock and meeting you back in the fae lands. I should be able to by tomorrow Earth time."

"That soon?" Norivun's eyebrows shot up.

The hunter merely smiled mockingly. "Yeah, that soon."

"A day in Earth time is nearly a week in our time," Haxil interjected.

The Fire Wolf shrugged. "Then you'll have some time to kill."

"What about the spell?" I asked. "Who's going to cast it?"

"Do you speak Latin? Or know how to pronounce the words?" the hunter asked.

Norivun and I both frowned. "No." I shook my head. "I've never heard of that language."

"I haven't either," the crown prince added.

"Then I guess I'll have to cast it." The Fire Wolf arched an eyebrow. "Now, where should we meet?"

CHAPTER 27 - NORIVUN

The Fire Wolf gave us a portal key, explaining how they worked, and assured us that he'd meet us in a week's time to complete the spell that would destroy the warlock's veil of death.

Knowing we had time to kill, we returned to the inn in the Nolus capital, and since we traveled together, the six of us appeared at once.

To say the journey back was as hideous as the journey to the strange land of Europe was an understatement.

Nish snorted when we finally stood on even ground again. "Those portal keys are atrocious."

"Agreed," Ryder replied and smoothed back his braid.

"Anyone know what day it is?" I asked.

"I'll find out." Ilara mistphased before any of us could blink and returned not even a second later. "The hunter was right. An entire week has passed since we left."

"Where did you go?" Nish asked.

"The front desk. I asked the employee working," Ilara replied sweetly.

Haxil whistled. "Ock, you're fast. You weren't even gone a minute."

I smirked. "She's almost as fast as me."

Ilara laughed. "And to think I intentionally mistphased slower than I normally do just to stroke your fragile male ego."

I quirked an eyebrow. "Me? Have an ego?"

She snorted. "I know, *never*."

"And a fragile one at that. You're correct, *never*. My ego is quite robust, thank you very much."

She laughed again, and I suddenly needed to feel her in my arms, needed to scent her unique fragrance, and needed to quell the uneasiness that was rolling through me despite our playful words.

If another week had truly passed in the day we'd spent at Sven's cabin, that meant my wedding to Georgyanna was less than two weeks away, and the thought of not having Ilara as my wife until the day I died created a savage darkness to swirl around my soul.

"Come here." I pulled her toward me.

She readily slipped into my arms, a sour hint entering her scent as the laughter died from her lips. Worry was strumming from her on the bond, probably because she sensed my uneasiness.

My guards left discreetly, talking among themselves as they worked out their schedule for guarding our room. It wasn't until the door closed behind them and we were truly alone that I allowed myself to crush my mate completely to me.

Minutes passed as I held her, running my hands up and down her back, then around her toned shoulders and over her rounded hips. I buried my face in her neck, taking in her delectable roses and dew scent. She smelled of love, of hope, and of the home I'd never had.

"Are you okay?" she whispered as her fingers stroked through my hair.

"I'm getting better with every second that passes." I kissed her, needing to taste her lips while soaking up her scent. Her fingers threaded more through the hair on the nape of my neck, and even though I'd meant to kiss her and kiss her only, when she released a soft moan, my cock immediately throbbed.

Within seconds, our kiss turned frantic and raw, as though we both knew that time was running out, and it was possible our joinings would become lost and be a mere memory if my father's tyrannical plan was able to come to light.

Her breath hitched, and when I backed her against the wall, she readily jumped up to wrap her legs around my waist. I snarled and hooked her ankles at my back, just beneath my wings, as her toe began to caress the right membrane.

My cock threatened to punch through my pants when she gyrated on top of me, all while her toes continued their erotic dance.

"Fuck, yes," I managed through a hissed breath. I ripped

at her clothes, tearing through them with frantic fingers and charged magic. When her naked skin touched me, I stripped my shirt, the material ripping as it caught on my wings. "Must be. Inside you." My words turned guttural, my thoughts scattered. Her scent. Her feel. Her arousal.

Need her.

Need her.

Need her.

She clawed at the unusual pants I still wore, her worried scent now entirely gone save for the heady musk that clouded me in her arousal.

Need her.

Inside her.

Owning her.

Pounding her.

She didn't complain when my cock sprang free, and I thrust myself inside her within the same breath. Her back arched, her core tight, hot, and wet. She took my entire length until my shaft was seated completely inside her.

"Yes," she moaned. "Yes." She turned feral in my arms, her nails becoming claws and her teeth fangs.

But it wasn't enough.

I needed *more.*

Gripping her, I pounded into her again and again, each thrust hard and long as she took me entirely each time.

Her channel tightened as her arousal swam in the air around me.

Need her.

Need her.

Need her.

Each thought was timed with a thrust until the only thing that mattered in my life, in this realm, in all of existence, was the female in my arms.

"You're mine, Ilara. *Mine.*"

She gasped again when I thrust into her fast and hard. And all the while, she gripped my shoulders and bit my neck, demanding more, more, more.

My release roared through me as she screamed at the same time. I gripped her hips tightly, emptying myself inside her completely as she shuddered with her climax.

I saw stars. Felt the gods. Knew that my life would never again be complete without her.

And when we finally came down from that high, that visceral need to keep her safe and close again overtook me.

I wrapped my arms around her, burying my face in her neck, as my heart pounded. She shuddered against me as my cock stayed buried inside her while I soaked up her scent.

Our mating bond burned brightly. Her love pulsed toward me with every breath she took as she became limp with satiation in my arms.

I rocked back on my heels and carried her to the bed with our bodies still joined. My wings fanned out around us when I lifted the sheets and laid her atop the mattress before kissing every inch of her skin.

We might not have saved the continent yet. We hadn't even stopped my wedding.

But Ilara was mine, and I was hers, and damn anyone who tried to rip us apart.

❄

I PLEASURED my mate twice more before we finally ordered supper. None of my guards commented on our fuck session even though they'd probably known what we'd been up to despite the solid air Shield I'd cast around us to prevent any other guests or fae on the street from hearing my mate's screams.

Those screams were for my ears and my ears alone.

After we'd finally eaten, Ilara crawled into bed beside me as the light from the moons bled through the curtains.

She was naked, something I heartily approved of, but . . . a frown tugged at my lips.

"What's wrong?" she asked, yawning before she leaned up on her elbow to place her hand on my chest.

"You don't have any clothes."

"Are you complaining?"

I snorted. "No."

She yawned again. "Good, cause it's your fault my yellow top is in tatters." She eyed its remnants on the floor. The clothes the Fire Wolf had given me were in a similar state. *So much for the memento.* "It's too bad. I liked that top."

Despite her playful words, my frown deepened. "As the future queen of the Solis continent, you should have hundreds of silk slips to choose from each night, so it doesn't matter if I tear them in two. You shouldn't only have one set of clothing."

"But I'm not the future queen of the Solis continent. Georgyanna is."

I growled. "Fuck Georgyanna."

"Agreed, but what if I don't like silk slips?" Her fingers skimmed along my chest, amusement strumming through our bond.

I nipped at her fingers when they reached my chin. "You know what I mean." A rumble of discontentment vibrated through me. "I don't like it. It means that I'm not providing for you. You need an entire wardrobe of new clothes. All of those tunics that Cailis had packed for you will no longer work. If you call your wings forth, you'll tear through your entire wardrobe in no time."

She cocked her head. "You know, I spent many seasons growing up with only one top. We never had a lot of rulibs. Sometimes a single set of clothes was all I had for a full season. It was all my parents could afford."

I angled closer to her. "Even before the crops began dying?"

"Yes, even then."

"But our continent is usually prosperous. How could you have been so poor as a child?"

Her nostrils flared. "Vorl enjoyed taking more of his cut than he was due. We could never prove it, but we never had many rulibs despite my parents working hard."

My dragon rumbled within me. "Fucking Vorl."

Anger fired hotly through my veins. My mate. My *queen* had grown up in near poverty due to that despicable male of a fae. Staying in the dungeons wasn't nearly enough punishment for him. I'd see to that when we returned to Solisarium, because while I'd had succulent meats on my plate each night, Ilara had gone to bed hungry more times than I could probably bear knowing.

"He'll pay for that."

She sighed. "I'm just thankful he's no longer in charge of our village."

"He never will be again, and you'll never go to bed hungry anymore."

She brought her fingers to my lips, and I nipped them as a stirring of longing pulsed through my chest. Blessed Mother, I couldn't get enough of this female.

"Don't make promises you can't keep. If the spell we found doesn't stop the dark magic that's poisoned our land, we'll all be going to bed hungry."

I frowned as she closed her eyes and nestled beside me, because as much as I didn't want to accept her words, I also knew that she was right.

SINCE WE HAD a week until we'd meet the Fire Wolf and attempt to stop what the warlock had done in Isalee, we all agreed that the time would be best spent searching for a connection between my father and the warlock he hired or having Ilara continue to imbue life into our continent's dead fields.

So after buying Ilara new clothes the next morning, we settled on that plan.

"Let's do both," Ilara said as she placed her hands on her hips. A new turquoise cape with wing slits swirled down her back, and the black pant suit she wore hugged her curves in all the right places. *Damn.* "I'll keep working on the fields, trying to heal what I can, while you search the castle for something that links the warlock to your father."

I finally dragged my gaze from her enticing waist. "That would require splitting up," I growled.

"True." Ilara inclined her head as my guards stood around us. "But you have to remember the bargain we made. It's been weeks since I've tried to fulfill my side of it."

My gaze shot to her wrist, alarm skating through me. "Are you feeling the effects of avoiding your side of our deal?"

She made a sheepish face. "I think I'm beginning to. I woke up a few times during the night when painful shocks began to emit from the mark." She ran a finger along her inner wrist, to where that leaf had glowed briefly before disappearing after we'd sealed our bargain. "It happened again this morning when we were shopping, but it was stronger."

"Mother Below," I muttered. "The gods aren't giving you much of a break."

She shrugged. "No, they're not, which means I have to go."

I scowled, and she inched closer to me until her scent began to cloud my thoughts.

"I'll be fine. It's winter. All of the Isalee fields are dead, and none of the laborers work in them anymore. Nobody will know I'm there. Besides, we're fully mated now so you'll be able to feel where I am. Surely, you'll derive some comfort from that?"

While I knew she was right, I still grumbled. I didn't want to be parted from her, not for one moment while my father's fae were hunting her, even if our bargain demanded it and even if I could feel her now and know her whereabouts.

"We'll keep her safe, Nori," Haxil said.

"Trust me," she added gently. "I'll be fine. Nobody will know I'm there, and if someone does happen to see me or suspect something, I can mistphase out immediately."

Haxil crossed his arms. "I'll accompany her."

"As will I," Sandus added.

"No, you *all* will," I growled. "If I go back to Solisarium, it's best if I'm alone. I'll stay hidden under one of my illusions so no one will know I'm there."

Ryder nodded. "Agreed."

Nish turned to my mate. "So, when do we go, Princess?"

AFTER ILARA and my guards left, I mistphased back to the castle to see if I could find a connection between my father and the warlock. I knew that unless I did, nobody would believe me when I accused my father of starving and plotting against his own fae, and the council would never side with us to have him removed from the throne.

But finding a connection proved just as hard as I thought it would be.

I returned day after day, searching relentlessly in the

castle while Ilara worked in the fields. But everywhere I checked only proved to be a dead end.

Within the castle, there was nothing. Not in the bank ledgers, our vaults, my father's private study, the hidden safes that had been built into all of the wings. Nowhere. All of it showed not an ounce of proof.

My father had been thorough, just as I'd suspected he would be.

Essentially, there was no trace of his deceit. No trail of rulibs to tie him to the warlock. No parchments or ledgers that captured what he'd done. Not even carefully removed payments over the years that were unaccounted for. The funds he used to pay the warlock were entirely off the books.

I growled in frustration as my sixth day of searching was coming to an end. Come morning, we were meeting the Fire Wolf, but I had nothing to show for my week in the castle. I'd been hoping to have a lead that would implicate my father in his misdeeds, but I'd literally accomplished nothing.

I WAS JUST ABOUT to mistphase back to the Nolus capital when Balbus and Haisley rushed up to me. Since I was in my private room, I'd dispelled my illusion, and I could have sworn they had a knack for knowing when I was present.

An eye roll was already in the works from me. This morning they'd cornered me when I'd appeared unhidden in my chambers. Of course, it was due to Georgyanna and a new petty venture she'd come up with. While she hadn't hurt any fae directly following our last encounter, she'd taken it upon herself to find other ways to needle them and irritate the fuck out of me. She truly was a vindictive witch.

"What's she done now?" I asked with a sigh and calmed my magic from the mistphase.

Balbus frantically shook his head as Haisley's face paled.

"It's not Georgyanna, my prince," Balbus said as he came to a stop just before me. "It's Daiseeum, Ilara's former lady's servant."

My brow furrowed. "What about her?"

Haisley twisted his hands, his face a mask of horror. "Oh, my prince. Oh, it's horrendous!"

Balbus nodded, his jowls jiggling as his features became a mask of fright. "She's gone missing, my prince. I fear Daiseeum's the castle's latest victim."

CHAPTER 28 - NORIVUN

I mistphased back to the Nolus capital immediately and
told Ilara and my guards what had happened.

My mate's heart thundered so loudly I could hear
it as she began to pace in our chamber. "We have to find her.
Now. Oh gods, Norivun, what if the warlock's already killed
her?"

Ilara's fear was so potent I could taste it. It drenched our
room at the Nolus inn in a sour cloud and made fury gather
around my soul.

"We'll find her," I growled and fisted my hands. "I'm
going to scry for her."

"But how will we get to her before he"—she choked—
"before he . . .?" She came to a stop in front of me. Her
midnight hair spilled over her shoulders as her white wings
flared. She'd been keeping her wings visible more and more.

Snarling, I closed the distance between us and pulled out
a piece of fabric from my pocket. "Haisley gave me this. This

clothing belongs to Daiseeum. Haisley said she wore it yesterday, so it should allow for a fresh trail." I extracted my yellow crystals. "I'm going to scry, and when I find her, we'll save her. Got it?"

She nodded swiftly as tears filled her eyes.

I disappeared into the bathing chamber to scry once more and call upon every ounce of magic I had to find the lady's servant, my father's latest victim, before it was too late.

Magic heated the room as I enacted the ancient spells that I'd stumbled upon in my last year at the Academy of Solisarium. Scrying wasn't common. Most didn't have enough magic to activate the aged spells, but through trial and error, I'd found what'd worked and concentrated completely on what was needed.

My crystals glowed. My blood flowed down my arm. Magic soaked into every pore of my body as I called upon the power to guide me to the female who would be dead by the morrow if we couldn't locate her.

Seconds turned into minutes. Sweat beaded on my brow as I chanted faster and faster.

And then an image came to me.

A stone room. A chamber. No, a dungeon.

My brow furrowed as I searched for a firmer location. *Where? Where are you?*

Chains. An altar. Burning candles.

A robed figure appeared, Daiseeum before him. A breath lifted her chest. *Still alive, thank the Mother.*

The figure tilted his head back. Gray skin mottled with red veins appeared on his chin. He lifted his head higher until the scrying vision shifted to reveal a stained-glass window above. It was small, at the very top of the room.

My breath sucked in.

I knew where those windows were.

"Fuck," I said under my breath as I collapsed onto my haunches and breathed deeply.

I jumped to a stand and burst into the room where my guards and Ilara waited. "I know where she is, but we have to go. *Now*. The warlock is there. He's going to sacrifice her at any second."

I whipped all of them in my magic and mistphased all six of us to the hall right outside of the castle chambers where those cells with stained-glass windows were.

Dank air swirled around us when we all reappeared on even flooring. Stone walls lined the hall, doors on all sides.

Ilara swirled around, her eyes wild. "Where is—"

A scream wrenched through the air.

"No time," I growled.

I followed the sound, exploding through the door like the hounds guarding God Seemus's back.

Daiseeum lay on an altar. The lady's servant was in restraints, struggling against them.

A robed figure stood before her. A huge blade in the male's hand lifted high as he poised it above her.

I hissed, and the warlock swirled to face us.

Ilara snarled in fury and flew toward her lady's servant on a gust of her air affinity just as the warlock released a curse.

A sizzling spark raced through the air, right for my mate.

Ilara ducked in blurred speed, moving like the wind as the warlock threw curse after curse at her.

A snarl ripped from me as my guards and I flew forward, but my mate had turned into a huntress, her limbs flowing with an inferno of power as she leapt, ducked, and rolled on her way to Daiseeum. All the while, she wore a mask of fury, her features twisted into absolute rage as her warrior affinity swelled around her.

Another curse flew from the warlock, flying right by her ear. A bellow ripped from my chest, but Ilara was still ahead of me, and the warlock was more focused on her than harming me.

Ilara reached Daiseeum just as I shot a warning to my guards to stand back. Magic pulsed in my gut as I flung the door to my creature's affinity wide open.

In a flash of power and absolute might, I released my dragon.

My massive form ripped through the stone walls and old chamber as though it were tissue paper. A roar of fire flew from my lips, incinerating anything it touched. Rocks flew as my guards dove to pull Ilara and the lady's servant out of the way while this underground part of the castle began to crumble.

The warlock's eyes widened when his hood flew back. His face was gaunt, pale, skeletal, and sickly looking. Just as the Fire Wolf had described.

I released another bellow of fury and channeled all of my dragon's fire toward the dark sorcerer.

Fire rolled in my throat when I opened my mouth wide.

The mottled skin around the warlock's face wrinkled when terror shone in his gaze.

A blast of my molten fury shot toward him just as he whipped his cape around him.

My fire hit where he stood, obliterating everything in that space.

But when the smoke cleared as Ilara, Daiseeum, and my guards hacked and coughed, the charred remains of the warlock weren't to be found.

He wasn't found at all.

The bastard had escaped at the last possible moment.

CHAPTER 29 - ILARA

Daiseeum couldn't stop crying as we all worked to calm her down and soothe her frayed nerves. Scorched stone and soot filled the air, dust motes everywhere. My former lady's servant oscillated between tears of hysteria at nearly being killed, amazement that we'd come for her, happiness at seeing me again, and terror at what would happen when the king learned of my return.

I tried not to let any of my trepidation show as she sobbed and rocked back and forth. But we'd just encountered the creature we were up against, and he was anything but weak. I would be a fool not to feel concern over the power that warlock had wielded.

Smothering that fear, I pulled Daiseeum close and tucked an arm around her. "Don't worry about me or any of that. You're safe now, and we intend to keep you that way. Norivun is assigning you a guard. You're not to go anywhere in the castle without him, understood?"

The servant stared at me, then gripped my hands. "Yes, m'lady." Fresh tears filled her eyes, and her knuckles turned white when she squeezed harder. "I shall never forget what you did for me tonight. Never."

I hugged her briefly, then let go, not because I didn't relish seeing her again but because we had to move. The huge hole that Norivun's dragon had blasted into the castle's underground levels had created a crumbling structure. From the shouts above, the entire castle knew that something destructive had been unleashed within its depths. No doubt, the castle commander was forming the guard at this very moment, and once they beheld the obliterated hall of cells, castle staff with constructo affinities would be called in.

This area was still salvageable and could be saved . . . if the constructo fae got here soon.

"Daiseeum, you're not to breathe a word of Ilara's presence here to anyone," Norivun said as the rise of distant boot steps grew louder. "Understood?"

She bobbed her head, her eyes still wide. I had a feeling nightmares would be plaguing her for the foreseeable future. "Yes, my prince. I would never. On the Mother's Honor. I will protect our queen until the day I die."

A satisfied gleam coated my mate's face as my former lady servant's words hit me. *Our queen.* She had just referred to *me* as her queen. Not Queen Lissandra. Not Georgyanna. *Me.*

"We must go." Norivun's magic again clouded around us as he pulled all seven of us into his affinity. His illusion shrouded everyone just as the castle commander burst through the door.

"Mother Below and all the gods!" he proclaimed when he saw the mess, altar, and teetering walls.

Every guard behind him came to a sudden stop.

"Call the constructo fae *now*!" the commander bellowed.

We didn't stay around to see what happened next. In a wink of mistphasing magic, we all disappeared.

We returned Daiseeum to her home, and Ryder volunteered to stay behind until the servant's newly assigned guard could arrive. While I didn't think the warlock that had almost killed her would be returning anytime soon, I was glad the crown prince wasn't taking any chances.

Once back at the inn on the Nolus continent, the scope of what we'd done, and who we were up against, hit me like a million volts of lightning. I collapsed on the bed as soot from my clothing billowed around me.

"That warlock is so strong."

Norivun grunted. "Indeed. He's more powerful than I realized he would be. The Fire Wolf was right."

I called upon my cleansing magic and whisked the grime away, but my mind kept turning, my thoughts racing a million millees per hour.

Pushing up on my elbows, I watched my mate. Norivun stood before me, also cleansing himself with his magic. I pulled my bottom lip into my mouth, sawing away on the flesh. "Do you think Daiseeum was targeted intentionally tonight?"

Fatigue lined his eyes, and with a start, I realized the toll the night had taken on him. I hurried to assist him, my hands fluttering over him and peeling off his clothes. I used my own magic to wick away all dirt and sweat from his skin that his tired magic had missed.

When I finished, he gleamed like a golden god, and Mother Below, my lady parts began to tingle.

This male. Everything about him called to me.

He smirked, his nostrils flaring. "To answer your question, I was wondering the same thing. It's too big of a coincidence that Daiseeum was taken by the warlock my father hired."

I planted my hands on my hips. "Do you think the king targeted her in hopes of hurting me?"

A grim frown grew on his face. "Knowing my father? Yes."

I bared my teeth. "I just thank the gods that my family is safe. If Cailis was still able to be found—"

Norivun silenced me with a kiss, then the feathery touch of his air affinity stroked down my back. "She's not. Nobody in your family is at risk. For now, they're safe. Come." He peeled back the bedsheets. "Tomorrow will be a big day when we meet again with the Fire Wolf."

❆

THE NEXT DAY, I was a ball of jittery nerves when we stood in Whimseal's midday market near the clock tower. Snow flew in the air as the wind raged. Despite the wintery weather, the market was busy as fae bustled about.

It was a well-known location in Isalee's capital. There was only one clock tower, so Norivun had deemed it the best place to meet since he figured asking the Fire Wolf to arrive at a specific spot in the Isalee field would prove too difficult for a foreigner to find.

"Do you have the looking glass?" I asked my mate.

I knew Norivun hated looking glasses since they could document things around us. More than once, the king had used them to cast the crown prince in a bad light, but Norivun had made an exception to his *no looking glass* rule today. We needed the council on our side, which meant they needed to see what was truly buried within the Isalee field. Only a looking glass could show that.

Norivun tapped his pocket. "I do."

I eyed the time and began to tap my foot. "Do you think he'll be late? He's due here in three min—"

No sooner had those worried words left my lips when the Fire Wolf materialized beside us. A tiny portal key was in his hand, but the second he fully appeared, the key obliterated into dust. In his other hand, he held an ax.

The massive black ax, along with the Fire Wolf's foreign raven-dark hair, amber eyes, and huge build, made me take a step back. He was as intimidating today as he'd been the first day we'd met.

The crown prince crossed his arms as his guards fanned

out around him. All of them eyed the ax, and given the heightened energy growing around the prince and his guards, if one of the prince's illusion spells hadn't been cloaking all seven of us, I had no doubt our presence would be causing quite a commotion.

"Relax," the Fire Wolf said, the ax still pointed toward the ground. "This weapon isn't for you."

I arched an eyebrow as the prince's aura dimmed slightly. "I should hope not," Norivun replied.

"Trust me, if I'd wanted to kill you, you'd be dead already."

Norivun glowered, which got a chuff out of the Fire Wolf. Ignoring the theatrics, I nodded toward the clock. "Right on time."

The hunter shrugged. "Best not to be late when meeting with royalty."

Norivun smirked, and a faint smile ghosted the Fire Wolf's lips.

"Were you able to secure lava rock from the Isle of Malician in the underworld?" I asked.

The hunter pulled a piece of ebony rock from his pocket. It was so black that it seemed to suck the light surrounding it into itself, and I could have sworn that magic pulsed around it. "I was."

My lips curved up in relief. "How did you obtain it?"

The Fire Wolf tucked it back into the pocket of his unusual pants. "Not important. What is important is that we have it."

Norivun grunted. "Shall we?" He eyed the ax again as his

mistphasing magic clouded around all of us. After a good night's rest and consuming an entire tray of food this morning, the fatigue that had been lining his face the night prior was gone.

The hunter nodded. "Thought you'd never ask."

In a flash of Norivun's power, we arrived back in the Isalee field. Cold air immediately raged around us, the snow flying so violently that it cut into my skin.

I cast an air Shield around us, blocking the wind entirely. Norivun gave me a nod of thanks, then turned to the Fire Wolf. "Ready?"

The hunter set his ax in the snow, and I could have sworn that magic pounded around the black blade. The Fire Wolf then withdrew a yellow crystal from his pocket, along with a piece of parchment that held a copy of the spell I'd discovered in Sven's personal library, the strange Latin words swirling across it. I studied the crystal. It looked identical to the crystals Norivun used when scrying.

I pointed at the Fire Wolf's yellow gem. "Your crystal . . . is that from Harrivee's floating meadows?"

The hunter canted his head, fingering the stone. "I have no idea. I inherited it when—" He shook his head. "I don't know."

Norivun held his palm out. "May I?"

The hunter's expression smoothed, becoming impossible to read. A second passed in which he still held the crystal tightly in his palm. Another second passed before he released it, his fingers opening reluctantly.

The yellow gem bounced onto Norivun's awaiting palm, and the prince held it up to the sunlight that penetrated my air dome. "It *is* from Harrivee. It's the same kind of crystal I use. Tell me, how did you come across it? We usually don't allow our gems to leave the Solis continent, especially the ones from Harrivee's meadows."

The Fire Wolf held his hand out for it, his jaw working. "I honestly don't know. Like I said, I inherited it."

Despite the crystal coming into a foreigner's possession, Norivun returned it without a word, then clasped his hands behind his back beneath his wings. "I'm guessing your crystal will be used to channel our magic and combine it?"

"Yes," the hunter replied gruffly. "If we're going to break through the warlock's netting and destroy it completely, I'm going to need all of our magic. This spell is complex." He hefted the ax up. "And a final cleave from this should do the trick. Hopefully."

Strong magic pulsed from the ax, and a part of me wanted to touch it while another part begged me to recoil.

"What is that weapon?" I took a step closer to him. "I can feel its energy."

"Full of questions, you are." The Fire Wolf shifted it farther away.

"It's her greatest quality," Haxil said as he crossed his arms.

The hunter shrugged. "This is a blade from the underworld. That's all you need to know. I'd advise you not to touch it."

Norivun and I shared a side-eye before I gave a respectful bow. "As you wish, but before you start, we'd like to activate a looking glass. What we're attempting to do in this field needs to be documented."

The hunter shrugged. "Fine by me."

My mate extracted the looking glass from his pocket, and then whispered the spell that would levitate it and allow it to record our actions. It rose from his fingertips, and its mirror-like surface began to glow.

Once the looking glass was suspended above us, its magic holding it in place as it recorded everything we were doing, Norivun gave a curt nod. "That should do it."

"You'll all need to join hands." The Fire Wolf indicated for us to stand in a circle, then moved himself to the center. "You'll have to open up to me and trust me."

An unsettled feeling slid through me. To allow someone access to our magic meant dropping our Shields entirely.

Norivun's nostrils flared, and I could only guess that he was scenting the hunter for any trace of deceit, but since our bonded link didn't pulse with growing worry, I knew he believed the hunter meant us no harm.

Norivun backed up, then slid his hand through mine. "Haxil, Ryder, Sandus, and Nish, I ask that you drop your Shields, just this once."

They all glowered but gave swift nods, then joined hands until all of us stood in a circle. All at once, they lowered their Shields.

The force of their collective auras hit me like a tsunami.

Calling upon my own magic, I had to force my Shield to lower. Ever since Georgyanna's attacks while I'd been training with Matron Olsander, I'd made it a point to never lower it.

The second all of our Shields were down, the air changed. Raw, potent auras simmered around us, nearly crackling with intensity.

The Fire Wolf's lips kicked up. "Nice. That should do it."

The hunter took out the underworld lava rock and set it carefully in the soil, right over the heart of where I'd felt the warlock's power. Following that, he hunkered to the ground and laid the parchment out in front of him. Then, with the ax in one hand and his yellow crystal in the other, he began to chant the foreign Latin words.

The hairs on the back of my neck abruptly stood on end.

Air within my dome began to shudder as though a phantom wind called to it.

Prickly sensations needled along my skin, and then—

My breath sucked in when the magic residing within my gut began to fly out of me. I gasped, almost doubling over from the force of it, as Norivun gripped my hand harder as a grimace twisted his features.

All of the guards appeared similar, everyone grunting or sweating under the epic pull of the spell the Fire Wolf was wielding. It was similar to what Drachu had done to me, but not painful, and something told me the spell wouldn't rob me of my life, that it would stop before such an event occurred.

The lava rock abruptly exploded, creating a huge tunnel

deep into the soil. Its circumference was at least a wingspan, and I inched farther from its edge while keeping my hands joined with my mate and his guard.

The yellow crystal the Fire Wolf held glowed, sparks emitting from it, then a portal appeared before him, burrowing into the soil and going down, down, down.

More and more magic was pulled from me, the strength and feel of the spell holding me in its embrace, like a powerful hand had wrapped around me, caging me in until I couldn't move, couldn't think.

We were all vessels, all empty beings holding the magic the spell demanded, and it took *everything* from us.

The words the Fire Wolf chanted grew stronger and more forceful. Energy strummed around him, the parchment in front of him lifting and hovering midair.

His channeled portal burrowed even deeper until it came to a twist of black webs and oily strands buried deep within the land. My eyes widened when the congealed mass slowly began to lift, like a sea creature's writhing tentacles rising from the depths of the abyss.

Minutes passed as my magic grew more drained. Sweat poured down the hunter's face, and I could only guess he was giving just as much of his magic as we were.

Slowly, the black web of coiled strands and never-ending darkness began to surface. It was so black that it was as if I stared into Lucifer's soul.

I instinctively recoiled when the heart of the warlock's netting rose in the tunnel created by the lava rock, and then was fully revealed. The rest of the ground bulged around it but held, only the heart exposed. Its web-like structure fanned out, stretching into the soil and traveling to who knew how far on our continent. The webbed netting crackled and writhed, as though it were a living creature, and all I could think about was how many lives had been taken to form it and fuel it.

Fire glowed in the Fire Wolf's eyes as he beheld the warlock's terrible power. His hands trembled from exertion, and his shoulders tensed as veins in his biceps bulged.

He reached for the ax, the power from the weapon causing a ripple of magic to pulse around us. With the ax gripped between both palms and the yellow crystal hovering over the veil's heart as our magic was channeled into holding it, the hunter lifted the obsidian blade. It gleamed in the sun, like a thousand black stars were encased within it, and then with a blurred swing through the air, the ax fell right on the heart of the web as the Fire Wolf roared the final words of the spell.

A *huge* crack cleaved the writhing heart in two, and then a shockwave of magic burst through our circle.

Wind like a hurricane whipped my hair behind me.

My body flew back, only the strength of the prince's and his guards' grips holding us together.

The very air from my lungs ripped out of me, and my heart throbbed in my chest as blood pounded through my veins.

The magical dome from my air affinity shattered as though a hundred knives had torn through it.

Winter wind abruptly raged around us in the same

second that the thousands of writhing black veins extending from the veil's heart obliterated.

Hundreds of pieces of black netting that had slithered through the soil disintegrated as though they'd never been.

The force of the warlock's magic breaking was as powerful as the release of that ax's might. It rippled through the land, the soil undulating beneath my toes as the putrid black strands disappeared.

For as far as I could see through the raging storm, the magic from the spell echoed, and then the huge tunnel before us re-filled, black and moist soil taking its place, the ugly gray dirt gone.

My life-giving affinity surged, sensing the shift in our land.

A second passed before I could suck in a breath of air. Norivun's hand had clamped down on mine so tightly that my bones shifted.

All of us still stood in the circle, death grips on one another as my eyes drooped, and my magic felt as if it'd run dry.

A burning sensation came on my wrist, and with wild eyes, I lifted my sleeve. The single petal that the bargain had burned into my skin glowed and then vanished. I shot a look toward my mate. The same happened on him. The broken heart burned and then was gone as was his bargain with the hunter.

Our bargains were complete.

"We did it," I whispered.

The crown prince gave me a tired smile, satisfaction gleaming in his gaze.

The hunter panted, that wild, fiery look still on his face, and if I didn't know better, I'd say that he'd just enjoyed that epic display of power. Standing slowly, the hunter lowered the ax as his chest lifted rapidly with each breath.

He gave all of us a cocky grin. "Thank you. I think that did the trick."

He snatched the hovering yellow crystal from midair and whispered a few more words. In a blink, the pull on my affinities stopped.

Still reeling that our bargain had been completed, I hunched over. Nish and Haxil did the same, both sucking in breaths of air.

"Blessed Mother!" Nish proclaimed as he gulped. "I've never in all of my life ever—"

A shift in the magic around us cut off his words.

The hairs on the back of my neck stood on end anew.

All of us turned wide eyes toward the same area of raging snow just as a figure materialized out of thin air.

A figure with a face hidden by a hood.

Hands covered in gray skin with mottled red veins shifted the robe back.

A snarl tore from the Fire Wolf's mouth just as the warlock revealed his face.

Fear pounded through me when the same warlock that had tried to murder Daiseeum stood before us.

"It's him!" I immediately called forth my affinities to

create a protective dome around all of us, but my air affinity didn't respond.

I was entirely tapped out.

My magic was *gone*.

The warlock's thin lip curled as his black eyes assessed us. "Which one of you destroyed my veil?"

CHAPTER 30 - NORIVUN

I spun away from the warlock just as he released a curse. It shot through the air, heading right for the Fire Wolf.

The hunter jumped to the side at the last second, swearing under his breath, as he ducked and rolled.

All of my guards fanned out, swords in hand as they tried to surround the warlock, but with our magic depleted, we all moved so damned slowly.

Cold winter wind whipped around us, snow everywhere, since Ilara's air Shield had disappeared when the spell had run us dry.

Snarling with fury, I called upon my magic, my affinities, something, *anything*, but the spell had drained me completely. I was entirely without magic.

Fuck!

My limbs moved as though I was weighted down. My arms felt as if they'd been tied to stone bricks.

Fear stole through me when the warlock moved like the

wind. Despite vastly outnumbering him, we were no stronger than magicless children, and the warlock was pure power.

In a blink, he was behind Ilara, and he pulled a wicked-looking blade from within his cloak.

My heart felt as if it'd stopped.

I ran.

Bellowed.

Roared with fury.

But I was too slow.

Ilara spun to face the warlock just as he sliced the blade through the air.

Helplessness consumed me when my legs didn't move faster. It was the same as when I'd been a child, and my father had raised his hand to my mother. I hadn't been able to stop him either.

The warlock slashed right at my mate.

I roared again, but his attack didn't slow.

The knife whistled through the air. At the last second, Ilara crouched to avoid the blow, the blade missing her by a hair's breadth.

Savage fury fired through me when the warlock raised his weapon again just as my guards and I arrived at Ilara's side.

In a blink, the warlock was gone.

Chest heaving, I whirled around to see the warlock reappear by the Fire Wolf.

The warlock's arm swiped out, catching the hunter in the stomach. A flash of red appeared through the Fire Wolf's clothing as he let out a hiss of pain.

Faster than the wind, the warlock was before us again.

Dear gods.

Magical spells flew from the warlock's fingertips, glowing curses shooting toward us one after the other. In a heartbeat of stunned realization, I knew he'd been holding back. Seconds prior, the warlock had been toying with us, enjoying the scene as we stumbled over our feet as his superior magical capabilities stayed in check.

But now he wasn't holding back.

Dozens of spells arced through the air, the force of them coming so fast I only had a chance to blink before they were upon me.

It took all of my training, all of my skills, to avoid one after another.

Flashes of movement showed my guards and Ilara doing the same. Thank the Mother she had a warrior affinity. Despite her magic being depleted, I knew the inherent tie to her strength and speed was still within her.

Ilara moved with fluid grace as she wore a mask of determination.

I jumped to her just as a curse flew in my path. It burned through my sleeve at the shoulder, leaving a gaping hole where it had touched. If it had hit me in the chest, my heart would have been obliterated.

"Ilara!" I called to my mate, desperate to get her out of here.

"We need to mistphase!" Nish yelled.

"I can't!" Haxil replied as he dodged another blow. "My magic's gone!"

"And we can't fly," Ryder bellowed. "Ilara's wings are gone, and the Fire Wolf isn't able to."

"Carry them?" Haxil roared.

"My magic's too depleted to have the strength," Sandus called.

I gritted my teeth. We were running out of options. All of my guards kept trying to attack the warlock, but their movements compared to his were laughable.

The warlock was too strong. Too powerful. This was why my father had hired him. This was what the Fire Wolf had warned us about. Warlocks' magical capabilities wielded from the dark magic they'd ingested from their living sacrifices made them godlike in their power.

"We must—" the Fire Wolf heaved. He was still doubled over, and I wondered how deep his wound had gone. "We must join hands. It's our only chance."

The warlock's lips twisted into a terrifying smile as all six of us leapt toward the hunter. At the last moment, I called the looking glass to me, and the magical device flew to my outstretched hand before I shoved it in my pocket.

A slew of curses rained down on us just as we joined hands, but the hunter held a tiny portal key, and in a whisper of words—

We disappeared.

WE REAPPEARED BACK at the marketplace, slamming into the ground near the clock tower. Blood still gushed from the Fire

Wolf's belly wound, and Ilara immediately leaned down to assess him as his gleaming black ax hung limply from his other hand.

"He needs a healer." She glanced up at me with frantic eyes.

The Fire Wolf coughed, then shook his head. "No, I don't. I'll be fine once I'm back home. I only came here to drop you all off." He coughed again.

"But your wound—"

He cut her off with a smile and a sly shake of his head despite his pale complexion. "If you think a belly wound is going to kill me, then you don't know me very well." He nodded toward me. "I take it my work is done here?"

"Yes." I gave a grim nod. "Thank you for everything you did, and thank you for . . . not leaving us."

The Fire Wolf inclined his head, and it struck me anew that the hunter had chosen to save us. He could have left at any time with his portal key, but he hadn't. He'd known that would have sealed our deaths.

"I owe you a life debt," I added.

The hunter smirked. "I may call in on that someday."

Before any of us could respond, the Fire Wolf held a new portal key in his hand, and in a whisper of words, he vanished.

SINCE MY MAGIC was so depleted, I couldn't hide us from Whimseal's fae under an illusion spell or mistphase us back to the Nolus continent.

"We need to conceal Ilara," I growled as the fae in the streets began to notice us. I shielded her with my body the best I could.

Luckily, the Fire Wolf had portal transferred us to an alley just east of the clock tower, but we weren't entirely hidden from sight. More than a few passing fae on the street had glanced our way. It was bad enough that some had seen us arrive with the foreigner, worse when a few recognized me just as the Fire Wolf had disappeared.

I had no doubt word would return to my father. He'd inevitably put the pieces together—if his hired warlock didn't report to him first—and realize that we'd foiled his plan by defeating his warlock's magic with the help of a subject from another realm.

Nish gave a curt nod and disappeared around the alley's corner as the rest of us stayed as hidden as possible. But *fuck*, I still felt so depleted, so weak.

A snarl tore from me.

Ilara placed a hand on my arm, her cobalt gaze piercing and her grip strong despite our vulnerable state. Black hair tumbled around her shoulders. She looked fierce and defiant.

Pride surged through me just as she said, "We're alive, and the veil that's been suppressing our *orem* is gone. We won."

Despite loving her so much in that moment that I wanted to crush her to me, I suppressed that instinct and shook my head reluctantly. "We haven't won even though we fixed the suppressed *orem*. There's no saying my father won't hire the same warlock to enact that horrible spell once more and create the veil all over again. He may not be able to do it anytime soon since he'll be starting with nothing, but until my father is dead or that warlock is gone, we're still vulnerable."

"What about the looking glass?" She peered toward my pocket. "Did it record everything?"

I pulled it out and whispered the spell to activate it. The mirror began to glow, and then replayed what had just occurred within the Isalee field. Ilara shuddered when the warlock appeared in the lifelike rendition. "It's intact."

"Thank the gods." Her jaw clenched, and she picked at a fingernail. "Do you think it's enough proof to convince the council of what the king's done?"

"It's enough proof to show that the *orem* didn't die by natural means, but I don't know if it's enough to implicate the king."

"Will they believe us anyway?"

I pressed my lips into a thin line and worked my jaw. "They might or they might not, but right now, it's all we have. We'll have to hope it's enough."

A fierce breeze flowed through the narrow street just as Nish rounded the corner.

My guard held out large hooded cloaks to all of us. "Bought 'em at one of the market's stalls. Same fellow I've bought cloaks from before. Long hoods on 'em. This'll hide Ilara and all of us until we're somewhere safe."

Ilara gave him a grateful nod and donned the garment, bringing the hood up completely until her face was entirely hidden.

Once satisfied that my mate wouldn't be easily identified, I pulled her close. "We'll need to find an eating establishment and lay low. Once we've rested for a few hours and consumed sustenance, we should have enough magic to mistphase back to the Nolus capital."

Ryder gave a grim nod, his cheekbones razor-sharp. "And then what, my prince?"

My arm wrapped tighter around my mate. "Then I marry the true rising queen, and . . ." My lips pressed together as anger stirred within me. "Then we tell the council what's occurred and confront my father."

CHAPTER 31 - ILARA

Our magic was so depleted that it took four hours until we had just enough power to mistphase out of Whimseal and back to the Nolus continent. Following that, it took three full days until our magic was fully restored, and our affinities flowed hotly and brightly through us once more. We didn't dare leave until then. None of us were willing to confront the king until we were fully capable of defending ourselves.

But I kept thinking about the queen. I imagined by now that King Novakin knew of the destruction we'd wreaked on his veil, and the queen had probably paid the price.

An ache settled in my chest. She'd suffered so much under his hand, and that needed to stop, but we couldn't act until we were strong enough.

So we laid low at the inn. We kept to ourselves. Who knew how far the Solis king's reach went. Even though we were on an entirely different continent, I understood

Norivun's concern that the king was hunting now for *all* of us.

"Today is the day I marry you," Norivun said when we woke on our fourth morning.

Sunlight streamed in through the window, and even though that statement made my heart trip, the underlying sense of doom that I'd been feeling since we'd made the decision to fight the king didn't ease. Still, I tried to tease and make light of his comment. After all, one's wedding day was supposed to be joyous, not fearful.

Curving my lips up, I replied, "You do realize that you've never properly asked me, right?"

Norivun arched an eyebrow, that silver wing flashing in the early sunshine. "Is that what it takes?"

Covers lifted as he hopped out of bed, and I got an eyeful of his broad shoulders, huge wings, and taut backside. My belly tightened, and a stirring of longing washed through me.

His nostrils flared, and a knowing look entered his eyes. Dropping to one knee, he held his hand out. "Ilara Seary, daughter of Mervalee Territory, rightful Rising Queen Victor, Bringer of Life, and Mate of my Heart, will you be my bride?"

I held back a small smile. "Is that my newest title?"

"It is. Do you like it?"

My heart skipped despite his cheeky words. "You do realize you're proposing to me naked, don't you?"

He glanced down at the impressive appendage dangling between his legs. "Yes, why in fact, I did realize that. A rather delightful bit of air is swirling around those parts at this very moment."

I snorted a laugh, unable to help it, and he gave me a sly smile and stood before slipping into a pair of trousers.

Once half-dressed, his face wiped clean of his teasing expression. He bent onto one knee again then clasped my hands, his look entirely earnest.

"I love you, Ilara. I always have. I always will. I will protect you with my life, and we will rule our kingdom together. I would have no other at my side. You are my life, my heart, my mate. I would be honored if you would be my wife . . ." He paused, his throat bobbing in a swallow, before he added hesitantly, "My *eternal* wife."

My breath hitched. "Your . . ." Surprise filled me, which I knew he detected through our bond. "But that's entirely permanent, my prince. We can never, ever part. You would be joined to me for eternity. Our souls would be one."

He paused, his gaze searching mine. "It's what I want. Is that something"—his throat bobbed again—"something you also desire?"

Tears pricked my eyes as his love and savage devotion flowed into me. "You'll be stuck with me forever. Not even your father could break that bond. Not even if he changed Solis law about marriage. That's an ancient bond. If we do that, there's no going back."

"I know."

"Is that why you want to do it, so your father couldn't annul our marriage?"

"Partly. It guarantees that I'll never marry Georgyanna, but I'd also want you as my eternal wife even if I wasn't bound to her in an arranged marriage."

My tongue felt as if it grew too thick to speak.

Norivun squeezed my hands again. "We don't have to. We can simply marry in the traditional sense and fight my father's rule if he tries to change the laws. We could—"

I jolted forward, capturing his face in my hands as I pressed my lips to his. Tears filled my eyes. When I pulled back, a sob threatened to escape me. "I want to be your eternal wife. I only want you. I'll only ever want you, and eternity still isn't long enough."

A fierce light lit his eyes, and with a growl, he molded me to him. "You're mine, Ilara Seary."

"And you're mine, Norivun Achul."

His lips lifted, immense satisfaction spreading across his face.

OUR WEDDING CEREMONY was small and entirely without frills. It was nothing like the royal Solis weddings of the past, the ones that took place every few centuries and were a week long and involved numerous parties and appearances, all leading up to a grand ceremony. A wedding that the crown prince was scheduled to have with Georgyanna in only one week's time.

Salty air drifted through my long dark hair as Prince Norivun Deema Melustral Achul waited at a cliff's edge overlooking the Adriastic Sea with only his guards and an officiant from the local clergy as our witnesses.

My feet slipped across the pebbled dirt, my heart bursting with what was to come, and my only true regret was that my friends and family weren't here.

But come tonight Norivun and I would be eternally bound, we would return to Solisarium, and we would expose the king to the council members and Solis citizens and stop his tyrant rule.

Later, we could properly celebrate this monumental union with those we loved.

When I reached the crown prince, a primal need shone in his eyes, and bursting satisfaction billowed toward me on the bond. The officiant draped the sealing cloth over our skin, joining my and Norivun's hands, and a pulse of magic swept over me.

"You're sure?" the officiant asked as the magic from the ancient sealing material heated our hands. "Once you do this, there's no going back."

My gaze never once left my mate's as Norivun's attention locked onto me.

"Yes," we replied simultaneously.

"Then we shall begin." The officiant began to chant words in ancient elvish, words that were long dead yet created by a powerful, extinct race. The magic from the ancient ones swirled around us, growing stronger and seeping into every pore of my body.

I sucked in a breath, my pulse quickening as the sealing cloth's hold held firm.

Switching back to our tongue, the officiant said, "I place this binding cloth upon you as a symbol of your intentions before the universe and all of our gods and goddesses. You are sealed now before the gods. Let us begin."

The soft material felt like a cocoon over my skin as tears pricked the backs of my eyes.

Norivun's nostrils flared, his gaze never once leaving mine, as his guards watched with bursting smiles.

With the cloth tied, the officiant placed a binding stone atop our entwined hands. "We join today to celebrate the eternal joining of Prince Norivun Deema Melustral Achul and Lady Ilara Seary, son and daughter of the Solis continent, as they stand before us, rightfully choosing to be bound by the gods and goddesses, declared to the realm, and sealed by the universe in a matrimonial ceremony of unbound magic."

The officiant began chanting the ancient elvish words again, a sealing ceremony that had bound not only elves, but fae, for all time. It was a spell so intricate, so absolute that it would seal me to the crown prince even after we took our last breath and joined our ancestors among the stars.

My lips parted when powerful, potent magic washed over me like a heavy shroud. Pulsing need strummed toward me on the bond from my mate. I pushed my love back into Norivun, just as potently, just as strongly as he did to me.

He was my mate.

My love.

The only one who could ever truly be mine.

And when the ceremony came to a close, and the final clash of magic sealed our fate, I gazed up at the crown prince of the Solis continent, once my most hated enemy, yet now my most cherished mate.

"You may declare your final vows before the gods and goddesses," the officiant stated.

The prince's lips curved as his eyes gleamed with triumph. "You're mine, Ilara Seary, for now until the end of eternity."

I squeezed his hands in return as the cloth heated around us. "And you're mine, Norivun Achul, for now until the end of eternity."

A pulse of magic burst across the back of my hand, heating and igniting.

"I hereby declare you eternally bound and joined," the officiant said as he released the cloth. My eyes widened at the swirling silver mark that was inked onto my finger. It was the supreme symbol that united all of the gods and goddesses—a circle with an array of connecting swirls and stars.

The same had inked itself onto Norivun's finger. The officiant nodded toward our eternal marks. "You are sealed before the gods and goddesses in a manner so absolute that you will be forever joined by the stars. May the universe bless your union."

A skittering of magic burst across the sky, like a thousand stars alighted so brightly that their shine was visible even during the day.

"Did you see that?" Haxil said under his breath, awe in his voice.

"The gods and goddesses approve," Ryder replied, the same wonder coating his words.

"Ock, as they should," Nish said smugly.

"You two are destined to change the realm," Sandus whispered.

My heart thumped harder at what that blessing meant.

Norivun growled and pulled me to him, his lips pressing to mine as immense joy surged through our bond.

When he finally pulled back, I was breathless as an undercurrent of determination slid through me. The same savage light shone in his eyes and flowed toward me on our bond.

We were permanently joined.

Eternally bound.

Forever mated.

Our souls had become one.

"Are you ready to return home?" he asked softly.

I gave a fierce nod as magic swirled inside me. "Indeed. Let's find the king."

THE FINAL BOOK IN FAE OF SNOW & ICE

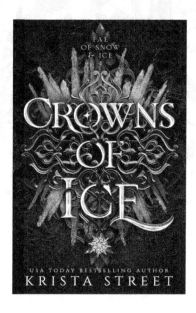

The time has come to return to the Solis continent.

With my mate at my side, my strength strong and imbued, Norivun and I venture back to the capital to fix all of the wrongs that have not yet been made right.

But victory won't come easily.

Choices must be made.

Lives will be lost.

And in the end, only the true royals will rise.

ABOUT THE AUTHOR

Krista Street loves writing in multiple genres: fantasy, sci-fi, romance, and dystopian. Her books are cross-genre and often feature complex characters, plenty of supernatural twists, and romance in every story. She loves writing about coming-of-age characters who fight to find their place in this world while also finding their one true mate.

Krista Street is a Minnesota native but has lived throughout the U.S. and in another country or two. She loves to travel, read, and spend time in the great outdoors. When not writing, Krista is either chasing her children, spending time with her husband and friends, sipping a cup of tea, or enjoying the hidden gems of beauty that Minnesota has to offer.

THANK YOU

Thank you for reading *Wings of Snow* book three in the *Fae of Snow & Ice* series.

If you enjoy Krista Street's writing, and you live in the USA or Canada, sign up for her new release text alerts. Krista will send you a text message when she releases a new book. To sign up, simply text the word **ALERTS** to **888-403-4316** on your mobile phone.

Message and data rates may apply, and you can opt out at any time. Visit Krista's website to learn more or to sign up for her newsletter if you live outside of North America.

www.kristastreet.com/contact

And if you enjoyed reading *Wings of Snow*, please consider logging onto the retailer you purchased this book from to post a review. Authors rely heavily on readers reviewing their work. Even one sentence helps a lot. Thank you so much if you do!

To learn more about Krista's other books and series, visit her website. Links to all of her books, along with links to her social media platforms, are available on every page.

Printed in Great Britain
by Amazon

36694076R00219